THE VENUS
TRAP

OTHER TITLES BY LOUISE VOSS

LOUISE VOSS

THE VENUS TRAP

THOMAS & MERCER

This is a work of fiction. Names, characters, organizations, places, events, and incidents are either products of the author's imagination or are used fictitiously.

Published by Thomas & Mercer, Seattle

www.apub.com

Amazon, the Amazon logo, and Thomas & Mercer are trademarks of Amazon.com, Inc., or its affiliates.

ISBN-13: 978-1477822159
ISBN-10: 1477822151

Cover design by bürosüd° München, www.buerosued.de

Library of Congress Control Number: 2014950387

Printed in the United States of America

THE VENUS TRAP

Chapter One
Day 1

I am usually awakened by the sensation of a small thumb prising open one of my eyelids, and the plaintive, hopeful word '*Doors?*'

Megan's been doing this to me since she was a toddler and it's one of our family traditions. This morning, however, I slowly open my eyes unhindered—although I have such a shocking hangover that a bit of assistance wouldn't have gone amiss. It takes me a moment to remember that Megan isn't here, that Richard's taken her to Italy. This should be my 'me' time, ten days' respite from bedtime negotiations, smuggling vegetables ('veggitroubles') into spag bol, arranging play dates, swirling neon pink icing onto cupcakes.

I can't think why I've got such a banging headache. Perhaps I celebrated my parental freedom too enthusiastically. The room roils and tilts around me, pulsing to the vibrations of pain inside my skull. Nausea slops and sloshes through my body and I have to lie absolutely still for it not to rise in my throat.

The headache isn't helped by the weird noise I can hear. It's a loud whining, scraping sound, as if a dog is trying to get into my bedroom. There are no dogs in this building—no neighbours, either, since old Hugh downstairs died. My flat is on the second floor, above Hugh's empty one and a boarded-up charity shop on the ground floor. The cat never makes that sort of racket.

The heating is on full. In July? There must be something wrong with it—or perhaps it's the toxic heat that my body is giving off.

Suddenly I feel scared, although I don't immediately know why. There is something deeply unsettling about being frightened in your own bed, in your own room. I wonder if it's just because I'm ill, and I hate being ill.

But I don't think it's that.

I am lying on my side, drenched in sweat, at the edge of the bed. On the floor next to me I see a metal mixing bowl, the one that Megan and I use for cake mix. It triggers some kind of Pavlovian response and I lift my head off the pillow and vomit into it. Most of it misses. I must have a bug of some sort. It's bad. I feel fuzzy-weaker and with less form than an amoeba. Groaning, I shove back a corner of the duvet to get up and clear up the sick, but something stops me, as if someone has grabbed me around the ankle.

With monumental effort I throw aside the rest of the duvet—and stare in astonishment and disbelief at the short chain running between my iron bedpost and the handcuff attached to my ankle.

What the hell was I up to last night?

I can't remember.

The fear rises harder and faster this time. I flop back on the pillow, which makes my head pound even more, and I think I'm going to be sick again.

At least I'm at home, in my own bed, I think to myself, probably irrationally. I reach for my mobile on the bedside cabinet—but it's not there. Damn.

I don't understand. I never drink so much that I have memory losses like this. It must have been a major, epic night involving a man—I'd hardly have handcuffed myself to the bedpost. I look down to see that I'm wearing my cream winter pyjamas, which is also odd, as these pyjamas are far too warm and sweaty for this time of year. Sun is blazing through my thin curtains. Definitely not winter PJ weather.

A horrible thought occurs: I'm chained to the bed, and my phone isn't where it should be—so how do I get out of this one?

There is another noise at my bedroom door, a renewed scraping sound, and a worse thought occurs: *I'm not alone.* The noise ceases. My mind races. There is silence for a few moments.

Then, to my horror, the door opens and a bulky man appears, holding two mugs of coffee and smiling uncertainly at me. I recognise him, vaguely. His head is too small for his body and his eyes are too small for his face. The shock of an unfamiliar man in my bedroom makes me bite my lip so hard that I taste blood.

'Morning, sleepyhead. I see you're awake at last. I've brought you some coffee. Sorry about the noise—I'm just doing a spot of DIY. I've fed the cat, by the way; it seemed hungry. How are you feeling?'

Suddenly something comes back to me: this man is called Claudio. I know him, but I don't like him. I'm sure I don't like him. It seems really unlikely that we came back here last night, had rampant sex involving handcuffs, and now he's bringing me coffee and doing DIY . . . *Did* we have sex?

'I feel terrible,' I blurt, staring at him as he walks into the bedroom and comes towards me with the coffee. 'Please . . . take this off.' I gesture towards my ankle. 'Why is it on there?'

Claudio looks rueful. 'Can't do that, Jo, not at the moment. Maybe after I've taken a few security precautions. Oh dear, you do look rough. And you've been sick. Let me get you some water and Nurofen.'

He puts the coffee down on my bedside table and the smell makes me gag. Then he picks up the mixing bowl and carries it into the en-suite bathroom. I hear the splash as he dumps the contents into the toilet and flushes, then the hollow sound of water on metal

3

as he rinses it out. I bite the inside of my cheeks and swallow hard in an attempt to stop myself being sick again. Panic swirls inside me like the flushed-away vomit, but something prevents it bursting out of me. Did he give me some sort of drug to make me forget? I am dulled, and I'm sure it's not by illness or alcohol poisoning. There is another layer of something heavy, coating and deadening my brain and my reactions.

Claudio reappears with the clean bowl and a tooth mug of water. His expression is diffident but there is a steely look in his eyes that makes me shiver.

'What's going on, Claudio? What are you doing here?' My voice sounds as thick as my head feels.

He sits down on the edge of the bed and pats my thigh. I recoil.

'Don't you remember? You started feeling poorly after dinner last night, so I brought you home. We're going to spend some time together, you and I. I want to be with you, Jo. We're so lucky to have this opportunity and I just want to make the most of it. Megan's away. I have a few days off work. We have time to really get to know one another. Isn't that great?'

I blink at him, realization slowly dawning. He stands up.

'But first I just need to finish off a few odd jobs.'

He walks into the hallway and returns a moment later holding two large sheets of plywood and an electric screwdriver. Apologising again for the noise, he thrusts open my bedroom curtains, pushes one of the sheets of plywood up against the window frame, and deftly screws it on with repeated brief high-pitched whines of the screwdriver. The room is plunged into semi-dark, the only light now coming from the half-open bathroom door.

Claudio turns to me. 'I'm going to do the bathroom window now. If you scream, I'll tie something over your mouth to stop you. Understand?'

Chapter Two
Day 1

That's when my heart starts thumping with fear, so hard that I can't breathe properly. It's as though my whole *body* is thumping and I definitely can't think straight—but I now realise what's happening. Even though I still don't believe it.

No no no no no no . . .

Things like this don't happen to me.

I open my mouth to scream blue murder—then remember what Claudio just said. If he gagged me now, I would vomit and choke.

My breathing is too rapid, too shallow, a percussive accompaniment to the snare of my banging heart. I grab my head in both hands and squeeze, as though that will contain everything, but it doesn't help. I feel sick again so I grab the cake-mix bowl. Claudio is in the bathroom. I force myself to slow down, calm down. Don't panic. Don't panic. Think. Hold it together. He can't keep me cuffed to the bed: I need the loo. I'll just rip off the wood when he's gone and scream out of the window.

I am clutching the bowl, gasping with fear and shock, when Claudio comes out of the bathroom into the dark of my bedroom, electric screwdriver held out in front of him like he's the

Driller Killer we used to laugh about at school. In fact I'm sure I remember Claudio himself talking about it, his skinny sixteen-year-old self obsessed with the banned video nasty. I never liked him. Why did I think he'd be any different as an adult?

'Relax, darling,' he says, flicking on the overhead light. 'I'm not going to hurt you. Not if you behave.'

I vomit into the bowl again, but the physical act of being ill doesn't for a second take my mind off the fear. I have to believe him.

'Oh dear, you really are poorly. I'll get you some Alka-Seltzer.'

'Just undo my foot, Claudio, please,' I beg, wiping away a thread of vomity spittle. 'I won't go anywhere. I'm too sick to scream, let alone run.'

He looks hurt. 'Why would you want to do either of those things? We're just having a little "us" time, that's all. Let me get you that Alka-Seltzer. Or would you prefer some Nurofen?'

He walks over to me and feels my forehead with the back of his hand. 'Oh dear,' he repeats, and takes the sick bowl away again to rinse out.

'Alka-Seltzer,' I whisper. When he hands me back the empty bowl I press the cold damp metal against my clammy forehead and hot cheeks, to remove the feel of his skin on mine.

He vanishes, returning with one of Megan's plastic beakers and handing it to me. It's fizzing, and the smell and sensation of the salty bubbles popping against my top lip as I raise it to my mouth threaten to make me puke again, but I manage a few sips and gradually start to feel very slightly better.

'Claudio.'

He sits down on the bed again and tries to push my fringe off my face. I bat him away.

'Claudio, I need the loo. You have to untie me. This is insane. You can't keep me tethered to the bed like a dog chained to a post.'

I curse my upcycled white wrought-iron bed, although I can even remember the thought of naughtiness with handcuffs crossing my mind when I bought it, on one of my regular forays to vintage antique markets.

Now I wish I didn't like vintage. If I had a modern, sleek bed with a built-in solid headboard there would be nothing for him to tether me to.

He laughs as though I've made a joke. 'Oh no, I'm not going to do that. Of course not. I understand completely. It's just a precaution until I get the place how it needs to be.'

I dread to think what he means by that.

'Once it's safe,' he continues, 'then of course I will undo you.'

'Safe?'

'Let me search your room. You will be here for some time, so I want you to be comfortable, and I want to make sure you won't . . .'

He tails off.

'Be able to escape?' I supply, thinking *This absolutely can't be happening to me.*

'Well, if you want to put it like that,' he says sulkily.

'Search it if you want. It's not like I've got a baseball bat under the pillow and a pistol in my knicker drawer.'

He jumps up with alacrity. 'OK. I will be as quick as I can, given your . . . predicament.' By which I assume he is referring to my bursting bladder rather than my involuntary incarceration. 'I'll start in the bathroom.'

I keep all my toiletries in a wicker unit with baskets for shelves, and I hear him dump each one on the floor and sift through it. Repeated thuds and rustles indicate that he is dropping contraband or potential weapons into a bin liner. I hear the gentle swish of what are probably pill packets—must be the strong painkillers I take when my slipped disc plays up—dropping into the bin liner, then the heavier clunk of something metallic, the scissors I cut Megan's

7

hair with, probably. A few lighter items drop in—I'm guessing things like tweezers and metal nail files. The rattle of matches in the matchbox I keep for the candles around my bath. How long does he think I'm going to be in here for?

How long will it be before I'm missed?

Something loud drops into the bin liner. I think it's my hairbrush. What does he imagine I'd do with that—spank him into submission? In his dreams. Or perhaps it's my hairspray, or aerosol deodorant. I doubt he'll allow any aerosols. My comb, the one with the sharp end, is on my chest of drawers: with any luck he'll overlook that and I can poke out his bloody eyes with it.

While he's out of sight I edge down to the end of the bed and yank at the handcuff on my left ankle. It's futile, so I shuffle back up towards the pillows and finish the rest of the Alka-Seltzer. If he'd put it in a glass I could've smashed it and used that as a weapon. His attention to detail is quite impressive, and I wonder if he has been planning this. He must have been—it's unlikely he'd have two sheets of plywood the right size to cover my windows knocking around in the boot of his car.

'What time is it?' I call out weakly.

'Twenty past two,' he replies cheerfully, and more things drop into the bin liner.

I'm shocked. I've been asleep for that long? I suppose he could have gone out this morning for the wood and let himself in again, knowing that even if I woke up, I was immobilised. He must have given me something to knock me out—that's why I can't remember anything. So there must have been at least some planning.

'Did you give me that date-rape drug?' I call, and I hear him suck in his breath with annoyance.

'I haven't *raped* you,' he replies, sounding offended.

'That's not what I asked.'

'Rohypnol,' he concedes, as though it's a perfectly normal thing to do. 'You seem to have reacted badly to it. I'm sorry. I didn't think you would sleep so long or be so sick.'

I suddenly feel so furious with him that I can't speak. Fury and fear combined make my head hurt even more. Impotent tears spurt out of my eyes.

'This is crazy, Claudio. You can't do this.'

He doesn't answer. A few moments later he emerges from the bathroom holding my yellow metal bin in one hand and the full bin liner in the other. Damn. That bin is heavy—I could have used it to swing at his head. But he had obviously had the same thought.

'Now will you undo me?' I wipe my eyes and sniff, and Claudio briefly stops in his tracks.

'Ah, Jo, sweet girl, don't cry! Let me get rid of this and then you can go to the bathroom.'

When he opens the bedroom door to put the bin out I see a new, large bolt affixed to the outside of it. His screwing it on must account for the whining noise that woke me up. My door also has a lock, with a key that I usually keep on my side, but the key is missing. The sight of the bolt makes me shiver, and I go from being too hot to feeling freezing cold.

'I need a shower and some clean clothes. I stink of sick.'

'Have a shower, baby girl, while I check your room for you. I'll clean that sick off the carpet too.'

Check my room for me? Don't call me baby girl*, you freak.* I am planning to bolt myself into my bathroom where at least he won't be able to get to me. I will prise the plywood off the window with my bare hands and scream until someone hears me.

He finally extracts a tiny key from his shirt pocket and unlocks my shackles. I try to slide off the bed unaided but I stumble and fall backwards. He laughs and helps me up, and I have to let him,

9

because my knees are so weak. He smells worse than I do—halitosis and body odour.

'I think you'd better have a bath instead of a shower,' he says, and I resist the temptation to say, 'And you'd better have one too: you stink,' in case he sees it as an invitation to come and bathe with me. Thank God there are two bathrooms in this flat, so he doesn't have to use mine.

With his help I stagger into the bathroom and the first thing I see is that the little bolt is gone, the one I fixed high up on the door when I first moved to this flat, above Megan's head height so she couldn't lock herself in. He must have unscrewed it when I was unconscious. Bastard.

'You are going to let me have a bath on my own.' I frame it as a statement and not a question.

'Of course,' he says indignantly. 'A lady needs her privacy. Shall I run your bath for you?'

'No. Please go. I need the loo, urgently.'

To my relief, he lets go of my arm and leaves the room, closing the door quietly behind him. I put the plug in the bath and turn on the taps full, so he can't hear me pee. I step over the mess of dumped toiletries, cosmetics, and empty baskets on the floor, sit on the toilet, and relieve myself. More tears fall and I start to sob, silently. I don't want him to see me cry again.

Then I wipe my eyes with loo roll and look around. He's taken everything that could possibly be used against him—the bog brush, all my mascaras and eye-pencils, anything sharp or pointed, metal, or heavy.

Surely there's something he'll miss, I think, cleaning my teeth vigorously and then stripping off my sweaty pyjamas. I lower myself gingerly into the water with the taps still running. I'm cold now, and the bath is so nice. I dump in a load of my expensive lavender bubble bath, immersing myself in the hot water until my skin goes scarlet. As I'm washing my hair I try very hard to pretend I'm hav-ing a normal bath, on a normal day, and that the sounds I can hear from my bedroom are just Megan playing with her Barbies on my bed, or dragging my dressing-gown cord across the duvet for Lester to pounce on. My dressing-gown cord! That could be a weapon. Am I strong enough to strangle him with it? Of course not. I'm so scared I can barely move.

How could I ever have thought Claudio was someone I could have a relationship with? If only I'd never bumped into him again after all this time. Just goes to show how bloody desperate I was—desperate enough to ignore for ages all the little signs that he wasn't right for me and think, 'Ooh, single man expressing interest in me? Yes please!'

Chapter Three
Day 1

I was on an internet date with someone else when I first bumped into Claudio. Must have been a couple of months ago. I'd been quite looking forward to this one, with a guy called Gerald (that in itself should have rung an alarm bell—I don't know any Geralds who don't call themselves the far more acceptable Gerry). He said he was five foot ten but was clearly at least six inches shorter than that.

It's not that I have anything against small men, as such. My ex-husband, Richard, is quite short—exactly the same height as me, when I don't have heels on. I'm five foot six and a half—although Richard always gave his height as five foot eight. It's just that if you're going to put a profile on a dating website, it makes sense to be honest about your height. I mean, it's not something you can get away with lying about. What if I'd been six foot tall? It would have been even more ridiculous. I suppose that Gerald did say that he was looking for a 'petite' woman, so I could have guessed he was never going to be a basketball player. Or perhaps he felt that I'd misled him, by being taller than he'd specified. Still—"five foot ten"? I don't think so!

In the event it wasn't so much Gerald's height, or lack of it, or his appearance. It was more his general demeanour. 'A face like a slapped arse,' as my ex-mother-in-law used to say. I felt sorry for him—no wonder he couldn't get a girlfriend.

As I waited in Pizza Express ten minutes before the appointed time, I felt the same thrill of anticipation that had become so addictive over the past few months. Would I really be lucky enough to find the one to spend the rest of my life with—the one to be step-father to my daughter—online? The odds were a lot higher than those of winning the lottery, and people *did* win the lottery. Some people, anyway.

I'd sipped my fizzy Evian, and then wished I'd ordered still water, in case the bubbles made me burp. Would we have chemistry? We'd got along fine on the phone. He looked OK in his photo. Anyway, I wasn't one of those shallow types who judged people solely on their looks. I'd spent most of my life fretting about my own appearance, so I was in no position. Inner beauty, that was my goal.

What if he thought I was a moose?

I'm *not* a moose, I told myself crossly. In fact, there was a man staring at me across the restaurant. It couldn't be Gerald, because he was with an old lady, but he definitely kept shooting glances at me and he wasn't at all bad-looking. Not gorgeous, but not hideous.

'Would you like to order some nuts or olives while you wait?' A waitress loomed up next to me with an electronic order pad, making me jump. 'Sorry, I should have asked you that when you ordered your water, but I forgot. I'm new, you see.'

'That's fine, don't worry,' I said, smiling at her. 'Olives would be great, thanks.'

The waitress, who was tiny and pretty and slightly breathless, turned too fast and banged right into someone. Her order pad went flying, skidding underneath my chair. I bent down to pick it up and when I emerged, the blood having rushed to my head, a very, very short man was standing there rubbing his nose. I think the waitress's head had collided with it, since she was rubbing her forehead too. Either that or she'd head-butted him, with uncanny prescience as to the emotional injury he was about to inflict on me.

I'd just handed her the pad and opened my mouth to ask if she was OK, when I was interrupted.

'Can't you bloody watch where you're going? You could have broken my nose!'

The poor waitress mumbled an apology and staggered off, close to tears. The restaurant was almost full, and all the other diners turned and stared, aghast.

I can't stand people who are rude to waiting staff. I was about to give him my dirtiest of dirty looks, when I realised with considerable alarm that this obnoxious little troll was my date.

'Oh!' I said. '*Gerald*?' Even under the circumstances, I did try to keep the disappointment out of my voice, I really did.

'Jo. Well, that's a good start, isn't it?' he said in a brittle voice, smiling uncertainly to reveal—dear God—sticky-out teeth the colour of rancid custard. His skin, so glowing and tanned in the photograph, was the pallid grey more commonly associated with coma patients. His shoulders sloped dejectedly and, like I said, he was extremely vertically challenged—about five foot four, I'd guess. With a red nose—although he couldn't exactly have helped that. His hair was almost colourless, as fine and wispy as a toddler's.

'Is it bleeding?' he asked anxiously, swiping beneath his nostrils with a stubby forefinger. I noticed he hadn't even bothered to check how the waitress was.

'No,' I said brusquely.

Gerald sat down opposite me and we shook hands over the table. There was a long, awkward silence, during which all the people at the other tables smirked knowingly and sympathetically at me. The man on the other side of the restaurant was still glancing over. I wondered if I knew him from somewhere, but I was too embarrassed to make eye contact with him. Gerald and I may as well have had a big neon sign flashing over our heads saying 'Losers on Blind Date'.

'You're very attractive,' he said eventually, sounding surprised.

'Thanks.'

'I love women with messy dark hair.'

Messy? It was meant to look curly, not messy. Still, did I care what he thought of me or my hair?

Yes, I did. Sadly. Even him.

'Is it natural?'

'All my very own,' I said brightly.

'So, you're divorced, are you? Do you want to get married again?'

I winced at his directness. *Not to you. Not if you were the last man alive, mate,* I thought. I opened my mouth to answer, and the answer would have been, *Yes, yes I do, more than anything. I want to recapture what I so recklessly threw away. I want to stop feeling so adrift, so lonely. I want to share my life with someone I love deeply, learn from my mistakes, move forward . . .*

'That's quite a personal question, considering we've just met,' I said instead. 'Shall we order? I'm not very hungry, so I think I'll just have some doughballs and a side salad.' I'd already been there ten minutes longer than I wanted to be.

'I'm allergic to dairy, yeast, and wheat,' he announced, scrutinising the menu, seemingly uninterested in the answer to his original question.

'Oh dear. Why did you choose Pizza Express then?'

He glanced suspiciously at me, as if this was an accusation. 'I don't eat out much. I've heard good things about this place. I thought it would be nice!'

'It *is* nice,' I said reassuringly. Who on this planet has never been to a Pizza Express before?

'Don't they have any steak?' He was markedly peeved now.

I realised that I had to do something dramatic. I had to leave, and very, very soon. My instincts were screaming at me to stay, to be the polite girl my parents brought up; it would only be for an hour or so—but what would be the point? I was never, ever going to see him again. Nothing he could do would ever make me fancy him. Surely he must have discerned the total absence of any chemistry between us? I would be doing us both a favour, saving us an hour of our lives—an hour that we'd never get back again—and about twenty pounds each.

I reached down and lifted up my bag from the floor, delving into it to retrieve my purse, just as the waitress returned with my olives.

'Can I get you a drink, *sir*?' she asked, scowling at him.

'I'll have a beer,' he said, shortly. Excuse the pun.

I couldn't be bothered to point out that beer is full of yeast. 'Listen, Gerald,' I said instead, blushing horribly. 'It's been interesting to meet you, but, really, I don't think this would work out.'

He gaped at me, as if he didn't understand. A wash of purple swept up from his neck to the roots of his wispy hair, which at first I thought was embarrassment.

I handed him a ten-pound note. 'This will more than cover the water, and the olives,' I said, but he didn't take it, so I left it under my side plate. 'I'm sorry. I don't want to waste your time, or mine. Um . . . bye, then.'

He was still glaring at me, his fists in two tight rolls. Then he shoved back his chair and stood up—at least, I think he did. It was hard to tell, his legs were so short.

I tentatively stuck out my hand to shake his for a second time, but when I saw the rage bubbling to the surface in his pale features, I realised that my best ploy would probably be to leave immediately.

I turned to go, but I was too late. To my utter and abject horror, he suddenly screamed, literally at the top of his voice:

'What, you can't even spend an hour of your precious time with me? WELL, JUST FUCK OFF, YOU STUCK-UP WHORE OF BABYLON!'

And he marched out, catching the hem of his jacket on the back of a chair as he went, sending it clattering to the floor. I sat back down again and buried my burning cheeks in my hands. I could see through my fingers that every last person in the room was staring open-mouthed in my direction, and for a moment I could not think what to do: run to the Ladies? Cry? Look around and shrug resignedly? Charge out after him and punch him in the mouth, or, more maturely, suggest he seek therapy for his issues with anger?

In fact, I did nothing at all, until I felt a gentle tap on my shoulder.

'Hi, it's Jo Singer, isn't it?'

I looked up to see the man who'd been staring at me from across the restaurant. He was tall, dark, and quite beefy, but his eyes were a little too small and his ears much too big. He looked familiar, but I couldn't think how I might know him.

'Well—it was. It's Jo Atkins now.'

'You're married? Then who . . . ?' The man looked pointedly towards the door, which was still closing slowly behind Gerald. It must have been very obvious that we'd been on a date, then. I was torn between relief that the man didn't for a moment think that Gerald had been my husband, and panic that he might think I was some two-timing tart to whom the epithet 'whore of Babylon' was entirely applicable.

'I'm divorced, but I kept my married name,' I said hastily. 'That guy was a sort of blind date. I'd never met him before. I can't believe he yelled at me like that; I'm mortified.'

It could have been my imagination, but it seemed that the man's face actually lit up at the news that I was divorced.

'*Really* . . . ? You married Richard Atkins, then? I remember you two becoming an item. Don't you remember me? I'm Claudio Cavelli. We were in the swimming club at the same time. And I was a friend of John Barrington-Brown's.'

It all clicked into place. I noticed that he hadn't said 'sorry' on hearing about my divorce, as might have been the polite thing to do. But then Claudio Cavelli, in my limited knowledge of him, had never been a particularly polite person. I wondered how he could have remembered Richard and me getting together, since that had been several years after we had all left school.

'Claudio! Of course. Sorry, I didn't recognise you. You used to be much thinner. Not that you're fat now, or anything, and it must be twenty years since I last saw you . . . twenty-five, maybe.'

I was gabbling. I did not feel at all emotionally equipped for meeting someone from my past, especially not someone associated with John. Someone who, it had to be said, I'd never really warmed to anyway. But I was so relieved to have a distraction from the awfulness of Gerald's outburst that I invited Claudio to sit down.

'I'll join you for a minute, but my mum's over there, so I won't stay long. She wanted to come out for some pasta. She can't eat pizza, you see: it dislodges her dentures.'

I glanced over to see a very thin old lady chewing very slowly, looking down at her plate with unwavering concentration.

'So, do you still live in Brockhurst, then?' I asked.

Claudio smiled again. It had to be said, though, he had a surprisingly nice smile. 'No, I'm in London, but I'm down here a lot visiting Mum. She has not been well recently. She lives in a nursing home.' The smile vanished, and the corners of his mouth drooped.

'I'm really sorry,' I said. We both looked at Claudio's mum again. She did not look at all well, now that he mentioned it. Her head was beginning to loll slightly as though she was about to fall asleep.

'What can you do, huh?' he asked, composing himself. 'Life's a bitch. Anyway, we're going to have some dessert and coffee in a moment—Mum loves the dark chocolate *bombe* they do here. Would you like to join us?'

I was surprised and, for a very brief moment, tempted. 'Thanks, Claudio, but I'll pass. I've got a babysitter at home, and I said I wouldn't be late. After the humiliation of just now, I think I'd rather just get home.'

Claudio seemed illogically disappointed, as if we'd been planning this dessert and coffee with his poorly mother for weeks and I'd let him down at the last minute. 'That's a shame,' he said, almost sulkily. 'It is so amazing to see you again.'

That's a bit over the top, I thought. Amazing? I didn't recall ever speaking more than a few words to him in passing when we were at school, or at swimming club. He'd always kind of given me the creeps, so I'd tended to avoid him when I could. But perhaps he was one of those people who looked back on their schooldays through such rose-coloured glasses that any connection with that era, however tenuous, was worth a detailed reminiscing session. I wasn't in the mood for one of those conversations about school discos and who'd snogged whom and when.

'Yes, you too,' I said, trying not to sound too discouraging. 'Perhaps bump into you some other time you're down here?'

'Well, why don't I take your phone number? We must go out for a drink sometime and talk about the good old days!' Claudio, enthusiastic again, had whipped out a ballpoint pen and had it poised over a red paper napkin. His expressions were changing like a weather vane in a high wind, and I found it confusing. I couldn't read him at all.

'Oh, right—yes,' I said, even though it was the last thing I wanted to do. I hardly ever even talked about John to Donna, his sister and my best friend, so I certainly didn't want to do so with some dodgy mate of his that I'd never even liked. I dictated my mobile phone number, but substituted the final 8 for a 3.

'So, maybe see you around,' I said, getting up and adding another fiver to the ten-pound note I'd left for Gerald earlier. I put both notes on the little silver tray containing the bill, which the waitress had discreetly slid onto the table as Claudio and I were talking.

'Definitely!' Claudio beamed, practically panting.

It was probably just my crushed ego from Gerald's very public rejection, but I felt oddly touched—if puzzled—that he, Claudio, had been so pleased to see me.

'And thanks for, you know, rescuing me just then,' I added. 'I didn't know what to do with myself when that awful man shouted at me, so you came over at just the right time.'

'Well, I would have talked to you anyway. To tell you the truth I was glad to see him go.'

Good grief, he fancies me, I thought, belatedly. I couldn't wait to tell Donna. I wondered if she'd even remember him.

'Bye, then, Claudio,' I said awkwardly, dying now to leave. The humiliation of Gerald's words kept repeating on me like a spicy meal, bathing me in fresh waves of embarrassment every time I thought about it. Claudio had at least taken my mind off it for a few minutes.

I am forty-three years old, I thought as I walked back to my car. How naïve was I to even think that I might meet someone nice, normal, and attractive? There were an awful lot of nutters out there . . .

I lie motionless in the bath for a long time, until my fingers prune and the water cools and stills around me.

'Jo? Are you all right in there?'

'Yeah,' I answer, like a morose teenager. 'Don't come in.'

'I'm just going to pop out for a while. Will you be OK?'

OK? No of course I won't. But I'm so glad to hear he's going out.

'I won't be long. See you in a bit.'

I hear him shut my bedroom door, the heavy clunk of the bolt being pulled across, then the sound of the flat's front door closing. I wait a couple of minutes then haul myself out of the bath, the effort making my head pound afresh. At least my stomach seems to have settled—I'm starting to get hungry. Surely Claudio can't be intending to keep me prisoner in my own bedroom? Maybe I should offer to cook us dinner or something. He seems to be under the illusion that this is some sort of bonding opportunity, a chance for me to reconsider my rash decision not to continue our burgeoning relationship. To think I'd thought that *Gerald* was the mad one!

I make a decision, the first really clear thought I've managed: I will try everything I can to forge a relationship with Claudio. I will attempt to figure out where this has all come from, why he could ever in a million years think it's a good idea.

As long as I don't have to have sex with him.

Please God, don't make me have to have sex with him.

Chapter Four
Day 1

Once I've dried off and listened at the bathroom door to make sure Claudio isn't still lurking despite telling me he's going out, I head back into the artificial light of my bedroom, rubbing my hair with another smaller towel.

I am brought up short by the utter mess he's left it in. It looks like I've been burgled—every drawer of my chest of drawers and bedside tables has been emptied out onto the floor to one side of the room, and my walk-in closet on the other side is ankle deep in not only clothes and shoes, bags and scarves, but also the boxes of stuff I store in there. All my bags have been searched and discarded and it looks as though every garment I own with pockets has been thoroughly rummaged through.

I feel utterly violated. The thought of him rifling through my underwear makes bile rise in my throat again and tears rush back into my swollen eyes. How fucking dare he!

I rush over to the dressing gown that still hangs on the back of the door, hope briefly flaring, only to be instantly dashed when I see that the cord is missing. As are all my belts, all my shoelaces, a large stone heart ornament that Sean gave me, my tennis racquet, my three bottles of perfume, GhD hair straighteners, most of my necklaces—all the leather beaded lariats—my only pair of stilettos, and of course my laptop.

For a moment it feels hopeless. I'm stuck here, with no contact with the outside world, and nothing with which to defend myself. I'm going to have to accept it, at least for the time being.

Then I think, no *way* am I going to lie back and let him intrude unwelcome into my life like this. No way can he go through my stuff, lock me in, keep me here. I will have to work out a way to be clever about it, to protect myself but lull him into a false sense of security . . . although I can't think how, not yet. But I have to.

I rush to the window and tear at the sheets of plywood with my fingernails, trying to prise them off, but there isn't a loose millimetre. Same in the bathroom. He's put about four times as many screws into it as are needed, and I have nothing to lever them off with. If only I could get hold of a knife. I don't know what I'd do first—try to free the window, or sink it into his fleshy belly. Stumbling back into my bedroom, I hammer with my fists on the wood but all it yields are dull muted thuds that nobody would hear. I scream and yell and sob and bang until I'm drenched in sweat again and my head is pounding afresh, but it's futile.

I sink back on the bed, panting, and look around me. It'll take hours to put this room straight. At least he's left the TV and radio. It will give me something to do, I suppose. I've been meaning to have a good clear-out for ages . . . not that I would ever have anticipated doing so under these circumstances.

A faded, scruffy A4 exercise book on the floor under my sweatpants catches my eye. I dress quickly in clean knickers, the sweatpants, and a bra and t-shirt, then pick up the book, one of my ancient diaries. I haven't set eyes on it for years and years—the contents of the box it was in have been lugged around from place to place since

I was a teenager. Funny how I've never felt the urge to re-read my old diaries, at least not the ones from when I was sixteen. The year my life got turned upside down—the first time.

I open the book at random and read a few lines, in my tiny but careful round teenaged handwriting:

If I can't even get my own way over the stupid dress—even though Dad bought it for me, it doesn't mean that I like it—then I might as well give up on asking for anything more ambitious, like security, or stability. That's what Dad was to us, and now he's gone, we're left <u>floating untethered across a vast sea of doubt and grief</u>.

Does that sound pretentious? I think it would be good in a poem. I'm going to underline it so I don't forget.

The entry is dated December 1986. Dad would have been dead for four months. I shudder at the memory of that year, my *annus horribilis*. Not that it seemed to stop me writing pretentious nonsense like '*floating untethered across a vast sea of doubt and grief*', mind you. I think I did actually end up using that in a poem somewhere. It rings a bell.

I hear the front door open again. My heart sinks and my pulse accelerates, making me feel more queasy. I close the diary and slide it under my pillow, then try to decide where to put myself. My bedroom is large—sixteen feet by fifteen feet, one of the reasons I rented this flat—so at least I will have a few seconds' grace after he opens the door. I try to calm myself down, but can't seem to quell the sudden violent shaking of my hands and legs. I sit down on the floor, feeling like a beggar child scavenging on top of a rubbish heap in India, adrift and vulnerable, except that I'm surrounded by my own possessions instead of by rubbish. It's only Claudio, I tell myself. You know him. You've met his mum. He says he's not going to be violent, if I'm not.

He unbolts the door and comes in, unsmiling. Arms folded, he sweeps a glare around the room, checking that nothing untoward has occurred in his absence. I follow his gaze from the still-secure window, to the mess on the floor, to my bed and—oh *shit!*

A small corner of the diary is sticking out of the side of the pillow. I close my eyes. *Please don't see it. Please don't see it.*

He sees it and pounces.

'What do we have here, then?' He holds it up and flicks through the pages, a mean smile curling at the corners of his mouth.

I try to affect nonchalance. 'It's nothing, Claudio. You've already seen it. It was lying on the floor with the rest of the stuff you dumped there.'

'I think I'll take that.'

I start up from the floor. 'No! Claudio, it's private! It's my diary.'

'I can see that.'

'Why on earth would you be interested in it? It's just a load of teenage ramblings. Please, don't take it.' I hear the desperation in my voice and try hard to quell it.

He opens the first page. 'Nineteen eighty-six. Excellent—the year we first met. This will be fascinating.'

'But it's private!' I repeat in a wail. I lunge for it but he snatches it out of reach above his head.

Then he puts it behind his back and restrains me with a heavy hand on my shoulder, keeping me at arm's length. His fingers grip my collarbone painfully.

'I don't think you understand, Jo. This will give us a perfect talking point. I want to know everything about you, everything. We have so many years to catch up on, to find out where we went wrong—and we have all the time in the world to do it.'

I lower myself down onto the edge of the bed, his hand still on me. My flesh is crawling. 'I'll tell you, then. Let me tell you,

25

anything you want to know. But please don't read it—you don't read someone else's private diaries. Surely you know that?'

He considers this, thrusting out his fat lower lip and tipping his head from one side to the other. 'Hmm. We'll see. I tell you what—I won't read all of it if you promise to talk to me. I've been out and bought enough groceries to last us at least a week, so we'll have plenty of time to chat. I'll take this for now, but I'm going to cook us a meal and we can chat over dinner, OK?'

Not OK. His grip loosens very slightly, and I twist away, leaping up to try to make another grab for it. This time he actually laughs at me as he shoves me hard back onto the bed.

'See you later, gorgeous. Shout if you need me. I'll be in the kitchen.'

And he's gone, with my diary, the clunk of the bolt shooting home behind him. I curl up into a foetal position on the bed, sobbing again.

How could I possibly not have had more of an inkling that Claudio was a total nutter? My instincts are *screwed*. I just don't listen to them, that's my problem. I mean, I gave him the wrong mobile number in Pizza Express so perhaps deep down I did think he was dodgy. Desperation and loneliness clearly over-wrote that sense of caution—I'd been so bloody impressed that he managed to track me down, even after not getting the correct number for me, that I chose to forget my qualms and instead started to really look forward to going out with him, actually tingling with excitement at the thought of our date. What an idiot.

⌒⌒

He first rang me a couple of weeks ago. I'd been in Megan's room checking on her before I went to bed. Even if I'd been feeling sociable I'd have ignored it anyway—my night-time ritual of checking on Megan was sacrosanct. It was only about nine thirty but I'd been miserable and tired that day, ready for bed. My skin was shiny with moisturiser and I was already in my nightclothes.

I close my eyes and run through the routine in my head, wishing with all my heart that I could be doing it right now. Straighten Megan's bunched-up duvet, retrieve Betty Bunny, who always slips—or gets pushed—down the slide. Richard bought Megan this high treehouse of a bed, reached by a vertical ladder and with a built-in slide for fast descent, but I don't like it because I can't reach Megan to kiss her when she's sleeping, and it's a nuisance to climb up to read her bedtime story. Megan loves it, because she feels like a princess in an ivory tower. Tuck Betty Bunny in next to Megan, who is often to be found thumbing her nose in her sleep, her tongue poking out and her fingers waggling weakly. I always wonder who she dreams about. She looks like her two-year-old self, and it never fails to make me smile. When she's a teenager, and then an adult, will I still get these flashes of her as a baby?

Will I ever see her again?

That particular night, I remember peeling a warm, reluctant Lester off the foot of her bed, lifting him up under the armpits like a child, his back legs paddling crossly at the interruption to his nap, when I heard a deep baritone voice on the answerphone.

It wasn't Richard's voice—and besides, he only ever called my mobile. Curious, I continued into the living room, more slowly, with Lester padding drowsily behind me, and pressed Play on the answerphone. Megan had forgotten to put away her little trampoline—it's one of those exercise trampette things—and as the answerphone tape spooled backwards, I stepped onto the trampoline and bounced gently, the open sides of my dressing gown flapping like giant wings. Lester looked at me as if I'd gone mad.

The machine clicked, and I held my breath.

'Er, hi, Jo, I hope this is the right number for you . . .'

I didn't recognise the voice. Who was it?

'. . . This is Claudio Cavelli. We met recently in Pizza Express—well, met *again*, I should say. You gave me your mobile number but I must have written it down wrong, because it didn't work. I have been trying to find out your home number but you are ex-directory, and it has been very difficult. I had almost given up, but then I paid to use 192.com, not the free service but the subscription one, and they have details from the electoral register. I found you that way. Anyway, I will call you again tomorrow, and maybe we can arrange that drink. It would be lovely to see you. Goodnight.'

I stopped bouncing. He'd paid money just to find my phone number? He was a reasonably handsome bloke—he couldn't be that short of potential dates. If I saw him on a dating website, I'd probably bookmark him, small eyes, lumpy head, and big ears notwithstanding. He had a nice smile.

I so clearly remember that moment, thinking *Maybe I should go out with him*. What was the harm? Just a drink. Just because I'd disliked him when we were teenagers didn't mean I would dislike him now. People changed so much. And he seemed so keen. It was flattering, especially after my recent disasters in the dating arena.

I decided that if Claudio was going to ring back, I would accept an invitation to go out for a drink with him.

Chapter Five
Day 1

I assumed that we'd be having dinner in the kitchen where the dining table is, but at 6.00 p.m. sharp—like I'm an OAP having an Early Bird Special—Claudio comes back in with a tray that he sets down on the bed. I have never been less pleased to see anybody, and I'm disappointed that I'm apparently not allowed to leave the room yet. As soon as the door opens, my heart rate doubles. Sweat springs out on my forehead and prickles my armpits.

'I've just made you something light in case your tummy is still a bit unsettled,' he says with a hint of pride, as though I ought to be impressed with his consideration. I glance at the tray. A poached egg sits messily on one of Megan's plastic plates, next to some spaghetti hoops and a slice of the sort of crap white bread that I never eat. I take a sip of the drink, also in a plastic cup, and make a face when I realise it's the sort of horrible cheap blackcurrant squash where all you can taste is sweeteners and carcinogens.

'I poached the egg the proper way, loose in the pan in vinegar,' he comments. We both regard the egg, which looks grey and straggly and utterly uninviting. I had been starting to feel hungry but now I feel sick again. The hoops have clearly been on the plate for a while as they're starting to congeal at the edges.

'Aren't you having any?'

Claudio shrugs. 'I'll get something later.'

I take a deep breath. 'Oh, that's a shame. I was hoping we might be able to sit down for a proper dinner together. You wanted to talk, didn't you?' I didn't mean it to sound aggressive but I'm worried it comes out that way.

'We can still talk.' He sits down at the end of my bed, looking constipated and uncomfortable, like he has something to say but can't spit it out. I put the tray on my lap and toy with a couple of hoops with the plastic picnic fork he's provided. My hand is shaking, which frustrates me, but I can't seem to stop it.

'I know this is a bit . . . awkward,' he says to the bedpost.

No shit, Sherlock.

'Well . . . it's certainly not conventional.' I'm trying to keep my voice light, conversational.

A long silence follows. The television is on in the background, a re-run of MTV's *Pimp My Ride,* so I focus on that. *Keep calm, Jo, keep calm. You're all right, so far. You aren't tied up or gagged any more. It's not like a real kidnap. He just won't let you leave, that's all.* And he's just sitting there staring at me. I can talk him round, I'm sure I can. If he tries to rape me at any point, I'll tell him I've got herpes, or syphilis, or AIDS.

But would that make him more likely to want to kill me? And what if he doesn't care what diseases I pretend to have, if he's planning to rape and kill me anyway and then top himself? He's a big man: I won't stand a chance if he tries to overpower me. I'm trying to recall what to do in these situations: a knee in the nuts, an elbow in the throat, fingers in the eyes.

Don't think about the odds of Claudio wanting to kill me, or of Claudio not *wanting* to kill me, but ending up killing me anyway because he doesn't know what else to do with me . . . Think about Megan cuddling up to one side of me in the mornings; Lester the cat to the other. Our own strange little family.

I eat another hoop and a string of vinegary poached egg, although it almost makes me gag.

'What do you want from me, Claudio?' I blurt.

I don't want to know the answer, but I suppose I need to know it.

He stares at me in silence for a long time, his face in eerie shadows cast by my bedside light, and I force myself to look back at him, to challenge him. His skull beneath his sparse, cropped black hair is a weird, distorted shape, with an unbecoming lumpiness at the side and above his forehead, like a baby Elephant Man. I noticed that on our date the other night. He won't look good once he finally goes completely bald. His cheeks look doughy and pallid. I can't believe I ever found him even remotely attractive.

'I want you to love me,' he says simply.

I'm blindsided by this. I don't know what to say.

'Love you?' I repeat stupidly.

'I love you, Jo, and I want you to love me. I want to have a future with you.'

Bile rises in my throat again and I force myself to swallow it back down. It won't look good if I puke all over the tray, let alone over his romantic little vision, although that's all it deserves.

'But . . . Claudio . . . you're a bright man. You must know that this is—'

Insane? Criminal? The least likely way on earth to ever make me fall for him?

'. . . not the right way to get me to love you.'

He snorts derisively.

'What?'

31

'I knew you were going to say that,' he says, glaring at me. 'Next you'll give me a load of bullshit about how the only way would be for us to get to know each other conventionally, go on more dates, more dinners—only you won't mean it, will you, because you've already dumped me! It would just be a load of lies to try and fool me into letting you go, so save your breath because I'm not that fucking gullible.'

It comes back to me in a flash: he's right—I did dump him, last night. After our third date. Had he planned all this already, or was it a spur-of-the-moment idea? How did he know I'd have a bed that he could handcuff me to? I suppose he didn't, and I'm fortunate not to have been chained to the radiator instead.

I ask him a more obvious question: 'But how do you really expect me to fall in love with you when you've drugged me and you're keeping me a prisoner?'

He tips his lumpy head to one side as if he's contemplating the question. 'You'll never find anyone who loves you as much as I do, you know. You just need a few days to get to know me, and to know that I'm serious. Eat up now, before it gets cold.'

It's already cold. I put the fork down.

'No? OK, let's talk then. Let's start with this—'

He pulls a crumpled piece of paper out of his jeans pocket and smooths it out on his large lap. In the dim light I don't at first see what it is—and then I do. It's a page of my diary.

'*You've torn up my diary?*'

He frowns, offended. 'No I haven't! I just brought this page in so we could start a chat about it. It's the first page. You can always sellotape it back in, if it's all that important. But honestly, nothing happens! You won't miss it.'

Oh my God, I think. He's insane, or really cruel, and I'm not yet sure which.

To my horror, he starts reading out loud in a high, slightly mocking voice, squinting at the occasional word he can't immediately make out in my tiny cramped handwriting:

"19th December 1986. Horrible day. I hate my body. I spotted my reflection in the window of Snellers Music Shop, and the sight of it made me cringe. My shoulders were all hunched against the December air, bedraggled even though it wasn't raining, red nose, watery eyes. My duffel coat makes me look like an Oxo cube." An Oxo cube? Really? That's a bit of a strange comparison, isn't it? You reminded me of many things when you were sixteen, Jo, but I have to say that an Oxo cube wasn't one of them.'

He sniggers, as though he's made a hilarious joke. I hate him.

I can't speak, and he seems to take this as encouragement to continue.

"There was a bitterly cold wind cutting through my woolly tights and blowing up the front of my Laura Ashley dress. I hate that dress, too. It's got a frilly yoke, like a nightie, and puffy sleeves, and I've had it since I was thirteen . . ." What's a *yoke*? I thought that was an Irish word for a thingamajig?'

I drop my head. My eyes are full of tears again. 'Please go. Leave me alone.'

He looks hurt. 'I'm interested, Jo! Come on, talk to me.'

'I don't want to.'

I don't want to. Richard and I used to talk to each other for hours, recounting stories to help each other sleep, or just for the sheer pleasure of it. This feels like a twisted, horrible parody of something that I now realise was sacred to me. Something I hadn't realised I missed so much.

He stands up suddenly and throws the torn-out sheet of diary at me. 'I asked you a question: what's a yoke?'

I have to bite the sides of my tongue to produce enough saliva to be able to speak; fear has dried me up and shrivelled me.

'It's a . . . I don't know how to describe it. A panel across the front of a garment.' I gesture with my hands across the top of my chest to indicate where, not meeting his eyes.

'So why did you hate your body then? I always thought it was really nice. And where were you going that day? See—I haven't even read it. I want you to tell me about it.' Claudio settles back against the bedpost, crosses his legs, and folds his arms, ready for a story.

Slowly, I set the tray with the almost-untouched food aside and smooth out the sheet of my diary. The sight of it gives me a pang. Even though I've not looked at it for years, it takes me right back, sitting writing it in my little attic bedroom in Brockhurst, my mother downstairs empty-eyed in front of the television, a huge gap in our lives where Dad had been. The gap had swelled and ballooned and pressed all the air out of the house until all that was left was stale, recycled grief.

I read the two pages to myself, refusing to look at Claudio. The writing is *really* tiny. I remember doing this intentionally to put off potential snoopers—little could I have imagined who that snooper would end up being, more than a quarter of a century later.

I don't know anybody else that wears needlecord. I've been trying to persuade Mum to let me get rid of it for ages—apart from being horrible, it's much too tight across my boobs now. Everyone else wears acid-wash jeans or baby doll dresses, while I'm still stuck with the prissy sprigged monstrosity. I'd die if any of my mates saw me in it.

'That dress cost £30. It's got heaps of wear left in it,' is all Mum says whenever I whinge about it. She's generally pretty good about letting me choose my own clothes, but the Laura Ashley's a particular bone of contention because Dad bought it for me. I used to get embarrassed that my dad did spontaneous, un-male things like buying me clothes. He didn't even mind putting on an apron and making the dinner. But Mum loved it.

'I miss him, Jo,' she sobs. 'I miss him so much. Who's going to look after me now?'

I just hug her, but I'm thinking, 'So who's going to look after me?' I don't say it, though. There's no point. If I can't even get my own way over the stupid dress—even though Dad bought it for me, it doesn't mean that I like it—then I might as well give up on asking for anything more ambitious, like security, or stability. That's what Dad was to us, and now he's gone, we're left <u>floating untethered across a vast sea of doubt and grief.</u>

Does that sound pretentious? I think it would be good in a poem. I'm going to underline it so I don't forget. I said to Mum the other day, about the dress, 'But it's so babyish,' and all she said was, 'Yes, well, you're my baby, aren't you?'

At least she smiled when she said it.

I hate Christmas, too. Even before Dad died, I hated it. Why does Mum's name have to be Carol Singer? It's so embarrassing and you wouldn't believe how much stick the swimming club boys gave me when they discovered.

It would be so much better if I only had a boyfriend, one who had a huge welcoming house with a Christmas tree that touched the ceiling, and enough turkey to share with me and Mum. A boyfriend like John Barrington-Brown. He's SO gorgeous. If John and I got married, then me and Donna would be sisters. How amazing to have your best friend as your sister too! Is sixteen too young to get engaged?

And then there's the small problem of John's current girlfriend Gill. Cow.

I'm still blushing from when I bumped into John on his lunch break from Safeways. Because I wasn't wearing a slip, the bunchy fabric of that hateful dress kept crawling up inside my thighs, and every ten paces

35

I had to stop and shake it out. I'd just extracted it for the umpteenth time, in a particularly unladylike fashion—knees bent outwards, bottom slightly sticking out, hand stuck up inside my duffel coat to reach the climbing dress.

Naturally that was the moment when John emerged from the supermarket's staff entrance, looking edible in those tight black trousers he wears for his job on the cheese counter. There's a little stripy hat that goes with the uniform, too (I know that from all the many hours I've spent lurking around Aisle 9 spying on him) but sensibly he'd removed that before venturing out in public. I hoped beyond hope he hadn't spotted me fishing around in my duffel coat, but he was already smirking.

'Well, look—it's little Jo. What have you bought?' Little Jo? How patronising! He tweaks the WHSmiths plastic bag dangling from my wrist. I've already forgiven him.

I blurted out, 'Oh, just Caravan of Love. *I must be the last person in the country to buy it . . .' and to my abject horror John yanks the bag off my arm and peers inside. I felt sooo humiliated, like he'd pulled down my pants or something—in fact, the way he did it made me imagine him undressing Gill. But it still gave me a shiver of something unexpected.* <u>Deep inside my needlecord folds.</u>

He cackled with laughter when the record was revealed instead to be Europe, The Final Countdown, *and I hoped desperately that he wouldn't tell all his mates.*

'The Housemartins? Yeah, right, pull the other one!'

Then of course I made things worse by stammering, 'Oh, um, silly me—that's for my cousin's Christmas present. She loves that song. I actually meant to buy Caravan of Love *but they'd sold out . . . .'*

John looked at me, his tawny eyes with their spiky black fringes blinking dangerously. Then his gaze slid down across my massive, horrible chest.

'Hmm,' was all he said. 'That's a very—flowery dress.'

I cringed and wished I'd done up the toggles on my duffel coat again after undoing them in WHSmiths, where the <u>fevered muggy breath</u> of the Christmas shoppers made me too warm.

'I know. I really really hate it, only my jeans are in the wash.'

I felt like I was being disloyal to Dad, by saying I hated the dress. But this was John. Dad would understand, I'm sure.

Then bloody Claudio turned up. He's such a weasel. I don't know why John likes him so much. He once pinched my bum and offered me a fag in the park. I hated him even more than ever, for interrupting my precious time with John. John's voice went all rough when he talked to Claudio:

'All right, Cloud? Give us a fag, I'm gagging.'

Wonder what John's parents would think if they heard him talking like that? They're seriously posh. They hate that Donna won't answer to her real name, Donatella—they think that Donna is very infra-dig. But she's insisted on it since she was seven.

Then John and Claudio just started walking off! John did look back, though, so I opened my mouth to say 'Bye,' and 'Send Donna my love,' but he'd gone before I could get the words out.

I watched him go. He always wears this really thin burgundy leather bomber jacket and he was pulling it closer to him, his cloudy winter breath huffing out around him. I half-expected him to blow smoke rings into the air, the way he had when I watched him smoking in the park. I wonder what it would feel like to have those beautiful curved lips pressed against mine?

On the phone later I tried to tell Donna that I thought John was sexy, but she just snorted.

'His feet smell worse than anything you could ever imagine,' she said. 'And he's got mossy teeth.'

I don't care. I still love him.

'So?' Claudio asks eventually. 'What's it about?'

It gave me a shock, seeing his name on the page. He must have known, he must have read it already.

I grit my teeth. 'It's about my crush on John. A dress I didn't like but kept wearing because my dad bought it for me. My mum, missing my dad. He'd only died a few months before then.'

Claudio doesn't express any sort of sympathy. There was clearly only one point of interest for him, and he's probably pissed off that I didn't mention that he featured. 'You were mad about John, weren't you?' he says, sulkily.

'Yeah.' No point in denying it.

He sighs, long, heavy and bitter. 'John always got the girls.'

Then he stands up, picks up the tray, and walks to the door, unlocking it and backing out.

'I'm tired. I'm going to watch TV in bed.'

Thank God he's not planning to sleep in my room, or Megan's. I would rip his throat out if he slept in Megan's room. I grit my teeth as I imagine his malodorous body sullying the purity and softness of her floral cotton sheets. But he is far too tall to fit into her three-quarter-size cabin bed that you have to climb a ladder to get to, even if he wanted to. His fat arse would never fit down the attached slide. And the thought of his head on her pillow, seeing what she sees before she goes to sleep— the whirling lions and zebras on her magic lantern, the butterfly stickers on her wall—makes me feel murderous. I'd almost rather he slept with me.

I feel heady with relief that he's finally going. The air in my room stinks of him. I don't tell him that the TV in the spare room doesn't work—he's probably got an iPad anyway. I suppose I'd better give him the wifi code if he asks; otherwise he might come back in here to watch whatever it is he wants to watch . . .

'But I'm going to leave you with a clearer answer to your question from earlier: it's *incentivisation*.'

'What do you mean?' A new trickle of fear snakes its way up inside me. I'm not even sure if incentivisation is a word—but it's not the semantics that are scaring me.

'It's just over a week until your daughter comes back. So you have seven days to tell me you love me, in a way that I believe you really mean it. No bullshitting.'

I shake my head incredulously. He's crazy.

'How do I do that?'

He shrugs. 'You can do it. Tell me your memories of all the other men you've known, then cleanse yourself of them. Photos, reminders, gifts. Help me plan our future. It can happen, if you let it. I have a lot to offer you—you'll see. We could be great together. But you have to let me in.'

Never.

'And if you don't,' he says almost casually, leaving the room but not quite closing the door behind him so that there is just a crack through which he speaks, like Jack Nicholson in *The Shining*. 'If you don't convince me that you love me within seven days, I will kill you.'

Chapter Six
Day 2

When I wake up at five in the morning, my head feels less muzzy and painful, but panic immediately surfaces, spurting in like water through the walls of a cracked viaduct: when will people start looking for me? Who knows what will have happened by the time anyone realises I'm missing? Perhaps nobody will realise, not until Richard gets back. I'm a freelance medical writer, no office to go into, no colleagues to miss me—I used to share an office with my journalist friend Steph but we gave it up just last week, because of the cost. I'm not due to see Steph or Donna and I don't speak to them that often on the phone these days. There's no reason for them to call me. Mum only rings me once a month from Scotland. Megan is unlikely to call me—she rarely does when she's on holiday with Richard, and that's fine with me because I know that it means she's having a good time.

Usually fine with me, I should say. Right now I'm wishing they called me religiously once a day because surely, after a day or two of my phone being switched off or unanswered, Richard would start getting worried? I never turn off my phone. I'm having a repeated fantasy in which he rings Donna and asks her to get hold of me, and then she can't, and she calls the police, and I'm rescued . . . but it's just a fantasy.

Fear rises in my stomach like a twister, ripping my insides apart like roofs being torn off barns.

Slow down.

Calm down.

Breathe.

I'm amazed I got any sleep at all last night. As it was, I lay awake for hours, turning Claudio's parting words over and over in my head. He wouldn't . . . He said he wouldn't hurt me . . . Would he . . . ? Surely he couldn't actually *kill* me! How would he do it?

How could I ever fool him into believing I love him when I don't? I've always been a useless liar: he'd see through me in a second—although, if he wanted to believe it badly enough, perhaps he might overlook my body language. Or could I rehearse a scenario in which I managed to convince him by practising declarations of adoration, lingering eye contact, little touches, all the things that besotted lovers do?

I doubt it.

Panic fluttered in my throat like a trapped bird all night and now exhaustion is giving me double vision. I switch on the radio and listen to low breakfast voices but they don't soothe me. How could they, when someone threatened to kill me last night?

All is quiet outside my room for some time. Then I hear the spare room door open and hear Claudio's ponderous footsteps past my room into the kitchen. Nausea rises inside me and I brace myself, wondering which Claudio I'll get today—the aggressive, snide one or the other one, the one who strikes me as someone who's bitten off more than he can chew.

It's the latter. When he brings me in some toast for breakfast he has the same expression as the cat has when it tries to stuff a live pigeon through the cat-flap or swallow a still-wriggling mouse. I wonder if he's regretting it already, realising that you can't possibly

41

force someone to love you if they don't. Particularly if you've already drugged and imprisoned them . . .

'Good morning, beautiful.' He hands me the toast, a diffident smile on his face. To my utter revulsion, he's still in his pyjamas, brown old-man PJs with more than a hint of nylon in their composition. The thought of all his skin so perilously close to the surface, just a thin layer of man-made fabric between us . . . I swallow hard.

'Did you sleep well?'

'No.'

There is an awkward silence.

'OK. I'm going to go and get dressed. I suggest you do the same. Then I'm coming back, and we'll talk again. I want to hear about your divorce.'

It sounds so blunt. I have to bite my tongue not to say, 'Mind your own bloody business.' I don't talk to anyone about my divorce, except my counsellor and my friends—not all of them, just my best friends. Just Donna and Stephanie.

'Why?'

He gives me a pitying look and I notice that stubble has sprung up all over his jaw, neck, and cheeks overnight. He must be one of those men who need to shave every day without fail. I hope he doesn't shave into the basin in my guest bathroom; imagining all those bits of black hair sticking to the porcelain makes me shudder. I don't like hairy men.

'I told you. I want to know everything about you. We have a lot of catching up to do.'

'Can I have my diary back, then, to help me remember stuff?'

He sticks out his fat lower lip and it glistens like an organ, like something private and internal that oughtn't ever be on show.

It strikes me afresh that if I hadn't been so desperate for a relationship, I wouldn't ever have given Claudio a second look. Why did I want a new partner badly enough to endure terrible dates with awful men like Gerald and Claudio? I should be able to be happy on my own. But I'm not, and now I've ended up here, aged forty-three, locked in my own bedroom by a deranged but apparently functional lunatic.

'Your diary's from eighty-six. You weren't married then, let alone divorced.'

'I know. But it's got . . . relevant information in it.'

I suppose it did have. Eighty-six was the year I first met Richard, the year he first fell for me.

He sighs heavily, as though I have made a great imposition, and moves to leave. 'Very well. I'll get it for you.'

'Thank you, Claudio,' I say meekly as he leaves the room.

What I don't understand is how I could have believed that this, any of this, would be better than being married to Richard. Especially up until last year, when I thought I was happily married. I had security, mutual trust, affection, validation. Yet I divorced the man whom I loved more deeply than I've ever loved anybody else, and he wasn't having an affair. He didn't beat me, or roll his eyes if I said something inane. He wouldn't dream of kidnapping a woman and attempt to make her love him.

I can't stop thinking about him. We told each other 'I love you' every day.

When Megan was a baby, Richard didn't wrinkle his nose at the mere suggestion of changing a nappy, nor did he feign sleep when she cried, leaving me to get up and give her a bottle. He'd get up and feed her himself, and I'd hear him singing to her. That song that goes *It's all about you, it's all about you, baby* . . . was a particular favourite. Every time I hear it, I think of him.

He bought me clothes and jewellery that, nine times out of ten, were things I would actually have chosen for myself. He did DIY around the house, expertly and without being asked. And he could cook—boy, could he cook. He cooked for me every single night, even though he didn't get in from work until eight thirty most evenings. Pale and hollow-eyed with exhaustion, he would pour us both a glass of wine, wrap the navy and white striped apron around himself, and set to in the kitchen, knocking up something delicious and often unexpected—tuna steak with chilli and water chestnuts, or a quick Thai curry with fresh lemongrass—'Ricky meals,' he called them, although he hated being called Ricky by anybody else.

To top all that, he'd been in love with me, and only me, since he was sixteen years old, apart from a brief relationship with a skinny girl called Chrissie when he was eighteen. He says he never loved her, though. She picked her nose in her sleep, allegedly.

It took me a lot longer than that to come round to his way of thinking, but that only serves to give him more credit for persistence and patience.

Well, that's one way of looking at it. The other way is to say that I should have trusted my instincts. I should never have allowed him to talk me into falling in love with him. But when you're twenty-one, and insecure, and your instincts have let you down so many times that you can only regard them with the deepest of suspicion, it's easy to accept that perhaps someone else knows what's best for you.

Perhaps by this reckoning, Claudio *is* the man of my dreams . . . After all, you could say there are similarities between his behaviour and Richard's. They both decided that I was the only one for them, and I didn't fancy either of them when I first met them.

This thought makes me feel sullied. I can't believe I even thought the words 'Claudio is the man of my dreams.' He's the stuff of nightmares.

I don't understand it. *I* wouldn't fancy me, if I was a bloke. They probably only fancied me when I was a teenager because I had massive boobs, and I don't even have those any more. It occurs to me that I seem to attract these needy, persistent men—but then I feel guilty for bracketing Richard with Claudio.

Richard was—is—a lovely man. He looked after me. He rescued me from myself. He gave me a home, stability, self-respect. We loved each other. So how could I have let it go all the way to separate houses and solicitors and signed divorce papers? His new girlfriend must be helping him regain his happiness, because he's putting back some of the weight that fell off him after my shock desertion. The stress-induced psoriasis that cracked the skin between his fingers is healing, and he's laughing again—or so I hear, via Megan.

I have a whole new file in my filing cabinet, with a plastic tab containing a little slip of card with the word DIVORCE written on it, splodged with my tears. And the answer to my question is: I'm not sure that I even know.

I thought I didn't love him any more; I really believed that I didn't. Funny, isn't it, how the mind plays tricks. What I'd like to attempt to get to the bottom of is this: was my mind tricking me into believing I didn't love him then, or is it tricking me now, by telling me that actually I did love him all along? Did I do the right thing by letting him go, or not? Which history am I rewriting?

Another of my sneaking suspicions about the whole thing is that perhaps it was just a manifestation of my seemingly bottomless capacity for self-destruction. Lots of people apparently have this. Maybe it's a defective gene.

There is a certain irony to the fact that we stuck together through the ten long years of pain and grief at not being able to conceive. The expense and heartbreak of two failed IVF cycles. The hours of discussions about adoption, fostering, surrogacy. The eventual and earth-shatteringly joyful revelation that we had conceived naturally, and our elation when Megan was born.

We went through all that—and then I left him. Either I'm mad, or I definitely do have that self-destruct button somewhere.

Chapter Seven
Day 2

Claudio reappears with my diary but whisks it out of my reach when I go to grab it. 'Don't snatch,' he says meanly. 'Apologise.'

Arsehole, I scream at him inside my head. 'I'm sorry, Claudio,' I say contritely, not quite risking fluttering my eyelashes at him. I still wouldn't put it past him to punch me in the mouth, or worse. There's a horribly volatile air about him—a phrase I once heard springs to mind: *madder and more unstable than a box of frogs on a one-legged stepladder.*

When he leaves again, I carry on reading it from the torn-out first page.

I wish I hadn't, though. I'm not sure there's any way I can talk to Claudio about this part of it. I'm mortified to think that he's already probably looked at it. What if it turned him on, got him going?

I can't think about that. I force myself instead to think that it serves as a reminder that I've been through really tough, shitty experiences before and survived them. Just about.

19th December 1986

I don't want to write about this, but I feel like I have to. What's that word that means something that makes you feel better for having talked about it? Am going to look it up in the dictionary.

Cathartic. Will it make me feel better? I doubt it.

I'm going to write about it like it's an English essay, just a story that I've made up. Mr Merwood would have a shock if I handed him this one to mark.

It was freezing cold. I walked down Endless Street towards home, my cold purple fingers fiddling with the plastic toggles on my coat to give me more of a shield between me and the biting wind, dreaming of the day that John realised he couldn't live without me.

It got really quiet, after the shops turned into houses. Every front room I walked past seemed to have a silently winking Christmas tree in the window, and the only sound was the plastic bag banging against my leg. I had hooked it over my wrist so I could walk with both hands jammed deep into my coat pockets.

When I reached the swimming baths' car park, I hesitated. There was a gang of teenagers messing about by the bins against the side wall of the pool building, smoking and pushing one another for no apparent reason. Swearing, of course, and laughing self-consciously, all of them wearing toad-coloured parkas with furry hoods and what looked like the tails of beavers trailing down behind their knees.

Mods aren't usually as intimidating as punks or bikers, en masse, but I felt scared straight away. The trouble was, though, in order to avoid passing them, I'd have to cut across the car park, which was deserted, and down the alley that's a shortcut to the end of our road.

Mum's always told me never to go down that narrow, unlit alley after dark—and I've never had any wish to, either.

I had to decide. I couldn't just stand there dithering—it would draw attention to myself. All my instincts screamed at me to keep away from the Mods by the bins. It's only a short alley: if I hurried, I'd be through it in thirty seconds.

That's what I thought, anyway.

The alley it was, then. I set off, head down, relieved that none of the boys appeared to have noticed me—I could still hear them faintly cursing and sniggering. A fragment of a song appeared in my head, chasing itself insistently round and round: 'It's my instinction, it's my instinction'—it's a song that's always bugged me with its grammatical inaccuracy and nonsensical lyrics. Was there even such a word as 'instinction'? Who sang it? It was around when I was about ten and still at primary school. Even then it irritated me.

Deep breath.

I went into the alley and suddenly, from nowhere, running footsteps came up behind me. They made me jump, and I forgot about the song. I glanced round, and moved to one side to let the runner pass. He was tall and skinny, with baggy jeans, but it was when I registered what was going on from his neck up that my heart started pounding so hard I thought I was going to faint. The man was wearing a balaclava, <u>his eyes two circles of horror surrounded by blackness</u>.

I still couldn't believe it. I forced myself instead to believe that this must be some kind of joke, and I waited for him to run past or rip off the balaclava, revealing himself to be a friend of John's, or even John himself, going 'Boo—scared ya!' Any alternative to that just did not seem possible.

But he didn't run past. Instead, he sort of lunged at me, pushing me against the wall and making my head bang against it. Then he started trying to kiss me, his tongue sticking out through the mouth hole in the woolly face mask in a really obscene way. His breath stank, and there was another smell, too, which took me a moment to place—damp wool. He must have been sweating into his balaclava even though it was freezing.

I shook my head to try to get away from his hideous tongue, closed my eyes, and then opened them again, in the ludicrous hope that I was just imagining the whole thing. My first ever kiss.

I'm crying my eyes out writing that.

But he was still there, and he still hadn't said anything, not a word. I leant against the wall to keep my balance, trying to think of my feet planted like tree roots into the ground, thinking that he wouldn't be able to rape me if I stayed standing up. But then it was like he read my mind, about trying to stay standing. I felt his hands grab the sides of my arms, twisting me around until my cheek was pressed against the rough bricks. I could smell chlorine from the nearby pool, and dog poo. He was forcing me to the ground. Even at the height of the crisis, I thought I would actually die if I had to lie in dog poo to be raped. He pushed and I fought, but he was stronger than me and I felt my knees begin to buckle. The plastic bag with the record in it flew off my wrist and across the alley.

Then it was like he suddenly had a different idea: he pressed one arm across the back of my neck, and his other hand shot down and then up under my dress. He was actually trying to pull down my tights. They were already too small for me, like the dress, I'd had them since I was in the Second Year, and the waistband was always annoyingly low on my hips. It meant that his cold hands touched my bare hot skin and I gagged, at the smell of the dog shit and the shock, my hands flailing to try to bat him away.

Finally it occurred to me to make a noise, to attract some attention, but the best I could manage was a pathetic little yelp, more of a feeble shocked 'eek' than a full-blown ear-splitting scream.

Or maybe it did work because suddenly, from nowhere, a boy in a beige macintosh ran into the alley. At first I thought it was an accomplice, and I bit my lip so hard that it started to bleed. My legs begin to give way and I thought, oh no, oh God, I'm really for it now.

Then there was the sound of a fist connecting with a stomach, once, twice, followed by a loud grunt from my attacker, who instantly released me and reeled back against the wall next to me.

The boy shouted at me to run. But even though my knight in shining mac was smaller and much younger-looking, about my age, the man in the balaclava reacted as if he'd *been told to run.*

There was this totally surreal moment when the three of us set off up the alley together, all running in the same direction like a starting gun had been fired: me and my attacker with a head start, Mac Boy chasing after him. But then he—the attacker—must have realised that all running off together was a bit, well, silly, and so after about ten yards he wheeled around a hundred and eighty degrees, pushed past Mac Boy, and sprinted back the way he'd come, into the swimming baths car park.

I ran without feeling my legs, aware only of a dull throbbing pain between them, until I reached the front gate, which was open, as was the front door. Mum was standing there, bathed in the yellow hall light, fidgeting from foot to foot, clearly very reluctantly listening to a reedy rendition of God Rest Ye Merry Gentlemen *sung by the small Women's Institute group of singers gathered around the doorstep. I hurled myself down the gravel path, almost knocking a lady in a hairy tweed coat into the lavender bush by the front door, and I didn't even stop to apologise. My whole entire being was focused on reaching the safety of my house. All I could think was, Why, oh why, did I go down that alley? If I'd gone past the Mods, I'd have been fine.*

So much for my bloody 'instinction'.

My fears about Claudio having already read it are confirmed when he returns about twenty minutes later, wearing jeans with creases in them and a boring button-down canary yellow shirt.

He looks very well groomed—he's had a shave, and his thick dark hair is gelled back off his expanse of forehead. Is he trying to impress me?

Without preamble he says, 'So that was your first kiss?'

How did he know which bit I'd been reading? Guessed, I supposed, since it came after the entry we 'discussed' last night. I hate him.

'I thought you wanted to talk about my divorce.'

'Jo, Jo, Jo . . . I told you, I want to talk about *everything*.'

I hate him.

He sits down again on the bed in his 'listening' pose, chin in hand, expectant expression.

I stand up. 'OK, I'll talk. But not facing you. It's not exactly easy to talk about, you know.'

He shrugs, so I go round to the far side of my bed and sit with my back to him. I notice faint white splatter marks around the legs of my bedside table, the residue of when I had to get the pest guy round to spray everywhere. Lester had fleas, and I had to get the flat fumigated.

'Where's my *cat*?' I say suddenly.

'It's fine. It's in the kitchen.'

'He's a boy. Lester. Have you fed him?'

'Yes, yes,' he says impatiently. 'I told you that last night. Anyway, let's get back to your first kiss. Stop trying to change the subject.'

Horrible, evil man.

'Not much of a first kiss.' I stare at the wallpaper, the big peachy rose print that I put on one wall to make the room more overtly feminine now that I was no longer sharing it with anyone. I had been thrilled when the landlord gave me permission to redecorate, and Donna, Steph, Megan, and I had gone mad with pastel shades, wallpaper paste, and Victorian ephemera. I loved it.

51

I used to love it, until now. Claudio's presence in my beautiful haven has spoilt it forever.

'Did they ever catch the guy?'

I shrug. 'Don't think so.'

Suddenly I feel something on my shoulder. His hand, tentatively touching me, not like the meaty clamp of yesterday. 'Must have been tough for you.'

I don't want his fucking sympathy! I make a noncommittal noise and twitch my shoulder out of his grasp.

'And did you find out who the boy in the mac was?'

'Richard. It was Richard Atkins.'

Claudio makes a girly, simpering noise. 'Awwww, how *sweet*. Little Richard to your rescue. That why you married him, was it?'

'I didn't know it was him until ages afterwards.'

'I'd have rescued you, if I'd seen it happen,' he says. 'Tell me how it made you feel.'

I try to imagine he's my therapist, Eileen.

I fail.

But I answer him anyway. 'What—the attack, or reading about it again now?'

'Both.'

I hesitate. It's so personal, it makes my toes curl. 'It made me afraid of ever walking anywhere on my own after dark. If someone was walking behind me, I'd freak out. If anyone ever pounced on my shoulders, just for a laugh or whatever, I'd scream. I feel—' My throat suddenly closes up.

'Yes?'

'The same now. You keeping me here feels the same.' I was going to add, 'I feel out of control,' but then realise that he'd probably love me to say that, because that's what he wants. He wants me to know that he's in control. I'm not going to give him that satisfaction.

'Have you read that diary again since?'

I shake my head. He'd emptied out a box of old school exercise books and the diary had been among these. 'I haven't seen it for years, and I don't think I've ever been able to read it back before.'

'I'm sure it's good for you. As you say, cathartic.' He sounds so smug and self-satisfied, like he's doing me this massive favour.

'It makes me feel sick.'

Sick, and disappointed at my sixteen-year-old self. Somewhere inside me I'd always had a small fantasy about having the opportunity to scream, really loudly—after all, it wasn't the sort of thing one often got the chance to do without the emergency services being summoned. And then, when any sort of emergency service would have been really handy, I hadn't been able to do it.

If I screamed like that now, would anybody come?

Chapter Eight
Day 2

He leaves shortly after that, muttering something about making coffee and going to read the paper, but it's clear that he needs a dump: after he's bolted my bedroom door, I hear him go into the guest bathroom and lock that door—like anyone could come in! But he strikes me as the sort of guy who habitually locks the toilet door even when he's on his own in a house. He's in there for a long time. He took my diary with him so he's probably sitting on the loo reading it. I don't think I'm ever going to be able to use that bathroom again.

What am I saying? I'm never going to be able to spend another night in this *flat* after this. Megan and I will have to move again.

I lie back on my bed, a fresh wave of hatred washing over me. Perhaps it's not even worth clearing up in here. But then I regard the mess on the floor around me and decide that I should. Putting things away might make me feel marginally better.

As I sit up again, something catches my eyes: the loft! This is a top floor flat, and the hatch is in the corner of my bedroom. I can't believe I've been in here this long and it didn't occur to me before.

I've only been up in the attic space once, to store a load of stuff when I first moved in. Donna and Henry were helping me move and

I think they were in charge of putting stuff up there, so I'm not a hundred per cent sure I would find anything useful even if I could get in—which I can't. The loft doesn't have a pull-down ladder and, obviously, I don't have a stepladder to hand. There's one in the flat, but it's in the tall cupboard in the kitchen and therefore not accessible to me. My chest of drawers is about three feet high, and the ceiling about ten. I'm five foot six, so if I stand on the chest, I won't even be able to see inside the loft, let alone climb in. So it's of no use at all to me, unless Claudio does by some miracle decide to helpfully provide me with a ladder.

As if.

I hear the toilet flush and him going into the kitchen. Presently, the smell of my Columbian coffee sneaks underneath the door on tantalising fingers, but he doesn't bring me a cup.

I spend the next two hours folding and putting all my clothes back in my chest of drawers. I can't hang my dresses back up because he confiscated all my clothes hangers, even the nice padded ones, so I fold them too and put them on the floor of my wardrobe. I work slowly and methodically and even set aside a bag of stuff that I never wear, to give to charity. It is soothing to have something physical to do, but all too soon, my heart leaps painfully into my chest as I hear the scrape of the bolt being unlocked again. I jump back into bed—I'm not sure why; perhaps because it's less confrontational—and am sitting up meekly when he comes in, clutching the duvet to my chest.

'I've brought you some lunch, darling.'

So it seems we're back to 'kind and concerned' mode, after the earlier 'snarky and aggressive'. He puts the tray down on my lap, with a plastic bowl, a mug, bread roll, apple, and a finger vase on it—mine, one that Richard bought me as a Valentine's gift once. The vase contains a rose that I can tell immediately is fake, and I wonder if the bowl contains plastic soup.

'Chicken soup,' he says proudly as if he made it himself, but I can smell that it's out of a can.

I clutch the edges of the tray to stop my hands shaking.

'How are you feeling now, my love?' His eyes are so full of pity I have to look away to prevent my expression antagonising him. 'Much better, thanks. Just been tidying up, but it made me a bit tired so I'm having a rest now.' I gesture to the much-clearer floor.

He beams. 'Excellent! I hope you like soup!'

'Yes. Thank you. I'm quite hungry. But I'll save the apple for later.'

I decide at that moment that I will stockpile food whenever I can. I'll keep anything non-perishable under my bed, if I can get away with it, in case he decides to stop feeding me. Or drops dead while I'm still locked in here.

He hovers beside my bed like he's visiting me in hospital, and we regard one another warily. I pick up the spoon—also plastic; for heaven's sake, what does he imagine I'd do with a regular spoon? Although once I start thinking about it, a few things spring to mind: stick the handle up his nose. Jab it into his eyes. Ram it hard into his testicles.

The thought of his testicles makes me lose my appetite, but I force down a spoonful of lukewarm cream of chicken.

He leans forward to watch me, planting his large hands on his thighs. 'I think you should have another afternoon in bed. You were so sick yesterday, you must still be feeling pretty weak.'

He's stalling, I can tell. I suppose he doesn't know what else to do with me.

'Do I have a choice?' I try not to sound testy. I'm torn between actually wanting to rest—as I do feel very dodgy still and I need to build up my strength, mental and physical—and dying to get out of this room already.

'Doctor Cavelli knows best,' he says, with what he probably imagines is a cheeky grin. 'But you could always just carry on pottering around clearing this lot up.' He gestures towards the remaining mess on the floor, now mostly books, shoes, old birthday cards, and board games, their contents spilled out and mixed up, a Scottie dog and a top hat lying next to Chinese Checkers and the components of Mousetrap. He spots it too and picks up the plastic trap.

'Mousetrap! I love that game. Hey, we could play later—how about that?'

'No!' I look down and meekly add, 'Thank you.'

'Oh. Right. OK then. I'll leave you to it. I'm going to cook a nice dinner for tonight. Is there anything you don't eat?'

'Um, no. Only anchovies. Can we eat at the table?' The thought of getting out of the bedroom into the kitchen lifts my spirits immeasurably. If I can just get out of this room, surely I can find something to hit him over the head with and escape?

Claudio hesitates. 'Let's see,' he says.

'Claudio, I can't stay in here forever!'

'You've been ill. I'm looking after you,' he replies stubbornly, not meeting my eyes.

'I haven't been ill. You drugged me and chained me to my bed-post.' I'm trying not to sound petulant but it's not working.

Claudio suddenly leaps up and thrusts his face in mine, roaring at me so loudly that my bowels turn to liquid and I almost soil myself. My knees jerk instinctively up and the tray with the bowl of soup and the lukewarm tea on it flips over and it all goes everywhere, soaking into the duvet.

'YOU WILL STAY HERE UNTIL I SAY YOU CAN LEAVE!'

I bite my tongue so hard I'm worried that I've actually bitten a bit off. But it's better than crying in front of him again. The scariest thing is that, for the first time, I truly believe he really is completely insane.

'Don't try my patience, Jo. I don't think you realise the sort of stress I'm under at the moment.'

I try to take deep breaths but they come out as shallow and fearful puffs. My tongue is agony.

'Sorry to hear it, Claudio. What is it? It is your work?'

I've been wondering why he's not at work—I'm sure he told me on one of our dates that he worked for a pharmaceutical company, in IT. No, wait, it's still only Sunday . . . I think . . .

'I've got the week off,' he says. 'To spend it with you. No, it's not that.' He opens his mouth as though he's about to say something else, then abruptly leans across and picks up the tray in one hand, then uses the empty plastic bowl to scoop up the dollops of soup sitting on the duvet like cat sick.

'Can you get me some clean sheets, please?' I ask him. 'They're in the cupboard in the spare room.'

He salutes with his free hand. 'Your wish is my command.'

'Let me go, then.'

There is a long, tense moment in which I immediately regret what I've said in case it provokes more aggression.

'Not until you love me,' he eventually replies, and heads towards the bedroom door. When he reaches it he turns back. 'By the way, if you even consider making a run for it when I open this door, or hiding behind it to leap out and bash me when I come in—I *will* keep you handcuffed to the bedstead. You will have to piss in a pot. I mean it.'

I nod submissively and he's gone, the now-familiar sound of the bolt shooting closed echoing in his wake. *Nice way to show you love me*, I think to myself.

Like an old, old lady, I push aside my wet bedclothes, climb out of bed, and plod over to my chest of drawers to get dressed. My legs are shaking violently and I still feel as weak as a newborn lamb. The thought makes me yearn to be in a field, frisking on fresh, green buttercup-studded grass in the morning sunshine. The sky would be the clearest blue and the sun would feel hot on my soft wool. At this moment, in the sickly yellowy light of my energy-saving light bulb, I feel more as though I've just been ushered into the slaughterhouse. I'd give anything to be in natural light and fresh air.

Will he really kill me if I can't prove I love him in a week?

Chapter Nine
Day 2

I must have still been feeling the effects of the drug because I did actually drift off to sleep again after Claudio brought in the clean sheets and I changed the bed. I felt exhausted after just that small exertion and the stress of Claudio yelling at me.

I fell into a vivid dream about Richard, Megan and I going on holiday to Balamory, the venue of the kids' TV show that Megan had a DVD box set of when she was three or four. Balamory is in reality Tobermory on the island of Mull, and we'd had a lovely week there about three years ago. In my dream we were back in our hotel, rain hammering on the windows and a grey sea boiling outside as Richard and I played Scrabble in the lounge, a room so grim and unwelcoming—gas fire, the sort of sofas you have to sit bolt upright in—that we christened it Suicide Lounge. Richard said there was nothing for it but to steal the Scrabble, play it in our room, and then take it home with us. They didn't deserve it, he said.

'But how will we take it without anyone noticing?' I asked, in my dream. I've never stolen anything in my life—too worried about getting caught.

Richard had grinned evilly. 'Tile by tile,' he said, tapping the side of his nose. 'Like in *The Great Escape*. Into the turn-ups when no-one's looking, then back to the room where we . . .' He mimed shaking the tiles out of his trouser legs and Miss Hoolie, a character from *Balamory*, called the police to have us arrested. I shouted, 'Good, yes! Call 999—I've been kidnapped!' Richard morphed into Claudio, and I woke up in a cold sweat.

The Scrabble in the lounge part of the dream had been true—Megan had mentioned it the other day, the last day before she left for her holiday, so it must have been on my mind. She had climbed into my bed—as usual, half an hour before she was allowed to—and said without preamble, 'Do you remember that time in Balamory when Daddy wanted us to steal the Scrabble?'

I hadn't remembered, but as soon as she said it, I did. My eyes immediately flooded with tears and I had to discreetly wipe them on the duvet cover while Megan played with the cat, wiggling her feet under the covers for him to pounce on. Just before the Scrabble incident we'd been out for a long, alcoholic lunch to escape the rain. Not that we even particularly cared that it was raining—our shared bi-annual holidays were sacrosanct to us both, a chance for uninterrupted family time, Richard banned from switching on his phone more than once a day so that work couldn't intrude. Sunshine would just have been an added bonus. Megan, aged four, had sat happily colouring and chatting to her felt-tips, while Richard and I polished off two bottles of wine and freshly caught sea bass.

I haven't thought about that for years, the holiday or the Scrabble. We used to play loads of Scrabble on holiday, and I can't see a Scrabble board now without imagining the accompaniment of a backdrop of sea and a chilled glass of wine.

There is so much I've forgotten about our lives together—I genuinely cannot understand how that could have happened. It's as if some evil scientist has wiped my brain clean of all our shared jokes, stories, anecdotes, rituals. It was only three years ago, for heaven's sake.

I'd forgotten them all, when the remembering would have saved us.

I'd forgotten how we both knew all the words to *Cool for Cats* and *Sultans of Swing*, and would bellow them, loudly and tunelessly, whenever either song came on the car radio, like that scene in *Wayne's World* where they're all head-banging to *Bohemian Rhapsody*, even though we were both in junior school when those songs first came out.

I'd forgotten how frequently we used to sing together, back in the old days. Neither of us can sing very well, but when we first became a couple, we used to lie in bed singing David Essex songs in Mockney accents, giggling and hamming: ''*Old* me close, don' let me go, no-oh *naw!*' Our mums had loved David Essex and one of the things we had in common was that we'd both grown up with his music in the background of our lives.

The bed was one of those tiny little doubles with a slightly rusty iron frame and a saggy mattress, which the vicar at Richard's mum's church had given us free of charge. Glad to get rid of it, probably. That was in the days before we had any money, in the mid-nineties. When Richard took me out to dinner for the first time, I was appalled that the bill came to twenty-seven pounds. It seemed the height of extravagance. How many thousands of dinners did we have, over all the years since, I sometimes wonder?

I can't do anything for a long time. I just lie there missing Richard and thinking about how I wish I had never set eyes on Sean, the catalyst for my disaster. My own personal marriage-wrecker. And now, six months after it's all over with Sean, I get *Claudio?* Give me a break!

Self-pity threatens to swamp me, so I make a conscious effort to rally. I remember when I was a kid my mum saying, 'If you're upset, go and clean out a cupboard.' Although 'upset' is an understatement in this situation, I take her point and decide to attack the remaining chaos on my bedroom floor.

As I'm sitting cross-legged on the carpet separating tiny components from board games into piles, there's a scratching at my door, and a tentative mew. Lester! Claudio must have left the kitchen door open. I crawl across to the door—it seems easier than standing up and walking—and lie down on my belly, whispering to him through the gap at the bottom.

'Hey, baby, how are you? Is he feeding you? Are you OK? Can you go raise the alarm for me, eh? *Mew once if you're in Cincinnati.*' I'm paraphrasing a line from *Anchorman* that Ron Burgundy says to his dog on the phone, and it almost makes me giggle. Not quite, though.

Richard and I love that movie.

In response, Lester slides a paw beneath the door and scrapes at the carpet by my face. I stroke the top of his soft foot and hear the low rumble of his purr, followed by a gentle flopping sound as he collapses onto the floor, pushing his front leg as far as he can through the gap. It is so comforting that it makes me cry. We lie like that for a long time.

Some time later I hear Claudio's footsteps coming out of the kitchen and down the hall.

'Hello, cat,' he says. Lester's foot vanishes from my view and I sit up, feeling light-headed. 'Jo, I've been Googling recipes for tonight. I'm just popping out to Sainsbury's. I thought I'd got everything I needed yesterday but I'm missing a few ingredients and you don't have them.' He says this like an accusation. 'Do you need anything?'

'Can you let Lester in here?'

There is a pause.

'Please?'

Another pause. 'Well, I don't see why not,' Claudio says, unbolting the door and opening it just enough for Lester to squeeze his narrow tabby body through. I'm so happy to see him that for the first time my heart doesn't sink when Claudio locks me in again.

'Hello, my baby, my darling,' I croon like the mad cat-lady I'm bound to end up as—assuming I even make it out of here alive.

I gather him into my arms and press his dusty warm fur into my face. He struggles and protests so I let him go; he is happier to weave around my legs until he flops down again, on top of an Aran sweater which in turn is covering up most of a manila A4 envelope that I hadn't noticed before in all the mess. I pull it out from underneath him and open it curiously, to find several typed sheets of paper. When I realise what it is, I make a sound that is half-sob, half-laugh. It's the copy I made of the printout of every single text that Sean ever sent me, over the course of our eleven-month relationship. I typed them up myself on my laptop, painstakingly transcribing all those emotions because I couldn't bear the thought of losing them.

Claudio's gone out. I hear the front door close then, faintly, the door to the street. I'm going to have another go at screaming. I don't think it will do much good but I have to try. My bedroom and bathroom are at the back looking down over a few small squares of unloved gardens, and the front of the building is on a busy road where there's a lot of traffic noise.

This flat was only ever meant to be a temporary base for me and Megan after the divorce, and one good thing about this situation is that now I am definitely going to move. I don't want to spend another night longer than I have to here, and I don't want Megan back here now that Claudio has sullied it for us with his sweaty hands and crazy delusions.

I wait five minutes and then go and stand by the boarded-up window, take a massive deep breath, and scream as loudly as I can, for as long as I can. I imagine a little huddle of concerned bystanders congregating in someone's back garden and it helps. They'll be listening intently: *'Did you hear that? That's a woman screaming. Doesn't sound good to me. Shall we ring the police?'*

'Yes, let's. Better safe than sorry . . .'

After a few minutes my throat is raw and my ears are ringing. I pause for breath and listen hard for the sound of sirens. But there is nothing. I try screaming 'FIRE!'—I heard once that this brings people faster than if you just shout for help because there's more of a potential threat to their own safety and possessions. Still nothing.

'Richard,' I scream instead in desperation. 'Help me! Richard!'

I will him to appear as if by magic in my bedroom. I feel his warm arms around me, and his lips against my ear, whispering soothing words.

'Oh thank God you're here! I knew you'd come!'

When I find myself saying the words out loud, I think that perhaps I have gone completely mad.

Richard is the man I loved more deeply than I've ever loved anybody else. But not more passionately. There have only been two men in my life I've loved with real passion, one of whom was John. That all ended in tears, and no-one else came close to inspiring that intensity of feeling in me, until I met Sean.

Sean is the reason that Richard and I didn't get back together. Sean is the reason I'm on my own now. Sean is the reason that I can't believe I will ever love anybody again. I sit down on the bed, exhausted and upset and beyond caring at the bitter, melodramatic turn my thoughts have taken. The vision of Richard has vanished from my mind, and I feel consumed with resentment for Sean. If I'd never met him, I wouldn't be in this situation now. If he materialised in my room right now I think I'd slap him.

I think of Richard rubbing my back when I was ill, and before I know it I'm crying again.

Even before Claudio weaselled his way onto the scene, this was not how I wanted my life to be.

When I get out of here, I'm going to have to do something to change things. I can't go on like this. I don't like this person I have turned into: she is not me. All I want is a family again. Security, stability, a future. I made a mistake and I want to put it right in any way I can, given that going back is not an option. Not too much to ask—is it?

Chapter Ten
Day 2

I met Sean two years ago, soon after Stephanie and I started renting an office together. Steph and I have been friends for years; she used to be my neighbour until she moved in with her glamorous footballer boyfriend. Since we're both freelance we decided that it would make sense to share an office—tax deductible and fewer distractions than working from home. Once we moved in, we then decided we spent far too much time sitting around eating croissants and gossiping and that we should both join the gym next door. We also thought that it would be a good way for her to meet a new man, since the men in our shared office complex were no great shakes, and she'd recently had another bust-up with the glamorous footballer boyfriend, who unfortunately loved himself as much as she loved him.

She had very exacting standards, being a sports journalist (her half of the office was full of books with titles like *Bestie, Foggy, Hizzy, Cloughie* and *Deano*) and thus accustomed to dealing with the more physically perfect of the male species. My first thought on clapping eyes on Sean was, honestly, that he'd be perfect for Steph. After all, I wasn't looking for anyone. I thought I was happy with Richard.

It's a bit embarrassing that Sean was my personal trainer. What a cliché. It's like having an affair with your tennis coach: the fit young man who comes into your life and expertly shows you how to make it better. But two years ago I thought I was only signing up for personal training, for a limited course of physical pain. Stephanie never got a look-in, and I bloody wish now she had. What price a tight arse, eh?

The first time I ever saw Sean, I was on the treadmill on a quiet Tuesday lunchtime. Stephanie had gone to interview Frankie Dettori for a feature she was writing, so I didn't have her to chat and puff to as I usually did. There was some tedious documentary about ants on the wall-mounted TV, so of course my eyes had drifted elsewhere, and there he was. He had the biggest shoulders I'd ever seen outside of a Chippendales calendar, his eyes were cerulean blue, and he even had dimples. He smiled a lot, not in a 'wow, it makes me happy to be this gorgeous' way, but in a warm, open way. I couldn't wait to tell Stephanie. He was so good-looking.

I could tell that his client, an ungainly blonde almost as tall as he was, felt the same as me—she gazed into his eyes every time she straightened up from her squats. I was jealous. I thought, 'I don't care how much it costs, I want to gaze into his eyes too.'

I didn't for a second want to lose Richard. We were still married then—happily, I thought, although the lack of sex and the long hours he worked did bug me—but I had never felt such a physical pull towards someone else. Not since John, anyway, and that had been well over twenty years ago. When I first saw Sean, I couldn't stop looking at him.

I went straight to reception and signed up for twelve personal training sessions. It cost a fortune, but I didn't care; we could afford it. There had to be some compensation for Richard working four hundred-hour weeks. The woman on the desk—my age, too much Botox—asked if I had a preference as to which trainer I wanted, and I said, trying to look casual, 'The one who's upstairs at the moment? He seems to know what he's talking about. I'd like him.'

She laughed, in a bitter sort of way, and said, 'Of course you would. That's Sean. *Everyone* would like Sean.'

I was so nervous before our first session. I bought a load of new Nike gear, cleaned my trainers till they sparkled, and just about resisted the temptation to get my hair blow-dried in Sean's honour. I'd told Stephanie I was having personal training—but when it came down to it, I found that I didn't want to confess my feelings for the trainer, as I'd assumed I would. That, right there, should have warned me that I ought to proceed with more caution—Steph and I always told each other about our little harmless crushes.

'Hello,' he said when I arrived, trembling, at the gym, smiling at me and holding out his large, strong hand for me to shake. 'Are you ready?'

Boy, was I ever ready. He took my blood pressure—that was nice, his hands slipping the little cuff up my arm, the pump squeezing it tight like an embrace. I wasn't quite so happy when he made me get on the scales, mind you. Still, I just closed my eyes and thought—

What did I think? That I'd lose my marriage? That Sean and I would be together forever? That I'd ever betray Richard? That heading down this road of insanity would end up with me a captive in my own bedroom? No. None of those. I don't know what I thought. I guess I wasn't thinking at all, beyond breathing in his pheromone-y sweet smell, and the sheer bulk of him. The only pain was in my abs, as I groaned and flailed in a pool of sweat on the red mat—and that was made bearable by the proximity of his hand, hovering over my midriff.

'Just a few more,' he'd say, in that firm but amused voice, which, coming from anyone else, would have made me want to punch them in the throat. I must have *really* liked him, to put myself through all that. Gyms are unpleasant enough when you're just pottering along on the Stairmaster in a big t-shirt, trying to ignore the glamorous petite girls in skin-tight Lycra. But having to lie there, puce and sweating, in front of a row of captive spectators on the tread-mills . . . now there's dedication.

The hour was over far too quickly. We hadn't talked much— I tried to quiz him, but it was hard to ask questions when I couldn't even breathe. I managed to find out roughly where he lived, though, that he was thirty-four, lived alone, did a lot of rowing in his spare time, and was a semi-professional pool player.

After the session, I could barely walk, and I had muscles aching in places I hadn't even known I had *places*. But all I remembered was his blue eyes, and the brush of his fingers on my skin whenever he was showing me the correct technique for a move. I floated home, lactic acid and hormones streaming in equal proportions around my body.

Ugh. I don't think I'm ever going to fancy a man again, ever. I don't want to think about Sean any more, or Richard . . . Yet some-how I can't seem to stop myself reading a selection from the first page of Sean's texts:

- *Hello beautiful! Just finished work . . . your gorgeous smile hasn't left my mind 4 one minute . . . I'm the luckiest man on earth, you are AMAZING! Love you, sexy beast XXX*
- *You are mine 2 . . . Didn't ever think I was capable of loving someone as much as this. You're amazing! X*
- *Went 2 sleep thinking of you, woke up thinking of you & dreamt of you in the middle . . . am I in love or what?*
- *I've only ever wanted 2 love & be loved by one special person . . . so lucky 2 have found someone as amazing as you! (sorry 4 soppiness!) XX*
- *You are the best and I love you so much . . . XXX*
- *SO lovely 2 be close 2 you again, you are so beautiful . . . will be thinking of you in my dreams angel! XXX*
- *I am completely loved up with you. What have you done 2 me!! I love being in love with you. Marry me someday angel! XXX*

The document makes interesting reading: the history of a relationship in bite-sized chunks, from infatuation to passion to desperation to frustration to . . . well, weary politeness, by the end, I suppose.

When he dumped me, I printed out two copies. It took thirty-five sheets of A4 to print each one—there were hundreds and hundreds of texts. Then I posted one of the copies to him. I wanted him to read them, to remember how he'd felt about me. I didn't know whether I wanted him to feel bad about it, or whether I hoped that they would somehow change his mind and rekindle the depth of passion we'd had.

Sean and I broke up six months ago, but I sent him a text just the other day. It's funny, but whenever I miss Richard, I text Sean instead. I suppose it's because in my head Sean is the reason I lost Richard, and I can't quite believe that here I am, alone, with neither of them. I can't have Richard, but perhaps, just perhaps, I could get Sean back again and then it would all have been worthwhile.

'*Remember the tower?*' my text said. '*Remember how cold it was? We kept each other warm. No need to reply.*'

But Sean, being a contrary bastard, replied almost immediately: '*Of course I remember. That was the best time in my entire life. XXX*'

We'd gone away for a long weekend, about three months after I left Richard, when Sean and I had recently become an official couple. It was the first time we'd been away together. Sean arranged it all on the internet—he had rented this odd little tower on the south coast, kind of like a windmill without sails, or a lighthouse without a light. It had a round kitchen and bathroom on the ground floor, stairs up to a round living room, more stairs up to a round bedroom, then more stairs to a tiny roof terrace. It was October and freezing cold. The tower had no central heating and our breath puffed out in clouds both inside and out.

The entire weekend was a blissful, romantic cliché. We spent the whole time walking on deserted beaches, through leaf-blown bleak woods, or huddled under the duvet with the rain lashing against the tower windows. It was utterly, utterly magical. We had sex in as many different places and at as many different times as we could: up trees, in sand dunes, on the kitchen counter, in the bath, on the roof terrace of the tower; dawn, midnight, lunchtime . . . I see it now like a scene in a movie, a wordless montage of togetherness. He told me he loved me a hundred times a day. He *cried* because he loved me so much, and couldn't believe that we were finally together; that he'd finally found the woman he was going to marry.

This is what I've been missing all these years, I'd thought, drunk on love and lust. *This is what I want to do for the rest of my life.* Sean would just have to stretch out a hand to me and before we could say a word we'd both be naked, and I'd be on him or him in me, gazing into each other's eyes, moving together . . . it was magical.

But I suppose that's not what love is all about. You can't spend your entire lives locked up in towers, ivory or otherwise, walking on beaches, having fabulous sex. You can't. Because there are children to look after, bins to put out, direct debits to sort, livings to be made. There is baggage: so much baggage! Guilt and regret and recriminations.

Obvious, really—but when you're in your tower, none of that matters. You think that because you feel that strongly then and there, you will always feel that strongly. You are invincible, because you have discovered what love really is.

Except that you are wrong.

I loved Sean, still love Sean, perhaps will always love Sean. But I want Richard back. Richard loved me more, and I pushed him away. I made an enormous mistake, and it's too late to change it now. It might be too late to change anything now.

Chapter Eleven
Day 2

If I can manage to convince myself that I'm here to help Claudio, I can just about keep the panic under control. I tell myself that he is a disturbed, lonely individual who is desperate for company and who I'm helping by talking to him. All I have to do is be able to fool him into thinking I love him. I've pretended to love people before—and in Richard's case, the pretence became reality. Claudio's not going to hurt me, if I can pull it off. He's not showing any signs of violence. He can't keep me here forever. He wouldn't really kill me.

Would he?

I'm still kind of annoyed that Claudio wasn't an internet date. It would be so much more . . . what? Credible? Interesting? Horrific? I could become the poster child for anti-internet dates. I could set up my own website and helpline. Whereas in fact the worst thing that ever happened to me on an internet date was Gerald screaming at me (which was, admittedly, quite bad).

Oh, and there was Dirk. That was pretty disastrous, but in a 'makes a good dinner party story' way rather than a 'life in danger' sort of way. Dirk and I had got along like a house on fire by email and on the phone. I'd seen photos and he didn't appear too hideous, but it was his astounding intellect that had really impressed me. *The brain is the body's biggest erogenous zone*, I kept telling myself, feeling a nascent tickle of sexual excitement after the first long telephone call. Here was a man who could teach me things I didn't know. He used words in conversation that I had to look up in the dictionary—'palimpsest', 'sublunary', 'nosocomial'—and I was far more impressed than I ought to have been. Particularly since anybody who actually manages to shoehorn those sorts of words into a casual sentence has got to be a total prat. But when I met him, my heart instantly plummeted. He looked like Elton John, short and podgy, with lots of teeth all clamouring for attention. Over insanely expensive cocktails at the Groucho, he was, within the hour, telling me about the night—not that long ago—he spent fifteen hundred quid on prostitutes and cocaine. Four prostitutes, all at the same time. I was shocked.

'Are you shocked?' he asked, perhaps hopefully, perhaps shamefacedly. I couldn't quite tell which.

'No, not at all,' I lied, trying to stop my eyes bugging out. Then he told me a story about when he got caught short whilst driving along the M62 and had to pull over onto the hard shoulder and do a poo over a fence. Not quite sure how he got onto that subject after the coke and hookers, but never mind.

'No kidding, Jo, it was the size of a wine bottle,' he said, in a matter-of-fact voice. 'I do have this big self-destruct streak,' he added miserably.

I didn't say anything, but I mentally agreed that he probably did. See, I knew lots of people had one; it wasn't just me. I ditched him the next day, declining his offer of a second date. He sent me a sad little text: YOU'D BE AMAZED AT HOW GOOD I LOOK WHEN I'VE DROPPED A STONE. Personally, I don't think I'd have been all that amazed. Plus, it made me think of the wine bottle again. Poor Dirk.

Anyway, Dirk and his wine-bottle-sized al fresco faeces fade into insignificance next to the horrors of Gerald and Claudio. Surely probability would indicate that my chances of meeting a decent man ought to be increased, not decreased, by the number of dates I've been on? I must have been on twenty dates in the last six months. It had become like a drug, a dependency. With the anticipation of every single date came the hope that maybe, if this one worked out, it'd prove that leaving Richard *was* the right thing to do after all, and not just another crashingly obvious example of my utterly crap instincts.

Like going out for that meal with Claudio when I'd already realised I didn't fancy him anymore.

I swear that if I ever get out of here, I am going to pretend that I met Claudio on a dating website, and then write an article about it for *The Daily Mail*. Medical writing can be so dry—I'd like to get into journalism. Try to get something positive out of all this. And I'm never going on another date ever again.

It's five o'clock in the afternoon and he's back in my room. He came in when he got back from Sainsbury's, carefully locked the door behind him, and put on some testosterone-y thriller movie that I don't recognise and couldn't be less interested in. Unbelievable! He sidled over and sat on my bed, almost as if he was hoping I'd snuggle into his side with a smile. When I shrank away to the most distant corner of the mattress, he sat uncomfortably upright to watch the TV, stubbornly gazing at the screen. He's mad. I wish there was a chair in here so he didn't have to keep sitting on the bed.

I've still got six days to convince him. I'm not going to spend all of them fawning over him: I'll have to work my way up to it, otherwise it definitely won't be credible.

The film seems to have been going on for*ever*. I have no idea what's happening and couldn't care less—there are a lot of shootings and explosions. I'd rather have *Bargain Hunt* on. I'd certainly rather not have Claudio polluting what little air there is in my bedroom. I am itching to scream at him to get out, but I can't. I can't speak. Maybe he'll leave when the movie ends, but it's clearly the world's longest film.

Time is a tricky customer. I find it hard to believe I've only been here for a day and a half, when I think about the number of times I've got angry at being held up by mere seconds: by the tap that you have to turn three times before any water emerges; the traffic light that remains stubbornly red for minutes on end; the call centre that plays you wavery classical music while you're on hold . . . All of these things, which are utterly out of my control. Shouting at taps or traffic lights never speeds them up.

I *could* shout at Claudio, though. I could change this.

My instinct tells me to do something, anything. But then the old fear comes sweeping back over me—what is the point of trusting my instincts? It's never made any difference before and I would only do the wrong thing. If I had decent instincts, I'd never have walked down that alley. I'd never have gone on that first date with Sean. I'd never have left Richard. I'd have immediately walked out of Pizza Express when I first set eyes on Gerald. And I'd certainly never have agreed to go out with Claudio.

Surely it's better to sit passively and mentally practise how to convince him of my 'love', than risk disaster by provoking him? I have to think of Megan. I have to be risk averse, for her sake.

But I can't. I can't just do nothing! My thoughts are whirling around in claustrophobic circles. I will think of something. I have to.

I look over at Claudio, who is doggedly watching the film whilst trying and failing to look relaxed. He is sweating, even though it is not particularly warm in here with the fan on and the sun blocked out. I almost—*almost*—wish he would flip out, just so the decision will have been made for me, and something will have happened.

'Are you hot?' I enquire.

He looks at me and an expression of pleasure, almost fondness, crosses his face. Does he really think I'm starting to care? He's deluded. But perhaps this might just be easier than I thought.

'Yes, it's very warm in here, isn't it?'

'Wouldn't it be lovely to go out?' I say, trying to keep my voice light. 'It must be beautiful outside. Just think of going to sit in a park with a rug and a picnic.'

It's not hard to make myself sound wistful. I can see it: families playing ball, a cool breeze on my skin, the prickle of grass stems beneath my bare feet, the sun reddening my face. Birds swooping and calling from the expanse of blue sky above me.

Of course Claudio is not part of this image, but he doesn't need to know that.

'It would be lovely. Obviously it can't happen.' He wipes sweat off his forehead, then wipes his hand on my empty duvet cover (the duvet itself is at the foot of the bed—far too hot for that). I make a mental note to turn it upside down and the other way round before I sleep under it tonight.

'Not yet, obviously. But soon, maybe?' I force myself to smile at him.

'Maybe,' he says. 'If you ever decide to be a bit nicer to me.'

'Give me time, Claudio. It's a big adjustment. I never was good at falling for people straight away. It took years for me to fall in love with Richard.'

I'm not sure if it's a mistake to mention Richard or not. His expression doesn't change.

'You fell for that Sean bloke pretty fast, didn't you?'

I swallow my shock. How the hell does he know about Sean?

'Sean?' I stall.

'Your ex-boyfriend, I believe?'

'How do you know about him?' It's a huge struggle to keep my voice steady, and I'm dreading the answer. What if he's been stalking me for months?

He laughs. 'You look shocked. I found a card in the filing cabinet in the front room. From him to you, dated last year. He mentioned how fast you fell for each other . . . along with a whole load of other slushy stuff.' Bitter, jealous voice. 'Mr Lover-Lover Man, by the sound of him.'

'Sean was full of shit,' I reply.

He's been going through my stuff again. I know the card he means, and he must have dug very deep to find that, because I hid it from Megan. I couldn't bear to part with it so I put it in the hanging file with my bloody utilities bills. Claudio's even been through my household finances? My life is in that filing cabinet: bank statements, IVF correspondence, divorce papers. He must know every little thing about me.

'You loved him, though, didn't you?'

'I thought I did.'

'What does he do?'

'Personal trainer.'

Claudio snorts derisively and I can't bear to talk about it any more. 'We're missing the film—what just happened?' Fortunately there is a big explosion on screen and Claudio's attention drifts back to the television.

'I don't know. Shhh.'

I'm only too happy to *shhh*. I sit there seething. I feel as though he's undressed me and is examining my naked body with a magnifying glass. I wrap my arms around myself and try not to rock.

What will I do if he gets fed up with my coldness and forces himself on me? I try to remember some of the moves from a long-distant self-defence class but find I've forgotten everything about that class apart from the fact that the instructor wore skin-tight Lycra that left nothing to the imagination, like he was using his lunchbox as a weapon.

I don't *ever* want to see Claudio's lunchbox.

Keep calm, Jo. You have to keep calm. There was that flicker of pleasure when I asked him if he was too hot—maybe I should start trying to flirt outright with him? I can't. Can I? Oh, I don't know! I need advice. I wish I could talk to Donna.

I think back to my dating experiences to see if I can extract anything valuable from them. Other men have acted as though they were in love with me after just a few dates, when they couldn't possibly have been. They just wanted to be in love with someone, and I vaguely fitted the bill. All those lonely, desperate men. And I have managed to find the loneliest and most desperate without him even needing to write an online dating profile!

Ironic, really—the most over-used line in men's profiles on the websites is 'I'm happy going out, but equally happy staying in, curled up on the couch with a bottle of red wine and a DVD.' (Apparently the women over-use the exact same line, only they still say 'video' instead of 'DVD'. Go figure.) I always immediately discount anybody who says this, on the grounds that they clearly have no imagination. Yes, it is a lovely thing to do with someone you care about. But why do so many people have to cite it as the ultimate example of social interaction? Or is it merely a euphemism for having sex on the sofa with the telly on in the background? And now here we are, not exactly curled up on the sofa, but watching a film in (reluctant) close proximity, Claudio's warped facsimile of a night in.

'Claudio, I'm hungry,' I say, and he looks sharply at me. I'm not at all hungry: I just want him out of my bedroom.

'Again? I'm going to cook later. It's too early for dinner now,' he says sulkily.

'Why don't we phone for a takeaway, save you the bother?'

Unsurprisingly, Claudio greets this suggestion with derision. 'I think not.'

'Would you like me to cook instead? I could rustle something up. A risotto or something. Or use what you bought.'

He hesitates and on cue I actually hear his stomach rumbling. Yes, I think, that was a good idea. After all, it seems that part of the genesis of this ludicrous situation is that he wants a girlfriend. He wants someone who'll stay, voluntarily. Having a woman cook for him would make him feel normal. Ha. What a sodding nutter. Was he this mad when we were at school, or has it happened since he grew up? I rack my brains to try to remember if he had girlfriends when I first knew him. I never saw him with anybody.

'Let me look in the fridge?'

He hesitates again.

'No,' he says eventually. 'I told you, I went out earlier and got some stuff for a curry. *I'm* going to cook us dinner. You need to rest. You're still not well. And I want us to talk more tonight, about the old days, when we were still at school.'

'You will let me have my diary again, then? I've got such an awful memory; I'll need it to remind myself of what was going on.'

He narrows his eyes at me, but he does go and get it, which gets him off my bed. That at least is a huge relief. When he brings it back to me and leaves again and I hear the bolt shooting home behind him, I leap off the bed, switch off the movie, and sit cross-legged in the middle of my mattress. He's left his stink behind, a miasma of BO that I can't get rid of. I don't even have any perfume to spray around the place.

Time to regroup. Why didn't I go for him? Throw the TV at him, take him by surprise by jabbing my fingers in his eyes? I had so many opportunities.

Because I'm scared of what he'll do to me in retaliation. I have a horrible realisation: that my excuse about faulty instincts is merely a way of kidding myself that I'm brave, when all along the truth is that I'm an absolute coward.

I can't help wondering what sort of a cook Claudio is. Under these circumstances, anything he cooks for me will taste like ashes in my mouth, so it's not like I care or anything, unless it involves anything I can use as a weapon. I wonder if he'll serve it up on Megan's plastic plates. I've got some wasabi paste in the fridge—if I can distract him long enough to get it, perhaps I could rub it into his eyes.

I'm just relieved he's left me in peace, and that I have my diary back, even if only temporarily. Every cloud.

Thinking those words makes me shudder. That's what John used to call Claudio—Cloud. One cloud is quite enough.

I do think it's important that a man is a good cook. It's such an attractive trait—apart from in psycho kidnappers, obviously. Longingly, I make a mental list of some of Richard's past repertoire of dinners, until my mouth actually starts to water:

— Skate wing on a bed of puy lentils
— Tuna steak with water chestnut and chilli sauce
— Garlic-stuffed lamb with celeriac mash
— Grilled halloumi cheese with fresh mint and baked sweet potatoes
— Roasted duck with a pomegranate salad and toasted garlic croutons.

Sean, on the other hand, was a rubbish cook. His idea of a good lunch was a packet of Nice 'n' Spicy Monster Munch with a warm Greggs sausage roll. I amuse myself briefly by compiling another list, of *his* top meals:

— Delivery pizza the size of a dustbin lid (regular toppings, unless being particularly adventurous, in which case, shredded chicken and BBQ sauce)
— Chicken in Quick Sauce, if trying to impress
— Large fry-up
— If in a restaurant: chicken, in any form
— No fish whatsoever, unless battered and from a chip shop
— Kebab
— McDonald's or Burger King burger.

I wonder how I'm even able to amuse myself in this situation. I'd have thought I would still be panicking. But what would be the point of that? I've tried to pull the wood off the windows but there's no way of extracting those screws without tools. I've tried screaming. I have no other way of contacting anybody.

It does help being in my own room, with Lester, and I know Megan is safe. I am also optimistically assuming that I won't be in here for longer than another day or two. I'm sure I can talk sense into Claudio. I'm going to do it at dinner tonight.

I don't want to think about Claudio, Sean, or Richard any more. I pick up the diary instead.

Chapter Twelve
Day 2

20th December 1986

I didn't get out of bed all day. Mum let me pretend I was ill. She even made me a sandwich with boiled egg chopped up and mixed with Bovril, my favourite. But I couldn't eat it. I was too embarrassed. I decided I was never going to get up again, ever. It was because the police had come over—Mum had insisted on calling them.

'I wish to report an assault on my daughter.' She sounded so haughty, and I knew it was because she was as embarrassed as I was.

Shortly afterwards two officers, a woman and a man, turned up at our house and sat like stereotypes drinking tea in the sitting room, their black uniforms taking up too much space and making me feel claustrophobic.

'Just tell us what happened in your own words, if you can, love,' said the woman PC, the hand holding her mug hovering indecisively over the coffee table, as she tried to think where she could put it without damaging the table's polished surface. I picked one of my English books off the floor—To Kill A Mockingbird—and gestured for the WPC to leave her tea on it in lieu of a coaster.

The hairy-eyebrowed constable pulled a small spiral-bound notepad out of his breast pocket. 'Wouldn't you like your dad to be here too?' he asked me kindly, glancing round the room as if Dad was hiding under the sofa or behind the TV, waiting for an invitation to join us. I didn't mean to make anyone feel even more uncomfortable but I couldn't help it. I said, 'Yes. But he's dead.'

The constable and Mum both looked pained.

'Oh, you poor thing.' The WPC patted my knee and glared at her colleague. 'Rightyho, let's crack on, if you feel up to it.'

I relayed the story, about the man's cold pouncing hands, balaclava, and cheap jacket, but when I got to the part where he touched me, I was stumped. What was the right way to say where he touched me? 'Bottom' was too far west. 'Front bottom' too embarrassing for words. Surely not 'on my vagina', even though that was anatomically correct. But other than 'vagina' I could only think of 'pussy', and one could never say that to a police officer. It was so humiliating.

'—on my . . . in my . . . he touched my . . .' I bloody struggled with the words every bit as hard as I struggled last night until, after what seemed like hours, the WPC came to my rescue. 'In between your legs?' she supplied.

Why hadn't I thought of that? Discreet, accurate, painless . . . Mum was scrutinising her fingernails with great interest, but I saw the tear roll down her face when I said yes.

When I got to the bit about Mac Boy coming to my rescue, I realised for the first time that I hadn't stopped to thank him.

'And what did he look like, this young man?'

The WPC sounded impressed and slightly wistful, as though she was wishing that a nice young man would swoop in and rescue her from something too.

'Um . . . he was short, about five foot four I think,'—at this point the WPC seemed to lose interest again—'Brown straight hair, a

macintoshy-type coat, you know, one of those beige ones with a checked lining. I think he goes to St Edmund's actually. He looked sort of familiar.'

'We'll need to speak to him. We'll have a word at the school, ask him to come forward.'

The thought of a headmaster standing up in assembly at the boys' school and booming, 'Will the boy who stopped someone from sexually assaulting Jo Singer in an alley please come forward now?' is too horrific to contemplate. It must have shown on my face because she added, 'Discreetly, of course, and mentioning no names.' Thank God for that.

The PC snapped shut his notepad and tried to slide it back into his breast pocket, but its spirals snagged in the thick black serge, and he ended up jabbing it in, creasing the cardboard cover. 'Thank you very much, Miss Singer. It's very brave of you to come forward. And brave of the lad who chased him off too. We don't recommend the public getting involved as a rule, but in this case, it seemed to do the trick. You're a lucky lass. We'll see ourselves out.'

I don't feel particularly lucky. I feel completely drained, as if someone's pulled out a plug in my heel. I miss Dad so much, more than ever, even worse than at the funeral. It is intolerable that he isn't here to make it all better.

The WPC stood up and congratulated me, like I'd just won something. 'Well done,' she said as she put her hat on and smoothed her black skirt over her thighs. That was when the doorbell went. I guessed it was probably Donna, wondering why I hadn't gone to training that night.

For one brief second I had this fantasy that it would be Dad standing there, his arms open wide to comfort me. But of course it was Donna on the doorstep, shivering but pink-cheeked, her sports bag in one hand and a Smiths carrier bag in the other. Her short wet hair had clumped into frosty spikes above the collar of her Barbour, and I could smell the chlorine on her from the hallway.

'*Crikey, Jo, let me in, it's freezing out here. Where were you, you skiver? Loads of people didn't turn up tonight, and Slug had a right nark about it. You're down for the fifty-yard backstroke in the B team on Saturday . . . Hey, look what I found in the alley! I don't want it, of course, but it's the sort of crap that you probably like.*'

She thrust the Final Countdown *single at me, and then noticed the big scrapes down the side of my face, and my swollen lip. 'Oh my God, Jo, what happened? Did you fall off your bike?*'

'*I don't want it,*' *I said, handing the Smiths bag back to Donna again. 'Get rid of it. Please.*'

Donna took it and put it in her sports bag. 'Come on, Jo,' *she said uncertainly. 'It's only Europe. It's a good song! Well, not bad, for an American hair band. Hairband! That's funny. They all look like they need hairbands.*'

I feel bad for what happened next. It wasn't her fault. But I sort of screamed at her, something about why she always had to make a joke out of everything. Then I ran upstairs and slammed the bedroom door so hard that a crack appeared down the middle of it.

I suppose I'll have to apologise soon. I don't even know if Mum told her or not. She hasn't rung me.

Some things just aren't funny, though.

Chapter Thirteen
Day 2

I can't read any more; it's really not helping. Don't I have any diaries from happier years? Perhaps I gave up keeping them after 1987, with some kind of prescience that my future self wouldn't want to revisit the girl I was then.

I have a sudden random flash of inspiration and dash into the bathroom. Somewhere I have a packet of Diazepam the doctor gave me when I sprained my knee doing aerobics. I could crush them up and slip them into Claudio's drink, return the favour. I don't remember seeing them in the pile of banned contraband that he unearthed yesterday. I haven't got around to tidying up the bathroom yet—but sifting through the packets and toiletries on the floor doesn't yield anything more potent than Lemsips and Bisodol. Damn. Where are they?

It's 7.00 p.m. and I'm scared, hot, bored, and fed up. It's suddenly got really stuffy in here even with the desk fan on all the time. The ribbons of cool air on my face feel like the only good thing in the world. Claudio is still cooking.

My room is almost completely tidy again, and I've put back all the contents of my bedside drawers apart from a load of paperwork

I'm now aimlessly sifting through whilst sitting cross-legged on the carpet in front of the fan, listening glazed-eyed to the radio. People chatting about films I haven't seen and probably won't ever. I'd forgotten I had this radio until Claudio dumped it on the floor with the rest of my stuff.

My throat is raw from screaming earlier.

I want to have a shower but I'm worried that Claudio will come in, having decided he's been 'patient for long enough', or whatever fresh hell is going on in his head. There's no lock on the bathroom door. The thought of him seeing me naked makes me feel so vulnerable that I imagine myself shrinking to the size of a drinking straw and slipping down the bath plughole. Right now I'd take my chances with drains and rats and claggy wads of hair.

I'm fretting continuously about whether he's serious in his insane proclamation, until dread has blunted and exhausted me.

I hear my bedroom door being unlocked and all my muscles immediately tense into fight-or-flight mode. Either would be good, I think grimly, but I'm too scared to do the former—Claudio is a big guy—and the second isn't an option. Not yet.

'Dinner's ready, darling!' He comes in, smiling, holding one of Megan's flowery plastic beakers.

'Little pre-dinner drinkypoos?' he chirps, and hands it to me. I take it wordlessly. 'I'll give you five minutes to get a tiny bit dressed up. Just knock when you're ready and I will escort my lady to the table!' He laughs like the maniac he so obviously is, and exits.

Oh shit. He really is insane.

I grab a brown spotty silk dress from the pile on my closet floor and put it on. It used to be a struggle to do it up—the top of the zip would sometimes snag the skin under my armpit—but I notice that it's already much looser on me. Shame, because I know I will never wear it again once I get out of here. I'll burn it, and everything else that I associate with Claudio.

Then I comb my hair with my fingers, slick some lip gloss on my lips, and powder my nose. When I see myself in the mirror I almost get a fright at the sight of the black circles under my eyes and the pinched expression on my white face. Overnight, several grey hairs have appeared on either side of my parting, and fine wrinkles that have nothing to do with laughter lines now decorate my cheeks. If I'm still here in a week, God forbid, I'll look about eighty.

Claudio comes back to escort me to dinner, which involves him tying my hands behind my back with one of my confiscated silk scarves. I submit meekly. I'm going to do things his way tonight. He shows me into the kitchen and pulls out a chair from the table. Or rather, I should say he shows me into my own kitchen and pulls out one of *my* chairs, from *my* table. He didn't untie my hands first so it isn't possible to sit naturally. I perch, leaning forward like I'm about to be executed.

Yet I feel heady with relief at getting out of my room into the familiarity of the rest of the flat, Lester weaving round Claudio's ankles. A new chair to sit in, different walls to look at, fragrant scents of ginger and coconut coming from the hob and, best of all, a summer evening outside a window I can actually see out of. Not a great deal to see as my kitchen window only looks out at the blank second-floor wall of the house next door, but at least it's real, actual light. I wonder why he hasn't boarded up the kitchen window too, but I suppose he's realised that even if by some miracle I managed to smash the double-glazing I wouldn't be able to do much else.

At least he hasn't harmed Lester, who actually seems to have taken to him. Furry traitor. If this was a horror movie Lester would be in deep trouble. I refuse to think that he might be.

Claudio pours me another plastic beaker of white wine, out of a wine box on the counter, and puts it on the table in front of me, where of course I can't touch it because my hands are tied. The first beaker is still in my room. I downed it in four gulps as I got dressed. I have to be careful not to drink too much, though.

He seems to have thought of everything, down to a wine box instead of a bottle.

'You look beautiful, Jo,' he says. 'I love your dress.'

He looks odd—defensive and simultaneously slightly thrilled, as if we were on a hot date. He's dressed up, too, in a cream linen suit over an open-necked blue linen shirt, so I presume he believes we *are* on a date. He must have gone home at some stage and brought back clothes, unless he'd packed a suitcase in advance and put it in the boot of his car . . . no, wait . . .

'How did we get back here from your place? Where's my car?'

'It's here. I drove it back the other night because you were . . . unwell.'

Unconscious, rather. Still, it was faintly reassuring to know that my car was outside.

'You have a change of clothes with you here?'

Claudio nods matter-of-factly. 'I suspected you might need looking after for a while, so I brought a few essentials.'

I resist the temptation to reel off a list: 'power tools, sheets of MDF, locks for every door . . .' Instead I look him straight in the eyes, those big brown eyes that I found so appealing up until the other night, and nod towards my full wine beaker.

'Claudio, how am I supposed to drink that with my hands tied? Or eat dinner? If you're planning to spoon-feed me, you can forget that shit right now.'

He hesitates, rubs his top lip with a finger. 'Of course I'm going to untie you. Just a moment.'

He walks over to the kitchen door, and I see that he's even fitted a lock to that too. It's shiny and new. He turns the key and drops it deep into the front pocket of his suit trousers.

'Oh for God's sake, Claudio, this is ridiculous! How long do you think you can keep this up?'

When he comes back across to me to untie the scarf I contemplate my options: the elbow in his balls, the fingers in his eyeballs, the frying pan across the side of his head—but then what? The key is still in his pocket so unless I knocked him out altogether, I still wouldn't be able to get out of the kitchen, and the front door was bound to be Chubb-locked too.

'I've made us a fresh chicken curry,' he says, avoiding my question. 'I've been really looking forward to our dinner together.'

OK. I decide to change tack, indulge him.

'I'm looking forward to the curry. It smells amazing.' I manage to smile at him.

He smiles back and all my internal organs shiver with disgust, but I think I manage to hide it.

'Thanks for dressing for dinner too,' he says, that horrible faux shy tone in his voice again.

'Nice to have an excuse to dress up,' I say through gritted teeth, even though it actually kind of was. Anything for a change from my bedroom prison. I had put on my smart kitten heels—not the suede stiletto ones, which he confiscated—and I had make-up on for the first time in three days.

I will try to get inside his head. I just pray he won't take it as encouragement and try to get inside me. The thought that only a week ago this would have been welcome makes me want to rip my skin off. I don't ever want to have sex again.

There's some music—just acoustic guitar and a voice—on in the background and I can't work out where it's coming from at first until I see an iPad on the kitchen counter by the toaster. I make a mental note of it as the only link to help from the outside world that I've yet seen. If I did manage to incapacitate him, I could send a Facebook message to Donna or Steph. I'm not a very active Facebooker, although I know that Steph is. She'd see it immediately.

'What are we listening to?' I ask.

He looks surprised. 'You're joking, right?'

'Er . . . no, why would I be?'

He stirs the curry and something about the set of his shoulders makes me realise I've upset him somehow. He has an odd way of standing and walking, buttocks permanently clenched as though he has something stuck up his backside. He's doing it now, and the fabric of his suit is trapped between his bum cheeks.

'I don't recognise this song,' I repeat, uncertainly.

Claudio lays down the wooden spoon—*my* wooden spoon—on my kitchen counter and turns to face me. He looks deeply disappointed.

'What's the matter, Claudio?'

'You really don't remember?'

I take a slug of wine—mustn't guzzle it; I need my wits about me—and shake my head.

'There's gratitude for you,' he whinges, in a high querulous tone like an old lady. His voice sounds like nails down a blackboard. He's trying to be jokey but I can tell I've mortally offended him.

'I'm sorry . . . what is it?'

He pours himself a good half-pint of wine, in the plastic cup that used to have a base with small LED lights that flashed red, green, and blue. Richard brought it back for Megan from some work trip to Vegas. The lights stopped working long ago but we kept the cup.

'Listen carefully. I'm sure you will remember it soon. I suppose it *was* a very long time ago.'

I listen. The song is OK, nothing special, some wishy-washy lyrics about loss and heaven, in which the singer claimed to be *always looking out for you.*

'It's nice,' I comment. 'Who sang it?'

He beams suddenly, and then his face droops again as he realises I really don't remember.

'I did. It's the song I wrote for you when your father died.'

I'm momentarily speechless. What song? I have no recollection of this whatsoever. There's no mention of it in any of the diary entries for that year I've so far read. In fact there are only a few mentions in passing of Claudio himself, just as one of John's gang.

'You wrote me a song?'

He tips his head to one side and closes his eyes, transported by his music.

'I think it's the best one I ever wrote.'

'Claudio, that was a lovely thing to do. I'm really touched. I'm sorry I don't remember. That year was such a blur, with everything else that was going on. When did you give it to me?'

He gazes at me, still disappointed. 'I put a cassette through your door. It must have been just before you started going out with John. I was so jealous when I found out.'

'Maybe I never got it?' I venture. 'I didn't even know you knew my address. Are you sure you got the right house?'

He jumps up again and busies himself at the hob, stirring rice and turning the gas off under the curry. 'Yes, I am,' he says curtly. 'You thanked me the next time you saw me in the New Inn. I thought you might have rung me up or something—I put my number on the tape—but you didn't. Then you and John got together.'

Wow. I'm surprised I didn't remember, not least because the act of writing me a song would have revealed Claudio's crush, and I had always been so flattered to learn that someone fancied me. But I have absolutely no recollection of any of it—the song, thanking him in the pub. I don't even remember ever having a single conversation with him, him liking me, none of it. He had just been someone who hung around with our crowd. It's so strange. My memory is bad, but it's not that bad. And I've not yet spotted anything in my diary about him other than a mention in passing. Perhaps it's him who's misremembering, or who has rewritten history. After all, he's clearly mentally ill.

'It was a very long time ago, Claudio. Over twenty-five years. And my memory has always been terrible.' I hesitate, not sure if what I'm going to say next is a good idea or not: 'I didn't know you liked me then. But I was so crazy about John that I suppose I didn't notice anyone else. He was the love of my life. Richard—my ex-husband—he liked me too, apparently, but I didn't know that either.'

'I remember Richard,' Claudio says, his lip curled. 'He used to hang around you like a pathetic little puppy.'

'*Did* he?'

'You must have noticed, surely.'

I shake my head. 'Everything from that time is such a blur. I suppose I was in a state about my dad, and I was obsessed with John. I was in my own little world.'

'When did you and *Richard* get together, then?' He says Richard's name as though it is the most abhorrent word in the English language.

'A lot later. After university. We started hanging out back in Brockhurst, just as friends, and things just sort of developed from there.'

I don't want to tell Claudio how it really was. How, shortly after the first few times Richard and I hung out, he confessed it had been he who had saved me in that alley, my little 'knight in shining mac', as I put it in my diary.

I remember when Richard told me. We'd been spending time together for a few weeks, having reconnected when I was working, temporarily, in the pharmacy at Boots. Richard had come in one day, all swollen and yellow from having his wisdom teeth out, and I think the state of him, looking so vulnerable and hideous, had made me let down my guard enough to agree to go out for a drink with him. It became a regular event. I was still hurting from losing John, even almost five years on, so Richard and I hadn't kissed or anything—I hadn't had any sort of romance at university, either, having rebuffed all advances. Yet I found myself warming to Richard, starting to gradually trust him a tiny bit, because he was generous and funny and kind.

He'd been walking me back to Mum's from the pub, and we passed the alley. Its dark maw gaped at me as we passed and even then, several years after the event, I couldn't prevent a shudder.

'It still scares you, doesn't it?' he said softly, once we were safely past.

I stopped. 'What?'

He put his hands on my upper arms and gripped me gently, his hazel eyes dark under a dim streetlight. 'Didn't you know?'

'*What?*'

For a moment I thought he was going to say that my attacker was his dad, or something ridiculous like that. I started to shake.

'I was there that night. I was the one who saw what was happening to you and ran in.'

I stared at him. Of course it was! I couldn't think how I hadn't realised before. I'd just tried so hard to block the whole thing out of my mind. I opened my mouth to speak, to say thank you— but what came out instead was a furious screech of ingratitude: '*And you never told me before?*'

Then I actually ran away, leaving him standing there looking hurt and stricken. I ran home, just as I had done on the night of the attack, so excruciatingly embarrassed that he had seen me like that, with a stranger groping me, that I refused to speak to him for three months. To my shame, I ignored his calls and his letters and the gorgeous love tokens he left on the doorstep for me—a book of romantic poetry, compilation tapes, a moonstone necklace that I still wear.

He later admitted that he'd been following me home that night, that he had quite often done so when he saw me out and about in town, even when I was with John. It made me feel for the first time that odd, confusing frisson of gratitude and discomfort that comes of being loved from afar.

I hate to admit it, but I feel flashes of it now with Claudio too. Just flashes—obviously I'd rather be anywhere else than here with him— but a tiny, tiny part of me thinks, 'Wow, he really loves me . . .' and down in the insecure depths of me, I'm impressed.

How sad is that?

Claudio looks around for a knife to slit open the plastic packaging of the chapattis he's bought, then remembers that he's hidden or disposed of the knife block and its inhabitants. I have to suppress a smile as he tries and fails to rip open the packet by hand, then with a normal knife, and eventually by stabbing the tines of a fork into the plastic. He must have wrestled with it for a full three or four minutes. Serves him right, the dysfunctional idiot. All the time his trousers are getting more and more bunched up around his arse as he gets increasingly flustered.

Finally he manages to extract the chapattis, which he shoves in the oven for a few minutes while he dishes up the curry on my two Pyrex plates—at least I'm spared the plastic flowery picnic plates. He puts one in front of me with a flourish.

'Yum,' I say, more enthusiastically than I feel. Although I had been starting to feel hungry, the sight of the yellow curry is now conjuring up comparisons with vomit and other such unpleasant-ness, and my stomach rebels. I pick at a piece of chicken with my plastic fork. 'It's really nice. Thank you, Claudio.'

He looks smug as he tucks into his own plate.

'It's so important, I think, for a man to be able to cook well,' he says, echoing my own thoughts from earlier. I bite my tongue to stop myself adding, 'It depends on the man.'

'Did your mother teach you?'

His face immediately changes, as if shutters have clanged down over him, and he actually turns red. I'm aware I've committed another faux pas but feel disinclined to explore it further. I suppose it's because his mum's so ill. 'Sorry.'

'Have a chapatti while they're still warm,' is all he says. 'What did you think of the food in that Greek place the other night?'

I think he's fishing, hinting so that I'll tell him this is in a differ-ent league or whatever, but again I feel disinclined to indulge him.

'It was good,' I said. 'Greek food can be quite bland, but it was tasty.'

'It was such a fantastic evening, wasn't it?' He's happy again, shutters raised.

I'm puzzled. He must be rubbish at reading signals. I'd been so emotionally distant that night that I was practically on the moon, whereas he seemed to have been *over* the moon.

'Do you remember,' he says nostalgically, as though reminiscing about a twenty-year relationship, 'we almost kissed?'

'No,' I reply bluntly. 'We didn't.'

He frowns. 'Yes! We held hands when we came out of the pub, and you had such a tender look in your eyes. I wanted to kiss you then but I thought I would wait until next time, build up the ten-sion a little more. We sort of kissed goodnight, though, didn't we?'

Well, you've certainly succeeded in building up the tension, I think to myself.

'That was the time before. The second date, when we came out of the restaurant.' *Not the third date, when you drugged and kidnapped me.*

He's right, though. We did hold hands then, and I had hoped he'd kiss me. What a crap judge of character I am.

'Claudio, listen. Things could definitely work out between us, but only if you let me out of here. Do you honestly think that I'm going to love you if you keep me a prisoner? Megan will be home in a few days. I've got a cleaner who comes once a week. My friend Steph will be expecting to meet me for lunch tomorrow.' (She's not, but he doesn't need to know that. In fact, I think she said she was going up to Birmingham to interview a footballer.) 'I talk to Donna a few times a week. She'll be worried if she doesn't hear from me.'

'I've cancelled your cleaner.'

'What? I don't believe you. You don't even know what she's called.'

Claudio looks smug again. 'She's called Ania. I saw the note you left for her last week, about dusting Megan's room. Then I texted her from your phone and told her that she is no longer required.'

I'm furious. 'How did you get into my *phone*? It's locked!' I want to throttle him, to inflict severe pain on him, to make him suffer the way he's making me suffer.

He shrugs and shovels in a huge mouthful of curry and rice. 'Easy. Saw the code you use when you texted Megan the other night in the restaurant: 8459.'

Does that mean he's gone through everything? Texts, emails, photographs? He's bound to have. I didn't think it was possible for my heart to sink further still, but it does.

'It's private, Claudio. My phone is private.' *Like everything else you've pawed over with your greasy mitts*, I think. My cards, my finances, my clothes, my toiletries . . . I want to cry. At least my confiscated laptop has a passcode he won't have seen and won't be able to figure out—it's my granddad's name.

He smiles and I have to sit on my hands not to launch myself at him. If only I had long, hard fingernails! I think longingly of the damage I could do.

'Do I have any texts from Megan?' I ask through gritted teeth.

'I don't know,' he replies shortly. 'I switched it off again.'

'Can I have it?' I know the answer to this already, and Claudio confirms it.

'No. I know you'll only use it to try to call for help, but let me tell you this: in the extremely unlikely event that you do somehow manage to leave before you've proved you love me,' he says, with the steely calm that frightens me to my core, 'I will take the wood off the windows and the locks off the doors and then fill the holes. I will put my pyjamas under your pillows and my clothes in your wardrobe. Everyone will think you invited me to stay over while Megan is away. I will tell the police we had an argument and you are trying to get me into trouble, that you're prone to making things up but I love you anyway in spite of your being a fantasist. They won't believe you. No-one will. I will deny everything. Then, I will track you down and kill you. That's a promise.'

Chapter Fourteen
Day 2

I remember, before our first date, trying to picture Claudio as somebody with whom I might have a future. It was hard, because I never really hit it off with him when we were younger, but I kept telling myself to give him the benefit of the doubt. He seemed really keen, and he wasn't all that bad-looking, from what I could remember of him the night that Gerald screamed at me. Unfortunately I kept getting flashbacks of how he looked at eighteen—spotty, gauche, too lanky, bad clothes—and that image kept superseding the picture of him coming over to me in Pizza Express twenty-five years later.

Although it makes me feel nauseated now, two weeks ago I was thinking about what it would feel like to get close to him, to feel the texture of his hair—he has good hair, thick and soft-looking. I suppose what I was really after was a combination of the best bits of Richard and the best bits of Sean together. Then I'd have the perfect man—especially if the combined person resembled John, too.

It almost makes me laugh to think how catastrophically wrong I got it.

I feel as if, before the third date with Claudio, I was a woman in layers. The top layer was the fun-loving, dating woman, up for a laugh and meeting new people, accepting compliments as her due, flirting as if to the manner born; the woman I'd described in my on-line profile. The layer next to that knew that she could, in certain circumstances, look quite pretty. Had even been described as being gorgeous, although she couldn't think how. The next layer still wore her wedding ring, on the wrong hand, because it was comforting to her. One more thin layer in was a woman who thought she looked hideous in—or out of—all her clothes, who couldn't bear to look in a mirror, who didn't believe anybody could seriously be interested in her.

As for the inmost layer—well, nobody except Richard or Sean has ever got down that far. That's the girl being assaulted in an alley, the girl crying over her dad's grave, the girl whose heart was broken by an amber-eyed sixth-former, the girl throwing up in the toilet.

I don't like that girl. I've hidden that secret heart in my layers, grown them around her, swaddling her with hard-earned maturity and experiences—but it seems that somehow she has fought free and lashed out at me again, worse than ever. But now it's as if Claudio has taken a giant machete and sliced me—her—into violent, irreparable halves.

My first date with Claudio was in town, at a bar close to the Millennium Wheel. I fancied a day out 'up London', as Sean would have said. Richard was picking Megan up from school for the week-end, and I had decided to go and see the Robert Crumb exhibition at the Whitechapel Gallery. I visualised a day full of mental stimu-lation, good cappuccinos, and mouth-watering *pain au chocolat* in street cafes full of attractive and funkily dressed people. Then, to top it all off, a date with a reasonably good-looking man.

I'd met him before, obviously, so I knew what to expect. It wasn't like an internet date. Although what I didn't know was whether or not we'd hit it off. But I decided to myself that if it was really dire, I could just feign an emergency at home and make my excuses. It crossed my mind that perhaps I ought to tell someone where I was going, but then I thought no, it would be fine, we'd be in a public place at all times, I'd known him since I was sixteen—even though I hadn't seen him for two decades in between.

I was quite tired by the end of my day out. The Underground was sweltering in the June heat. Londoners were weary and dusty at the end of another week, and the streets were full of people fighting their way home, or to pubs for an after-work drink. I wished I'd arranged the date for another day, but it was too late by then.

Coming out of the Tube at Waterloo, jostled from all sides, I suddenly had a moment of thinking that I wasn't sure if I could face it: the small-talk, the explanations, the twenty years of catching up, and of course the tentative enquiry as to who had ended the marriage. On internet dates, this usually comes with the second drink and is always asked casually, but with great trepidation. I'm never sure what the correct reply is—if I lie and say that my husband left me, does that portray me as a victim, or a nightmare harridan who was so unbearable to live with that her poor long-suffering husband walked out? And when I tell the truth, that it was my decision, there's a moment's hesitation, what screenwriters call a 'beat', and I can see my date thinking, 'Hmm, OK, so she left him, therefore she's probably unreliable, lacking in moral fibre, if she's prepared to break her marriage vows.' I don't know if men these days ever use the word 'flibbertigibbet'—I'm guessing not—but if they did, that's probably what they were thinking of me.

I told myself not to be so paranoid as I headed towards the Millennium Wheel, having made a quick pit-stop in the ladies' loo at Waterloo station to comb my hair and put on fresh make-up. Everybody knows that marriages break up all the time. Eileen's always saying that you can never tell what's going on in anyone else's marriage, even the apparently rock-solid ones. If a man I dated was prepared to judge me for being divorced, whether or not at my own instigation, then he clearly wasn't going to be a man I wanted to spend more than five minutes with.

My hands were clammy with nerves as I pushed open the heavy plate glass doors of the bar. I'd changed my mind about not wanting to do this. Now I really wanted it to work, I really wanted him to have changed since we were at school. Claudio was no oil painting but he was better-looking than any of the other men I'd been on dates with, and he seemed so keen on me.

I walked up to the bar, glancing around me, trying not to look too desperate. For a brief second I imagined that I was here to meet Richard after work, back in the days when he was a graphic designer in an office near Waterloo, and I was working at IPC Magazines as a staff writer on several of their women's titles. We'd meet in a bar like this one, sinking a couple of cold beers, chatting amiably and non-stop about not much—the new band he'd heard on the radio and whose CD he'd bought, which one of my colleagues was having an affair, where we'd go on holiday that summer.

I spotted Claudio straight away, sitting at one of the tables reading a menu in a manner suggesting that he needed something to do with his hands. He looked up, and I waved tentatively. His face broke into a huge but nervous beam, and he leapt to his feet, kissing me on each cheek when I approached. That night, he smelled pretty good, if slightly as if he'd been in an explosion in an aftershave factory. Underneath that was a faint note of that sour smell clothes get when they aren't adequately dried, but this was mostly masked by the aftershave.

'Jo! Hi! It's so great to see you at last. You look beautiful. Sit down, sit down. What would you like to drink?'

That's a good start, I thought, telling him I'd love a glass of Rioja. Teenage Claudio, as far as I could recall, would never have had the style to tell a girl she looked beautiful. He rushed off to the bar to get my wine, and I watched him go, dodging elegantly between the post-work drinkers. Even then I wouldn't have called him gorgeous, but he was attractive all right, by anyone's standards. And *way* more eligible than I'd have thought he'd turn out to be, based on his appearance as a sixteen-year-old.

I had a good feeling about it.

Four glasses of wine later, the feeling was even better. He was noticeably more relaxed and gazing into my eyes, asking me question after question about myself and what I'd been up to since we'd left our respective schools. Before I knew it, I'd told him all about Megan, and Lester the cat, and even a bit about Richard, and how long we were together. He didn't ask whose decision it was to end the marriage, just smiled sympathetically and said, 'You know, when the marriage vows were first thought of, hundreds of years ago, people didn't live for much longer than forty years at the most, so being married for life wasn't likely to be for more than fifteen or twenty, until death did them part. These days couples might be together for fifty or sixty years. It's an unrealistically long time to be with the same person, don't you think?'

Actually I didn't. A promise was a promise, especially before God—and I'd broken mine—but it was kind of him to say so.

Claudio told me about himself too, but only in reply to my own enquiries. He was working in IT for an pharmaceutical company in Feltham, had been there for four years but hoped to leave soon and set up his own IT business. He lived in Twickenham but had been spending all his weekends in Brockhurst lately, with his mum. Then he quickly changed the subject and asked me instead about my parents, where they lived, if we were close.

'My dad died when I was sixteen,' I said in a rush—it was still hard to say out loud, even after all these years. 'My mother remarried three years later. She and my step-dad live in Scotland, where he comes from. I don't see them all that often. But she's very happy.'

'Oh yes. I remember now that your father died. And you don't have brothers or sisters, do you?'

I shook my head ruefully. I wish I did. I wish I had a big strong brother up the road, to call me 'sis' and take me out for curries when I was particularly depressed. Someone like Richard's little brother, Ben. He's twenty-eight now, which is bizarre to think of—I first met him when he was about five or six. Not at all little any more, either; he's six foot four, and gorgeous.

'What about you? Where do you live? Do you have a big family?' I asked.

I couldn't remember anything about Claudio's family circumstances, only that he told me in Pizza Express that his mother had cancer. I was hoping that he was from an enormous extended Italian family. It would be handy if half of them lived in Brockhurst and half still in Italy. I loved the idea of Sunday lunch around a huge table with a large, noisy bunch of siblings and cousins and nieces and nephews running around. I so wished I came from a big family.

'Oh,' he said, rather distantly. 'No, just my mother. I think I told you she is not too well.'

Odd, I think, for an Italian to be an only child. Perhaps his father died when Claudio was a baby, and his mother never remarried? But I didn't like to pry. I didn't need to know everything on the first date. All the same, I was a little disappointed that he wouldn't be the one to fulfil my familial daydream. *Never mind*, I remember thinking, *he seems pretty good in all other ways*, and I liked him considerably more as an adult than I had as a teenager.

'I can't believe you've never been married!' I said flirtatiously. I didn't mean it as an accusation, more as a compliment, but an odd, almost angry expression crossed his face.

'Sorry,' I backtracked hastily. 'I mean, all the other Italians I know are really into family. I would have imagined that you would have a load of kids by now.' He looked away and I realised I'd put my foot in it again.

'I nearly got married once, about ten years ago. She . . .'

For an awful moment I thought he was going to say she died. I arranged my features into a sympathetic expression.

'. . . she left me at the altar.'

Bad, but not as bad as her dying. It wasn't difficult to maintain the sympathy, though—it must have been horrendous for him.

At least that's what I thought then. Now, obviously, I'm silently applauding the woman. She got out just in time.

'Oh, Claudio, that's awful, I'm so sorry.' A million questions ran through my head: Had he any inkling? Why? Who was she? How did they meet? Had they been together long?

I waited for him to say something and eventually, fiddling with the cocktail sticks piled next to the olives we'd ordered, he blurted, 'My mother never liked her anyway.'

'Oh dear. That's never easy.' I said that as though I knew what he meant, but I didn't. My mum loved Richard, and Richard's mum, until her death, loved me. I still miss her.

'Do you remember my mother? She remembers you.'

'Does she?' I pictured again the thin, hunched lady chewing slowly, but nothing came back to me from the past. 'Perhaps if you showed me a photo of her from when we were teenagers I would.'

'She always said you had the face of an angel. I think she was as disappointed as I was when you married Richard.'

I blinked. That was a bit dramatic. 'Oh! Does she know we're out on a date tonight?'

He nodded enthusiastically. 'I rang her up to tell her. She was thrilled! As soon as she's feeling a bit better she said we should all go out for a pub lunch.'

'Lovely,' I said, sort of meaning it.

The rest of the date proceeded without incident. It was only later that I realised he had successfully deflected any further mention of the ex-fiancée without me finding out anything at all about her. Perhaps she's actually buried under his patio.

Chapter Fifteen
Day 3

Unsurprisingly, last night's dinner didn't exactly go with a swing after Claudio's repeated threat to kill me. I refused to eat another mouthful or speak another word except to demand to be taken back to my bedroom. Now that I am locked up again and lying sleepless at 3.00 a.m., I try to rationalize what he said. Obviously, it's ridiculous to think that he could convince the police that I was a fantasist and that he really did live here in this flat. One chat with Megan, Donna, Richard, Ania the cleaner—anyone who knows me—would confirm that he doesn't live here, and hasn't ever, and therefore is off his head and they'll arrest him. But the risk is that he will realise this too, and might really carry out his threat to kill me.

Odd thought, that I might be dead in less than a fortnight. There is a desperation in Claudio's eyes that makes me believe he could actually do it. He strikes me as a man with nothing to lose. His mum is terminally ill, he has no other family. He won't talk about her. I asked him how often he visits her, but he just ignored me. I get the feeling he can't face it.

I want to appeal to him that murdering me would not be a very pleasant fact for a dying, loving mother to have to deal with in her final months, but I don't dare. And anyway, that's assuming he'd be caught—and he's arrogant enough to believe he wouldn't. I don't know how clever he is. I need to leave clues in here, although it's tricky, since he's removed all the pens from my room.

I imagine the aftermath of my murder: the funeral, Richard, Donna and Henry, Steph, Mum and Brian all weeping at the front, the tragic Facebook page that someone—probably Steph—would set up to give people details, a smiling photo of me that everyone comments on . . .

I don't allow myself to picture Megan as part of all that. The thought of her little woebegone face is in a place that's far too agonising for me to allow myself to go. But it does give rise to a fresh determination: *This will not happen.* Nobody will be going to my funeral any time soon, because I won't be having a funeral. For Megan's sake I resisted the temptation to top myself all through the really dark days of the divorce and then the split with Sean. I'm certainly not going to let some twisted loser do the job for me now, after all that.

Actually, there is a ray of hope. Assuming it's now Monday—which according to my calculations it must be—then I'm due at Eileen's at 2.00 p.m. for my counselling. She knows I would call to cancel—I'd never just not turn up. I'm sure she'll ring me when I don't show. The question is whether she'll be concerned enough to do anything about it when I don't reply. Claudio won't know about that. It's not even in the calendar on my phone because I never forget.

Every week when I go to Eileen's house there are several scrunched-up tissues already in the wastepaper basket next to the sofa. This always makes me wonder who her previous client is, and what is so bad about her life—somehow I'm sure it's a woman—that she needs to get through so many tissues each time. It disturbs me. I find myself thinking about this person at odd hours: in the bath, when I wake up in the middle of the night because Lester's scratching at the bedroom door trying to get me to let him in, in the condiments aisle of Tesco's. I have a weird feeling that I'd recognise her if I bumped into her. *By her tissues she shall be known*—that kind of thing. Even though they're just plain white Kleenex, from the box that Eileen leaves discreetly on the table. But the ones in the bin seem saturated with somebody else's sadness. They are screwed up small, like a face in pain.

I'd give anything to be in the condiments aisle of Tesco's right now.

I feel sorry for Eileen, having to sit opposite an endless stream of needy and doubtless tedious personality disorders day in and day out. I wouldn't like to do that, and definitely not in my home. Eileen's own house is always immaculate, and I take tantalising peeks through the open doors I pass on the way up to the back bedroom she uses as a consulting room, admiring the chic Edwardian decor. Occasionally I think that her house is just an elaborate set, that she doesn't actually live there but arranges it like a show home in order for her clients to feel comfortable as they make their way up to the Sofa of Emotion, to winkle out and worry at all the narcissistic little hurts and perceived slights inflicted on them over a lifetime of pain.

I do cry there myself, occasionally, but in a controlled sort of a way—I never get through more than one tissue. I don't like to cry, even though Eileen asks me why I'm holding back, when she sees me staring hard out of the window and biting my lip. I suppose it's because I'm afraid of really letting rip the way I do at home—if I started, I might not be able to stop. I don't want to add to the snowballs of tissues already in the bin.

In our sessions, Eileen keeps coming back to that couple of years in the mid-Eighties: to the attack, and John, and Dad. I really wasn't sure that I could see the relevance, not for ages, although as the months have gone by, I can grudgingly admit that yes, Richard was a father figure, and Sean represented the passion that had been missing from my life since I lost John. I suppose, if I get out of here, I ought to take the diary in to show her.

I wonder what Eileen will make of this, of Claudio. If I get out of here alive I'll be keeping her in business for years to come. But it does make me think that perhaps what she helped me to figure out is not so very far from Claudio's warped logic: Claudio's losing his mum, the only other woman (I assume) he's ever loved, and his only chance of happiness now—he thinks—is to make me love him at any cost. He believes that if he can't have me, no one else can, either. Likewise, I lost Dad and John, so subconsciously made a mess of the rest of my relationships with men.

There's no way I'm going to get any sleep tonight.

I switch on the bedside light and slide the diary out from under my pillow again. At least Claudio hasn't demanded it back yet.

Chapter Sixteen
Day 3

24th December 1986

I *went to visit Dad's grave today. Haven't ever done that before but suddenly I really wanted to get out of the house. Mum was sitting in Dad's old armchair sipping sherry, even though it was only two o'clock. She seemed OK though, engrossed in an afternoon movie with Rock Hudson. I told her I was going to Argos to buy Donna's present. Instead I walked all the way up the hill to St George's.*

I never thought there was any point in visiting his grave. Dad isn't there. He is—I sincerely hope—somewhere much better. The idea that I can communicate with him in any meaningful way when he's just a pile of ashes under the ground is ridiculous. Yet somehow I really wanted to go. Maybe because it's the first Christmas without him. Maybe because I miss him so much. Or maybe just because I feel like I ought to?

When I got there, I wasn't sure what to do. I felt a bit self-conscious, even though there was nobody else in the churchyard. Dad's grave is one of a few dozen small neat squares of slate, surrounded by crumbling and listing tombstones, centuries older, their inscriptions worn smooth. Someone—presumably Mum—had left a bunch of chrysanthemums there some days or weeks earlier. They were long dead now, colourless and crispy, drooping through the holes in the top of a square tin vase. It was a cold, damp day and I could feel the chill of the earth through the soles of my shoes. I felt bad that I hadn't even brought flowers. The place felt unbearably lonely.

I thought about the last time I had stood in that spot. It had been much warmer then, although I can't remember if I had worn a coat or not. In fact, there's hardly anything about the funeral I can remember clearly.

I remember that everyone was staring at me, with concern, sorrow, curiosity, pity. There were loads of people there, considering that neither of my parents come from large families. Friends, Dad's ex-work colleagues, from before he got made redundant, neighbours, a smattering of cousins, one great-aunt, Donna and her parents. But I felt that Mum and I were the main attraction, the star turn.

By the end of the committal, after the terrible bony splat of earth on the shiny ash-filled wooden urn, Mum's and my pitiful petals dropped in on top—after all that, I just wanted to wheel around, pull down the skin under my eyes, stretch my mouth sideways with my thumbs, stick out my tongue and scream 'yaaaah!' at the lot of them, because they all seemed to <u>expect</u> something from me. Perhaps tears would have done, but I couldn't cry, not then. The grief was buried far too deep inside me for tears to be any sort of relief.

Over and over, I just kept thinking 'Inside that little box are the remains of the man who laughed till he cried at that scene in Airplane! where Roger, Victor, and Clarence have a conversation about landing the plane:

"You have clearance, Clarence."

"Roger, Roger."

"What's our vector, Victor?"'

Such a trivial thing to think of, on such a life-shattering occasion. I wonder what Dad himself had been thinking, in his last hours. Probably nothing cogent, he was so full of morphine. Almost certainly not that scene in Airplane!

I remembered the two ducks that appeared above us as we all stood at the graveside. The ducks swooped back and forth overhead, chasing each other through the sky, banking and wheeling and looking as if they were having the most fun it was possible for a living creature to have, oblivious of the sorrow going on a long way beneath their wings. Ducks seemed to have the ability to have such a damn good time. They are the all-round sportsmen of the bird world: swimmers, divers, fast fliers. I would have given anything to be a duck that day.

Ducks, stares, and silly jokes from a silly film—not much in the way of gravitas for funeral memories. I can't remember the service at all.

And then there was Tracy Jackson and her mum Virginia, who was Dad's secretary for years. Tracy's a couple of years younger than me, and she was the biggest gawper of them all. She stared at me across the graveside so stupidly, and for so long, that I wanted to march across to her, across the wreaths and bouquets, and the sad little floral letters saying D*A*D, which Mum had insisted on buying on my behalf. I wanted to grind my heels into their useless pastel colours, and shout at Tracy Jackson to piss off and never look at me or speak to me again.

Back here after the service people milled around aimlessly, like they were looking for Dad. It felt all wrong that he wasn't there, being mein host, *keeping glasses topped up and warming vol-au-vents in the oven. Mum couldn't even pretend to make small talk and look after the guests—she just stood in the front room, drinking steadily and mashing a sausage roll with her thumb into a paper plate, as she accepted condolences with a blank but polite expression. I felt embarrassed for her. I tried to make sure that everyone had a drink, but as soon as I'd asked what someone wanted, I'd immediately forget again. I felt furious that people around me were chatting politely, even laughing. How dare they?*

All I could think about was Daddy, sitting on the sofa, smoking his pipe and chuckling at Morecambe and Wise; *Daddy, tinkering with his carpentry tools in the garage; Daddy, buying me a dress from Laura Ashley and handing it to me so proudly that I couldn't tell him that I didn't really like it. Daddy, on holiday in Devon that time when Mum got a fish-hook stuck in her heel on the beach, and he extracted it with such loving tenderness that I almost wished it had pierced my own foot.*

I remembered all this as I stood by his grave and it was like a great unstoppering of grief occurred; all the tears I hadn't been able to cry at the time came out of me now in great harsh sobs, the December air hurting my throat. I sank to my knees in the cold, wet grass, literally unable to bear the weight of it, tracing his name on the stone with my fingers like Braille because my eyes were too blurred to see it.

Nothing could ever hurt as much as this. Nothing.

Chapter Seventeen
Day 3

I have to stop reading because I'm crying so much I'm worried I'll wake Claudio up. I slide out of bed and sit in the bathroom sobbing as silently as I can into a towel behind the closed door. It's 5.00 a.m. and I imagine the sky outside streaked with apricot. I miss the sky. I miss fresh air.

Most of all, I miss Megan.

I don't normally, when she's away with Richard, because it's so fantastic to have some time to myself. To be able to have a lie-in, or read a book uninterrupted, to have time to think. The irony is that I can do all these things now, but under these conditions—all I want is to be free and for Megan to be here, bugging me.

I hear my bedroom door open and my heart sinks to the very ends of my toenails. Damn damn damn, he's heard me.

He comes bowling into the bathroom in his hideous pyjamas and actually tries to put his arm around me. I wriggle away from him and back myself up against the wall.

'Darling! What's the matter?' He's all peachy sweetness and light, like the dawn I can't see.

I hesitate, then decide it would be prudent not to further antagonise him.

'I miss Megan,' I sob, sliding down the bathroom wall to sit on the cool lino. I'm glad I'm wearing respectable nightwear—knee-length cotton shorts and a vest top. Move along, nothing to see here . . .

Claudio sits down on the edge of the bath and tilts his head to one side in what he probably imagines is a sympathetic pose, but which just makes him look thick. His bare feet are in my line of vision and they are horrible—hairy, fat-toed Hobbit feet. 'What would you and Megan be up to on a typical morning like this?'

This is not a typical morning.

I blow my nose on a sheet of loo paper and sigh, averting my eyes from the yellow crusty build-up of skin on his heels.

'We're often both in a pretty bad mood first thing during term time. She likes to chat, and sometimes we just don't have the time before school,' I tell Claudio, my voice thick. A sudden flash of memory pops into my mind and it actually makes me laugh, just briefly.

'What?' asks Claudio eagerly.

I don't want to tell him, but I suppose I'd better. Part of me wants to paint an awful picture of her so that he doesn't get any ludicrous idyllic notions about us three becoming a family. I settle for honesty.

'Living with Megan is like puddle-jumping. She's so happy one minute, then everything's a disaster the next. She hates being told what to do. If I ask her to clean her teeth, she'll say, "What are you, my *mother*?"'

Claudio bares his teeth in an 'I don't get why that's so funny' smile.

'She was in a right strop last week. She's always really tired and grumpy by the end of term. I sent her to her room for being rude and she slid a note out under her bedroom door. I thought, "Aah, bless, she's apologising"—I suppose it was sort of an apology, but when I picked it up the note said *Dear Mum, I'm sorry but you are Really geting* (with one 't') *onto my Nevers.'*

I'd laughed for the first time in weeks, the first belly laugh probably for months. I laugh again now, a thick, hiccupy laugh—but Claudio still doesn't get it.

'She's not always grumpy in the mornings, though,' I continue wistfully. 'The other morning she was totally sweet to me. She wanted to interview me.'

I close my eyes and transport myself back to that moment.

———

She had come into my bed, twined her arms around my neck, and murmured into my hair: 'I love you so much, Mummy. You're a lovely mummy, and a wonderful writer, even though your breath smells a bit phewy in the mornings. Can I interview you?'

'Thank you, angel. Those are very nice things to say. Apart from the breath bit. Interview me? What about?'

'Your job.'

'OK then. Fire away.'

She held an imaginary microphone in front of her mouth. 'So, Mrs Atkins. You're a writer?'

'That's correct.'

She pretended to scribble into a pad. 'Interesting. And what do you write about?'

'I write about medicine and hospital equipment. It's not usually very exciting,' I told her solemnly, thinking that if I could just hold onto this feeling, I'd be OK. I could survive, and perhaps even be able to believe that everything really was going to be all right again, some day. That feeling, of Megan's warm skin and adoration, the tiny soft hairs on her shins rubbing against my legs, and her head nuzzling into the space between my neck and shoulder. The cat was mewing from the kitchen. In a minute I would get up and let him out so we could play with him. We felt like a family.

'Time to get up for school,' I said, climbing over Megan and hooking my bathrobe off the back of the door. Lester was mewing more loudly now, hurling himself against the closed kitchen door.

'Can I watch TV in bed for a bit?'

'Not on a school day.'

'Oh, MUM! You are just so mean and unreasonable!' Megan slammed her fists into the pillows on either side of her, and the spell was broken. 'I'm NOT going to school.'

Oh well. I didn't mind. I could cope with the flashes of stroppiness when they were preceded by such sweetness.

'There's only two more days of school before summer. So you are,' I replied, doing up the robe. It reminded me of how Richard used to do up his dressing gown, in a brisk tight knot at his right hip.

Perhaps Megan had the same thought, because tears suddenly sprang into her eyes. 'I miss Daddy,' she wailed. 'Why did you have to get a divorce?'

I sat down on the side of the bed again, ignoring the cat's pleas. I reached out and held Megan's hand.

'You'll see him next weekend, and then you're going on your holiday to Italy and remember, another month after that you're going on your big adventure with Daddy, your even more special holiday! Aren't you excited? Disneyland, where Mickey Mouse lives? You're so lucky to have all these holidays!'

'But I want to see him now. And Mickey Mouse isn't real. Don't talk to me like I'm a baby.'

'Sorry. But you are my baby. Dad's working away this week, in Germany. Even if we were still together, you wouldn't see him until the weekend.'

'Huh,' she said, the seven-year-old cynic. 'I don't believe you. You're just saying that. Can you bring Lester here, please? I need cheering up. But don't feed him, because I want to.'

I was relieved that we seemed to be off the subject again. 'You'd better get up, then. He's hungry—listen to him.'

'Let me play with him first, just for a minute?'

'Oh, all right. I'll let him in.'

The truth was, I wanted him to come in too. It was part of our routine. Insane as it sounded, Lester goes quite a long way to filling the gap left by Richard and then, for me, Sean.

I plodded down the hall and opened the kitchen door, on auto-pilot. Same thing every morning: switch on the radio, fill the kettle, pour crunchies into the cat's bowl, make Megan's sandwiches. That part of our lives at least had been unchanged by the divorce—Richard was always up and out before either of us girls surfaced.

I miss it so much. Particularly now, when I can't plod anywhere except in here to the bathroom, four paces away. I think longingly of the simple pleasure of making tea and feeding the cat.

'Interview you?' Claudio repeats, breaking my reverie. I can't be bothered to explain, though. Fortunately, Lester joins Claudio and me now, climbing into his litter tray and starting to rake and shuffle enthusiastically. He's been a fellow hostage with me since Claudio gave in to my pleas to bring his bowls and tray into my bathroom yesterday. He—Lester—is delighted. He rarely uses the cat-flaps I installed in the flat door and the downstairs back door and has become a house cat anyway.

'That's something else that Megan and I do in the mornings. We hang out with the cat,' I tell Claudio as Lester squats, pointedly avoiding our gaze. 'He must be almost out of dry food by now. Please could you go out and buy some more?'

He looks at me suspiciously. 'I'll check,' he says. 'Bloody hell, it's getting it everywhere.'

Lester's post-poo paw raking has indeed become even more enthusiastic, and cat litter sprays around the floor. 'That's my cue to leave,' Claudio says, standing up. I could kiss Lester.

'If you bring me some more plastic bags, I'll scoop his tray out.'

'Yes, dear.'

I can't tell if he's saying it sarcastically or not.

In a self-pitying sort of way it occurs to me that Claudio is like a hideous fairytale mutation of a husband: I went to sleep one night with a lovely husband and daughter and awoke to find them gone and in their place an ogre with bad breath and nylon shirts who keeps me captive in the bedroom. But I can't even blame Claudio. He didn't wreck my marriage: I did that all by myself.

'Before I go, though, I want your diary back.'

I have to make a colossal effort not to let my eyes fill up again. 'Why?'

'You said you'd talk to me, but you hardly say anything. I'm going to have to find it out for myself.'

'I *am* talking to you, Claudio! I've just told you about Megan! Ask me whatever you want. But I need it. I've not had time to read more yet. Let's talk later—you were in the swimming club with me, weren't you? We could talk about that?'

I hope I don't sound too desperate. It's so hard to get the balance right of how I speak to him.

'Doug the trainer. Going to galas in a coach. I remember all that,' Claudio says nostalgically. 'Do you still swim? I haven't been swimming for years.'

I nod. 'Yes. Donna and I go every week.'

He laughs. 'You still see Donna Barrington-Brown? How funny.'

Why? I think.

'She's still my best friend. Although she's now Donna Hayden. She married a guy called Henry Hayden—he's a *policeman*.' I say this pointedly, but Claudio doesn't react.

'Well, I suppose you can keep the diary again for today,' he magnanimously agrees.

Big of you, arsehole.

He yawns. 'It's still really early. I'm going to go back to bed for a bit.' He looks pointedly through the open bathroom door at my rumpled bed. 'Unless I could . . . ?'

'No!'

'OK then,' he says sulkily. 'See you later. Glad you're feeling better.'

I manage not to snort. But at least he's still asking permission for intimacy, and accepting my refusals. I wonder how long that will last before he loses patience.

When he's gone, I climb back into bed and try to get back to sleep, but I can't. Megan fills my thoughts like a lost lover, and my yearning for her becomes almost physical.

It occurs to me that the morning Megan interviewed me was the same day as my second date with Claudio. It seems like ages ago but it was only last week. After I picked her up from school I asked her opinion on the outfit I'd chosen for the date, the tight red dress that Richard had bought me, high wedge red espadrilles, with a big clashy bracelet with lots of fat coloured glass beads on it. The look I was going for was smart, but slightly funky.

She came into my room, not even noticing what I was wearing but away like a greyhound out of the traps on a train of thought: 'Mummy, so, will you test me on money? We're doing that at school, I need to learn about my change, I can do it using sticks and blobs, go on, give me one, but nothing too difficult just something that I can probably do like maybe say if I had one pound of pocket money then I bought something in Poundland, some glitter pens or something for another certain amount then how much would I have left? That sort of thing.'

'Say you went into Poundland and bought some glitter pens that cost 79p, and paid for them with your one pound pocket money. How much change would you get?' I asked obediently, twisting round to check how my backside looked.

'Mummy. They wouldn't be 79p because everything in Poundland is ONE POUND.' She grinned, delighted at catching me out.

'Oh yeah. So it would. OK, Tesco's then.'

'OK, right, so I give the lady on the till my one pound which is ten sticks, and it costs 79 pence which is seven sticks and nine blobs or sometimes we call them chocolate bars and sweeties, so it's seven chocolate bars and nine sweeties but not Licorice Allsorts cos I don't like them, maybe Maltesers or something instead . . . ? No, not Maltesers cos that's chocolate so it might get confusing. Jelly babies. Seven chocolate bars and nine jelly babies. One makes ten which adds up to eight sticks . . . .nine . . . ten . . . that equals a pound . . . So that's—um—three sticks and one blob—31p?'

I just about managed to remember what the original sum was. 'No, sweetie, that's not right.'

'It is!'

'No—it was one pound take away 79p.'

'Yes—31p!'

'No—because 31 and 79 equals 110. One pound ten pence. The right answer is 21 pence.'

'That's what I said.' Megan's voice was crackly with outrage. I realised I'd better try to head off this new tantrum at the pass.

'Hey, Beans, guess who's coming over tonight?'

'Father Christmas and Taylor Swift?'

'Um . . . no. Guess again.'

'Sharon Osborne and Professor Dumbledore!'

'No. A real person, not from books or on TV. Someone you already know.'

'Sharon Osborne and Taylor Swift are real people.'

'Yes I know, but—oh, never mind: Zuzana!'

There was a pause. 'To babysit? You're going out?'

'Yes. I'm going for a drink with a friend.'

Megan's voice raised into a wail. 'Why can't I come?'

'It's a grown-up evening and you don't know my friend.' *Nor do I*, I thought, *not very well*. 'You'd be bored out of your brain. Anyway, you have lots of treats coming up.'

'Yes.' Megan sniffed. 'So does that mean it's my birthday next month, because you said me and Daddy were going to Disneyland for my birthday?'

'Nearly. It's July now, and then you're going at the end of August, in time for the first of September.'

'So, my birthday is on September first which means that from September to December I am seven and a quarter, then from December to April I'm seven and a half, then until June I am still seven and a half, and then from June until September I'm seven and three quarters! Which means that I'm seven and three quarters now because it's July so it's my birthday soon and can I have another make-over party but this time with the cinema too and maybe some pony riding? Daddy said I can.'

'But I thought we agreed he was taking you to Disneyland for your present?'

'Yes. But I need to do something with my friends too.'

'Well, yes, I expect so. So—what do you think?' I gave her a twirl.

'Ye-es,' said Megan, head on one side, scrutinising me. 'You look quite nice, Mummy, but . . .'

'What, sweetie?' I allowed myself a small daydream about me and Claudio really hitting it off, and going for weekends away to Paris on Eurostar. Oh, the irony.

'I think you need another colour. Red on its own is a bit boring. Can't you wear your pink scarf as well?'

'I don't think that would really go, angel.'

'Can I wear it, then?'

'OK, but only until Zuzana comes. Then you take it off and go to bed when she tells you. Yes?'

'Yes, Mummy.' She skipped off triumphantly, Lester trying to pounce on the tassels of my lovely pink scarf, which was trailing down behind her back. She was too quick for him, though, so he gave up and settled down on the bed, hoiked up his back leg, and proceeded to lick his own penis instead. All right for some.

I look at the clock—6.00 a.m. There's no way I'm going to get back to sleep now, so I obediently open the diary again and find the entry where I talk about the swimming club. I'm already dreading having to talk to Claudio about it later.

Chapter Eighteen
Day 3

29th December 1986

*T*hings I can do when I've got smaller boobs:

— *Wear a bikini*
— *Wear a vest top*
— *Wear wide belts (although would they make my bottom look huge?)*
— *Little lacy bras!!!!*
— *Wear strappy dresses*
— *Go jogging*
— *Stand on the poolside at training without my arms crossed*

I've been thinking about this one thing for months, long before the attack, but it's the memory of those cold, grabbing hands on my chest that has made me decide that I'm really, definitely, going to do it: I'm going to get a breast reduction.

They still don't seem to have stopped growing, even though I'm sixteen. They just get bigger and bigger. It's like living with a pair of starving hungry twins. I'm a 34H! I'm not sure bras come any bigger than that. I remember the first time I ever noticed them, in a photograph when I was eleven, at the last sports day of junior school, triumphantly winning the three-legged race with Hannah. Hannah was tiny and neat, and her shins so twig-like, it looked as though she would have just floated away if she hadn't been tethered to me. In the photograph, I am a huge galumphing elephant, dragging Hannah along to victory in my wake. But the worst thing about the shot was my terrible prepubescent breasts. They were small then, but still flapping about in opposite directions on my chest as I ran. Mum confirmed my fears by marching me down to Just Jane to get my first bra fitted the day after we'd got the photos developed.

From then on my boobs just grew and grew. It's like they too are taking part in some kind of race, straining towards an invisible finish line. It doesn't matter how I try to contain or hide them, there's no disguising their disproportionate size.

They are truly terrible. And since two weeks ago when I walked through that alley, it's even worse. They're like an obsession. I can't bear to look at them in the mirror, clothed or unclothed, and I definitely couldn't bear the thought of anyone else looking at them, either.

It'll be so great. Imagine not having to squash these things into my tight Speedo any more, or having to walk out of the changing rooms with my arms crossed. I might even shower naked after training like the other girls do, and not in my swimming costume! As long as the scars aren't too bad, of course . . .

Doug (aka Slug, or Sluggage) won't be able to talk straight at them any more. Ugh. Doug and his nylon navy tracksuit, spittly whistle around neck, chlorine-saturated bald spot on head. I won't have to worry that as soon as I get out of the pool, they'll all stare at my boobs. All those horrible boys, letching after me. Claudio Cavelli and Nigel Weston and Peter Henrich, all thinking it's fine to stare at me, because Doug does it.

That stranger touched them, squeezed them, and manhandled them, in the alley. Perhaps that was why he chose me to attack? He'd noticed them, sticking out in two big fat lumps even through my duffel coat. If I'd had neat little unobtrusive ones like Donna's, he'd have left me alone.

They have to go, these ungainly mounds of flesh. I feel like taking a carving knife and cutting them off myself. I was afraid before; afraid of the surgeon and the anaesthetic and the embarrassment of having doctors and nurses see my naked breasts in all their mammoth non-splendour—but now, none of that matters. Not after what that man did to me. I just want rid of them.

Plus, dare I say it, John might fancy me once I have the operation—another good reason to have it done, and soon.

I went to see Dr Hamber this morning, pretending to the receptionist that it was about that wart on my finger. I asked him how much it would cost, and if you have to be eighteen. When I got into his consulting room he made me lift up my shirt while he inspected my boobs, in their ugly grey bra, and my cheeks burned when I held the shirt in front of my face. I was so glad of its cover so that I didn't have to look at him. He's known me since I was a baby. It's weird.

'Yes, well, they're certainly large enough for you to have the operation on the National Health,' he said cheerfully, and I wanted to cry. My boobs are so big that it wouldn't even be considered vanity to have them reduced!!! He said I didn't have to be eighteen as long as I had my mum's permission, but that there was a waiting list of a couple of years so if I wanted it done sooner, I'd have to go privately and it would cost about two and a half thousand pounds.

Two and a half grand! I asked him to put me on the NHS waiting list and came home in tears, but when I told Mum why I was crying, she said something incredible: Daddy left me some money in his will! She hadn't planned to tell me about it until I was eighteen, but she thought I could use it for the op!! I hugged her so hard she squeaked. Then I rang Donna to tell her, and this was her response:

'You're off your head! Why? All that pain, and being in hospital, and having scars—are you sure?'

Then I didn't want to discuss it any more, not if she was going to be so negative. So we got onto the topic of how many verrucas Nigel Weston's got. You can see them when he tumble-turns next to us. His spotty back, bum, and legs rise up into the air and sink down again out of sight, like a whale blowing. Then when he swims off you catch a glimpse of a foot, the sole all peppered with black verrucas.

'Why are all the boys in this club so disgusting? Nigel Weston—acne and verrucas, mmm, attractive. And don't you think he looks like he's got a chipolata in his Speedos?'

'He fancies you,' I said, grateful that Donna could make me feel even halfway normal again. Although I'm a bit annoyed that she hasn't taken the news of my operation seriously. Bet she thinks I won't go through with it.

'Yeah. And Claudio fancies you. Aren't we just the lucky pair?'

We chatted for a bit longer but I wasn't concentrating. I just kept imagining myself with small, pert bosoms, and smiled down the phone to Donna without her knowing. At least something can make me smile.

Chapter Nineteen
Day 3

I thought he wanted to talk about the swimming club, but when Claudio storms into my room later that morning, slamming the door behind him and dangling the key menacingly, tantalisingly, in front of me in between his thumb and forefinger, I can see that reminiscing is the last thing on his mind. I've been sitting on the bed reading my diary, and I drop it to the floor with shock.

'You've been *lying* to me, Jo.' He looks furious.

I'm too frightened of him to refuse to reply. I draw my knees protectively up to my body and hug them tight. 'What? No I haven't! Why do you say that?'

He continues as though I haven't spoken. 'I won't have it, Jo, I just won't have it. We have to have absolute trust!'

Trust? Yeah, right.

'I don't know what you're talking about.'

He sits down next to me on the bed, not touching me, but putting his face so close to mine that even in the dim light I can see all the open pores around his nose and the stray hairs in his eyebrows.

'You told me you and Sean had finished . . .' he hisses.

'We have!' My voice is a squeak short of panic.

Frigging Sean, still causing trouble for me.

'That's not what it sounds like.'

'Claudio, you have to explain. Sean and I split up six months ago.'

He takes an exaggeratedly deep breath, as though I am a particularly stupid pupil and he is a long-suffering head teacher.

'Then why would he send you a text saying "Good to see you last week, kiss kiss kiss"? Last week *we* went out. Last week *we* almost kissed! How could you, Jo? How *could* you? I didn't have you down as a cheat, I really didn't.'

I sigh too. 'Claudio, I did see him last week, but it was for about five minutes. All that happened was that he told me he's got another girlfriend now. We just . . . bumped into one another when I was going into my office. He was coming out of the gym.'

This isn't entirely true, although it sort of is. I did see Sean last week, but not outside the gym—that was the time before. I'm not going to tell Claudio about it. It's too humiliating.

Instead I give Claudio an edited version of an encounter I had with Sean about a month ago.

'We bumped into each other. I asked him if he was seeing anyone else. He said "Sort of," and then changed it to yes, he was. That was it. I spoke to him for about two minutes. I don't know why he'd have texted me afterwards, but he always was a bit contrary. It was probably only because he feels guilty.'

I was an idiot to ask him. It would have been better not to know for sure. I mean, of *course* Sean would have got himself another girlfriend, almost six months after we broke up. He probably got together with someone within six days. He's the type who can't survive without adoration on tap.

I just hadn't been able to help myself.

He was running down the steps of the gym cramming a whole chocolate biscuit into his mouth when I saw him, which was good—he was embarrassed. Sean was a dreadful stuffer of food, a fister of cutlery. He would focus on a huge slice of pizza with the intensity of a cat about to pounce on a blackbird and then, instead of merely biting into it or—heaven forbid—cutting it with a knife and fork, he'd semi-fold it and slot it into his mouth sideways, actually turning his shoulders as if that would help to accommodate it. Then he'd have to sit, cheeks bulging, speechlessly trying to masticate, until it was reduced to a more manageable size.

'Uh-oh 'o,' he mumbled, not looking me in the eye, and covering his mouth with his hand as he tried to get the biscuit under control enough to articulate actual words.

'Hello, Sean.'

'You all right?' he managed eventually, poised with what was probably dread to see whether I was planning to walk straight on or stop to chat.

I braced myself for the wash of irritation I always used to feel when he stated those words, because it wasn't a genuine enquiry as to my state of mind but a token pleasantry, and it was as if he didn't want to hear the answer, unless it was in the affirmative.

Annoyingly, the irritation didn't come. I found that I was so overwhelmingly relieved to be in such close proximity to him that he could have come out with all the little Seanisms that used to bug me so much—'You all right?' 'up London', 'innit', 'eh?' . . . and so on and so forth—and I would still have wanted to grab him and wrap my arms and legs around him like a monkey clinging to a pole.

'I'm OK. How are you?'

'Yeah. All right.'

Then I asked, just blurted it out. 'So. Are you seeing anybody else?'

There was a long, long pause and then Sean said, to a nearby lamp post, 'Not exactly.'

Everything in my body seemed to stop—blood stopped flowing, heart stopped pumping, pupils didn't dilate, muscles didn't contract. I felt as if I'd turned to stone.

'That means yes, then,' I eventually said, knowing full well that it did. All 'Not exactly' meant was 'Yes, but I don't want to tell you.'

'Well. Sort of. But we haven't done anything,' he said in a hurry, in an almost plaintive voice, as if he was a teenager and I was his mother, catching him and the mystery girl rolling around semi-clad in his bedroom. 'I can't,' he added, sheepishly.

Can't? I thought. What does that mean? Can't physically get it up? Doesn't want to? (Unlikely.) Is still so much in love with me that he can't give himself to anybody else? In which case, why the hell did he dump me?

'Oh. I see,' I said, wondering if I was actually going to throw up then and there. I was shaking so much that I had to grip the strap of my handbag till my knuckles turned white. 'Gotta go. Bye.'

I shot away, almost running into the office and slamming the door behind me. Thankfully, Stephanie wasn't in, and the room was silent and empty.

It's so weird that I can miss Richard so much and yet not be upset that he's got a new girlfriend—Wendy, who, according to Megan, stays for 'sleepovers in Daddy's bed'. But the mere thought of Sean with another woman still makes me want to just die with pain.

I remember the list I wrote after that little exchange. I sat in my office for a long time, until cramp prickled at my toes and my head throbbed with the effort of not crying. I hadn't even bothered to unzip my laptop or get out my notebook—there was no chance of getting any work done that day. Eventually I took a sheet of paper off the printer and slowly wrote another list, in my neatest handwriting:

- *Is she older/younger/prettier/sexier/better than me?*
- *Was he lying when he said he wasn't sleeping with her?*
- *Does she know that he hates his skinny calves?*
- *Does he bring her Tea in Pants?*
- *Does she know how much he loved my bottom?*
- *Does she know that only six months ago he sent me a text saying 'I really love you' and then finished with me, a week later?*

Then I'd trudged home, locked the doors, run a bath, and lay in it for two hours crying like a teenager who'd just been chucked. Then I got dressed and went to collect Megan from school.

'So, honestly, Claudio, there's nothing going on between me and him any more.' *He just wrecked my marriage then fucked off,* I refrain from adding.

'I'm not sure I believe you,' he says, standing up and fitting the key back in the lock. Then he comes back and leans even closer. 'But if you ever lie to me again, Jo, you will be very, very sorry.'

Then he hits me really hard around the side of my head. Boxes my ear, I suppose. Hard enough that I keel sideways and see stars, tiny white dots like fireflies. I'm too shocked to speak.

He stands up. 'Like I said, Jo. You'll be very sorry.'

I don't even hear the door being locked and bolted again, over the ringing in my ear.

Chapter Twenty
Day 3

What actually happened last week with Sean was that he left a note stuck behind the windscreen wiper of my car: 'I REALLY REALLY MISS YOU.' My heart leapt with joy—tempered with caution, of course, because he'd done this before. I still seemed to run into him with alarming regularity in Brockhurst—it's another reason I'm glad Steph and I gave up the office, because it was right next to the gym—and he'd give me these long, longing looks and the little sad smile that said *I don't know what went wrong, I still love you* . . . I could assume—as Donna obviously did, when I talked to her about it—that this was just wishful thinking on my part, were it not for the further evidence.

The day after the note, I got a call from him. Last Monday, I think it was. Steph and I were in her flat having coffee. I'd been telling her about the first couple of dates with Claudio—wait, that's a point! She knows about Claudio! Perhaps she'll realise he might have something to do with it when she hasn't heard from me for a few days?

Anyway, when I saw the display on my phone screen, I froze.

'It's Sean,' I hissed in hushed tones, as the phone pulsed in my hand.

'Well, answer it!' she said, half-impatient, half-resigned. She was clearly thinking, 'Oh no, here we go again . . .'

I answered it. 'Hi, Sean.'

'Hi, Jo, you all right? Just drove down Elm Road, saw your car and . . . well . . . I wondered what it was doing there. How come you're not in your office?'

He was checking up on me, because my car wasn't where it should be? All those months after we split up, and when he's got a new girlfriend? How odd.

I wish he'd bloody well check up on me now. He could take Claudio out in a second.

'We've given up the office. I'm just visiting . . . a friend,' I replied then, not wanting him to know that it was only Steph, that I wasn't visiting a boyfriend. I felt like saying, 'What's it to you?' but my annoying heart was too busy singing, 'He's jealous, he's jealous, he still wants you!'

'So are you still there?'

'Yes. Why?'

'Wondered if we could have a chat. If I'm not interrupting anything, that is.'

I didn't know whether to dance around the room, or to tell him to sod off. This was really it this time—he wanted me back! He'd realised that there was no point going out with the Twelve-Year-Old (as I christened her, after I saw him outside Boots holding hands with her a couple of weeks ago. I bet she buys all her clothes from Gap Kids. No pub in the land would serve her without ID) and he wanted a real woman again.

I went over to the window and peered out—sure enough, there he was, standing by the kerb, suspiciously eyeing up my car and scuffing the toe of his trainer on the pavement as he talked to me on the phone.

'See you in a minute, then,' I told him and hung up, turning to Stephanie. 'He wants to talk to me! He's outside.'

Steph joined me at the window. 'Couldn't you have played just a *little* bit harder to get? Make him wait for at least ten minutes.' Then she added, 'In fact, do you really think you ought to go at all? I mean, you've been here before, haven't you? He's going to tell you how screwed up he is over you, and how much he misses you, and you'll get all excited—but then when you ask him to give you two another try, he'll say no, and you'll be gutted. Again. He's a textbook sufferer of Narcissistic Personality Disorder. I read all about it in *Cosmopolitan*. He can't commit, but he just wants everyone to be in love with him. And besides, you've got another date with the Italian Stallion bloke next week, haven't you, so why don't you concentrate on that instead? He might be the man of your dreams.'

I hesitated. She had a point—about Sean, that was, not Claudio. Despite fancying him, I was pretty sure even then that Claudio wouldn't turn out to be the man of my dreams, but I'd agreed to go out with him anyway. Just in case.

As for Sean, I already knew exactly what I was going to do.

'Oh, you know what I think: there's no point in trusting my instincts. It won't make any difference in the long run. What will be will be.'

Stephanie sighed despairingly. 'Well, I think that's very defeatist,' she said, uncapping a tube of hand cream and rubbing a smear into her fingernails. The smell of almonds filled the air.

'You can't help who you fall in love with,' I added feebly, checking my make-up in her mirror. 'Well, see you later. Don't watch from the window. You'll embarrass me.'

'Don't worry. I don't think I could bear to watch,' she said. 'Good luck. You'll need it.'

'Went to Eastbourne last weekend,' Sean said without preamble when I joined him on the kerb.

It was exactly a year since he and I had gone to Eastbourne for the weekend. I wonder if he remembered that. We'd had the most amazing time: playing pool, dancing in a tacky pier nightclub, having totally outrageous sex in the hotel, on the beach, in the car . . .

'With the Twel—your girlfriend?'

'Michelle. Yeah.'

My eyes instantly filled up. 'Sean. I so don't want to know that! It's a year since we went. Why would you tell me that you'd gone again with someone else?'

'No, but you don't understand. All weekend, I could only think of you. I missed you so much. We went to all the same places that you and I went to. We even stayed in the same hotel! I couldn't stop talking about you, not once.'

'That must have been nice for Michelle,' I said sardonically.

Sean dismissed this with a wave of the hand. 'Oh, she's not the jealous type.'

'Just as well, for her sake. Anyway, Sean, like I said, I really don't want to know.'

He reached out and touched my hand. 'Shall we sit in your car for a bit?'

I shrugged, glancing up to see if Stephanie was watching. Fortunately there was no sign of her.

'OK.'

We climbed in awkwardly and sat facing one another across the hand brake. He picked up my hand again and caressed it gently.

'The reason I'm telling you is this: it wasn't the same, going with Michelle. It was like going with a mate. We didn't even kiss, let alone do anything else!'

I shook my head, confused. It was clear that things had moved on between the two of them since last month, when he'd announced that he 'couldn't do anything' at all with her. Now it seemed that he could, but hadn't wanted to in Eastbourne. Perhaps he was waiting for her sixteenth birthday. Or for her to grow some breasts, or something.

'Everyone thinks I'm so happy and sorted out,' he continued, 'but I'm not. I'm so screwed up, I just don't know what to do. I keep thinking I should go away, on a retreat or something, or maybe go travelling round the world for a year.'

'I think that's a great idea,' I said grimly. 'Do it!'

Sean gazed deep into my eyes, still stroking my hand. It felt as though his touch brought back as many memories as there were nerve-endings on my palm.

'I couldn't,' he said. 'I've got . . . too many emotional ties here to think about leaving.'

Now he was really rubbing it in. 'With Michelle?' I said, just to check.

He smiled sadly. 'No. With you, of course.'

I was flabbergasted. 'Then why don't you want to give things a go with me, if that's true?'

He looked shifty. 'Well. It's a bit awkward, see. Michelle's stepmother is the bar manager at the gym.'

Unbelievable. I couldn't help being sarcastic: 'Oh well, in that case, you'll have to marry her, won't you?' I wanted to slap him around his big stupid head.

'Do you want a hug?' he said, ignoring my snarky comment.

Say no, say no, say no, my instincts begged me from somewhere deep inside. As usual I ignored their distant trumpeting, and nodded.

'Let's get out so we can have a proper hug.' Sean opened the door and leapt expectantly into the gutter, his arms open. It was so surreal. He always liked me to be up a step from him when we hugged, so our heights were better matched. I couldn't help thinking that the Twelve-Year-Old probably had to stand on a stepladder.

Still, I fell into his arms, and I had to admit it was like coming home. He enveloped me in a huge bear hug, my head fitting perfectly into the space between his neck and shoulder. We stayed there for a long time. I inhaled the warm smell of him and felt his body pressing closely against mine. Motorists and passing pedestrians gave us odd looks, this couple half on the pavement and half in the road. Meanly, I wished that the Twelve-Year-Old would drive past and see us (although, of course, she's probably not old enough to drive, is she? Perhaps she could cycle past instead. I imagined her pedalling along behind her dad, on a tug-along attached to the back of the big bike, like Richard used to do with Megan. Ha . . .).

'We had such an amazing relationship. I can't believe I didn't see it before. We had an incredible time, didn't we? Nobody could ever compete with you, Jo. I mean it. You and I were something else together, weren't we? But it's too late now . . .'

Sean was murmuring into my ear over the sound of the passing traffic, caressing me, holding me tighter and tighter, and I wanted it to last forever. I caught a glimpse of Stephanie at her living room window making hideous faces at me, but I pretended not to see her and closed my eyes. I kissed the side of Sean's neck and moved my mouth towards his—but he turned away at the last minute.

Suddenly I knew exactly what he was thinking: he was thinking, 'I'm not being unfaithful to Michelle if we don't kiss. It's just a hug . . .'

I broke away from him and stared at him. Time to stop pussy-footing around. 'So why are you telling me this? Why did you want to see me? Do you want us to get back together? I mean, I'm not saying I would, definitely'—this was my attempt to play hard to get—'but I might consider it. It might not be too late.'

He blushed slightly and stepped back onto the pavement so that he was taller than me again.

'But it is too late, Jo . . . I'm with Michelle now.'

Frustration, rage, and sorrow built up in me until I felt like jumping up and down with fury. He'd got me again, reeled me in like a fat stupid carp. I wanted to scream insults at him, punch him, kick him in the balls. This was the man who was wild with jealousy as I was going through the long, painful process of extricating myself from my marriage, which I thought I had to do because surely nobody could ever love me more than Sean did. This was the man who sobbed with abandon when I told him I was struggling with my decision to get divorced and thinking that the right thing to do was surely to at least try to give things a go with Richard. This was the man who begged me not to. This was the man who told me gleefully that he knew exactly how he was going to propose to me, just as soon as my divorce came through. This was the man who, right after that last wonderful weekend in Eastbourne, said he couldn't bear it any more and that he knew the right thing to do would be to leave me alone until I got the divorce sorted out and finalized, that he didn't feel comfortable going out with a woman who was not yet divorced, even if she had been separated for some months. This was the man who said he'd wait 'as long as it took' until I could be his, because I was worth waiting for.

This, then, was the man for whom I hurried through my divorce, quashing the nagging little voice in my head saying 'You haven't given you and Richard a fair chance to work things out.'

This was the man who, when I finally rang him up to tell him that my decree absolute had arrived, announced that I'd always be the love of his life, but that 'he couldn't handle it', and left me.

What I wanted to say to him that day was, 'You are a narcissistic, selfish arsehole, and I wouldn't go out with you anyway. I've met someone else, as it happens.'

But of course what I actually said was, 'Well. Good luck. See you around.'

So I'm not at all surprised that he's texted me since. I'm such a wuss when it comes to Sean, and because he really is a narcissist, he just wants to keep me hanging on indefinitely.

Bastard.

Chapter Twenty-One
Day 3

After Claudio's gone I lie there for a very long time, my ear throbbing, while the stars gradually subside. I wish I could get rid of the memories of Sean as quickly.

I have to make a conscious effort to get him out of my head.

I have to make a conscious effort to get away from Claudio. I force out the bitter thoughts of Sean and try to concentrate instead on my current predicament.

Last time I read my diary there was a mention of the fact that Claudio fancied me. I think it's weird that I had no recollection of it. I hadn't even remembered that he was a member of the swimming club too. I had better not tell him what scant memories I have of him. He's still upset that I didn't remember him writing me that stupid song. I decide again that I should perhaps try to flatter him a bit instead. Tell him that I had a secret crush on him when we were kids, but didn't realise how he felt. Would that work? It feels so deeply counterintuitive, but I need to start trying harder to get him to believe I could love him. I can't be too over-the-top, but if I play it right maybe I can let him think I'm thawing towards him. After all, I did really quite fancy him up until recently. It can't be impossible to 'fake it till I make it', can it? I remember times towards the end with Richard when he kept reaching for me and I kept backing away. I had no desire for him at all, not an iota. When I—reluctantly—used to kiss him it felt like licking a frozen pump, fearful and desperate.

I pick up the diary again. There is a section of its pages that are clipped together with a paperclip. When I first found it, I hadn't thought much of it, thought it was random, but now I've got to the page, I see the warning:

PRIVATE! EVEN MORE PRIVATE THAN THE REST OF THIS DIARY. PLEASE DON'T READ.

I suppose that must have been for Mum's benefit, although I don't know that she ever even knew I kept a diary. I was pretty haphazard with it, though. Weeks went by without me writing anything, and most events seem to be written about in retrospect, days or sometimes months after they happened. I think I had delusions of being a novelist around that time, so I probably looked at it as if it were my 'memoirs'.

I'm intrigued—what was going on in my life at that time that needed such rigorous censoring? But as soon as I start to read, I remember. It wasn't scandal or misbehaviour that I was trying to keep private. It was shame. Even now, more than a quarter of a century later, I feel it afresh. My other ear starts to burn in tandem with the one Claudio whacked.

I don't even want to write about this. Maybe it will help. But I would die if anyone ever read it. Just die.

I suppose it started after Daddy died. The first time it was a massive craving for sausage in batter and chips. But Grease + Calorific Awareness = Guilt, and it was only the taste I wanted. So I had an idea.

What if I went along to the Chinese chip shop, handed my money across the shiny metal counter, carried the hot damp heaviness of the plain paper packet home in my hands, smelling the mouth-watering scent of the chips and feeling the tingling of the vinegar inside my nostrils . . . What if, once home, I unwrapped the parcel, inhaled the full unfettered heavenly smell, added a snowstorm of salt and a spring shower of extra Sarsons, took a bite of the spicy, warm sausage in its delicious swaddling of batter . . . but just didn't swallow it?

I could just spit the mouthful out, into a paper towel, right before that point of no return when my saliva went into overdrive and the swallowing reflex became too overpowering (we did it in Human Biology). That way I'd get all the taste with none of the calories. Perfect!

The thing is, though, I underestimated just how powerful the swallowing reflex really is. As soon as that golden vinegary potato hit my taste buds, my mouth simply refused to let it go, zipping shut my lips, forcing me to swallow. My throat wanted that food, and so did my tummy. They weren't giving it up, not until it had reached its destination.

So that idea didn't actually work. I ended up eating every mouthful of two great fat sausages in batter, and a large portion of chips. Afterwards I felt so bloated, huge, a grease-soaked sausage myself in a 34H bra and Lee jeans that had to be undone at the waist. The food sat uncomfortably in my stomach, like it was saying to me, Look, I never wanted to be in here in the first place. What are you going to do about it?

It didn't take me long to realise that it wasn't too late to fix it. A clandestine trip to the bathroom, two saliva-slick fingers down my throat, and whoosh, problem solved. Slowly at first, and then in great liberating splurges of anti-calorie. Straight down the toilet, cut out the middle man.

143

Not quite as satisfactory as spitting into a paper towel, and harder work, but infinitely more rewarding, tastewise.

───────⌣───────

That night, the night of Balaclava Man, after Donna took her damp togs and my appropriated Europe single and went home—in a mini-cab, paid for by Mum, I later found out, 'in case he was still out there'— I was lying in bed, on my left side so as not to put any weight on my grazed right cheek. But my nose was all blocked up on the left, from crying, and I wanted to roll over. I tried lying on my back, but it made me feel vulnerable. Then I realised that I was starving. Crying always makes me peckish. On the day of Dad's funeral I ate sixteen mushroom vol-au-vents, one after the other.

I waited until all was silent downstairs, knowing that Mum would have nodded off on the sofa, the fire out, test-card on the television, nobody to tap her on the arm and say, 'Come to bed, darling, you're snoring,' as Daddy used to do. It never occurred to me to tell her to wake up and go to bed. It would have been presumptuous. I tiptoed down-stairs to the kitchen in my dressing gown and slippers.

I opened the larder door and conducted a quick recce of the con-tents. Not much that day, since it was a Friday, the day before our big Safeways shop-cum-ogle-at-John, but enough to make do with. I found four tins: a tin of custard powder, one of fruit cocktail, one of peaches, and one of prunes. I heated up a pint of milk and stirred in the custard powder. I love custard powder. It's the way it's pink, before it goes yellow, and it tastes gritty, pink and sugary. I poured it into a big mixing bowl and added the tinned fruit. If only there was some fresh cream in the fridge. I thought about adding a carpet of hundreds and thousands, and some glacé cherries, and bingo, I'd almost have a beautiful trifle— but decided that the aesthetics weren't really top of my agenda. I rinsed out and squashed the empty fruit cans as quietly as I could under the *hard rubber sole of my slipper before hiding them at the bottom of the bin under the sink. Then I washed up the custardy saucepan and wooden spoon, running the taps at little more than a trickle. Eventually I tiptoed down the hall past my snoring lonely mum and back to my bedroom, nursing the mixing bowl.*

It occurred to me as I sat in bed shovelling in the fruity custard that this was the same mixing bowl that Dad used to bring out whenever I was poorly. He'd perch on top of the covers next to me, holding the bowl underneath my chin for me to vomit into, stroking my sweaty hair away from my face. 'My beautiful girl, my beautiful daughter,' he'd murmur, even when I was bug-eyed, retching stinking bile.

That night I didn't need to stick my fingers down my throat. In fact I hardly made it to the bathroom in time before the whole yellow lot came up again, prompted only by the memory of the sour breath of that man in the balaclava, and his mean trespassing hands roaming over my fat helpless body.

I close the diary. I don't do that any more, thank God. But I still want to sometimes. I hate myself so much that I want to push everything good away, out of me.

That's the crux of it, really: I have never loved myself, so how can I love anybody else? Since John, I've *always* faked it. I faked it with Richard at first, and when I stopped faking it then I pushed him away. In hindsight I faked it with Sean—I thought he was the love of my life, but if I'm honest, I fell for him out of vanity, sheer vanity and boredom. The fact that a beautiful, fit, young man could love me in such an all-consuming way blinded me to the truth— that I was a conquest to him, a MILF, a sexy older married woman. When I extricated myself from my marriage, he ran a mile. I guess I hadn't been the only one faking it.

Therefore I can fake it with Claudio too.

I have to be able to—my life depends on it.

Chapter Twenty-Two
Day 3

I haven't heard the home phone ring all day, or the doorbell. Eileen hasn't checked to see why I didn't show up for my appointment—well, maybe she phoned, but she hasn't come round. I suppose why would she? She probably thinks I forgot. Stephanie hasn't come, and neither has Donna. This is how old people die alone in their houses. Minus the lunatic obsessed kidnapper.

For the past couple of hours I have been teetering on the precipice of hysteria, that feeling that something could set me off at any moment and I would either laugh myself into a heap or howl uncontrollably.

I've not had much of a sense of humour in the last couple of years. Although I think a lot of people forget, or lose the ability, to laugh daily once they're well into adulthood. My Eighties diary is full of stories about Donna and me laughing until our bellies ached and tears streamed down our cheeks, collapsing on one another's shoulders with merriment. But I only remember doing it before the end of that year. We've laughed since, of course, but not like that.

Surely Donna will come! She knows I'm never away from my phone for long. She would come and ring the doorbell, I know she would. My phone will be full of increasingly puzzled and concerned messages.

Although our friendship seems to have waned a bit since Richard and I split up. That kind of hurts, if I'm honest—when I need her more than ever, she backs off? I know she's busy with Henry and the twins, and Henry and Richard are friends—but she and I have been friends since we were fourteen.

We're still managing to go swimming once a week, though. On a Thursday—so when's that? Two days' time? I'm starting to lose track. No—three. It's Monday today, Eileen day. Whenever a radio announcer mentions the day or the date, I scratch it—literally scratch, with my fingernail, because Claudio took the pens—in a notebook I found in my room, because I can see it all getting hazier by the hour. The notebook is one of Megan's, with pink unicorns on the front and a few scribbles of hers on the first few pages.

We swim at the old pool in Brockhurst, the one we used to train at when we were kids. I prefer the more modern pool at the gym—the changing rooms at the old baths are so scummy, you think you'll catch a verruca the minute you set foot on the slimy, hair-swirled tiles, and there's always bits of detritus lurking in the bottom of the lockers, sweet wrappers and used tissues and, if you're really unlucky, somebody's forgotten dirty knickers—but I can't go to the one at the gym any more in case I bump into Sean.

Donna never even got to meet him properly. She was always asking to, but I have to admit I felt a bit embarrassed, when Richard and I were such good friends with her and Henry. I told her that it was too soon and too weird for them to see me with someone new. It was true—but if I'm honest I think the real reason was because I was a bit embarrassed to be seen with him. I thought he would compare unfavourably to Richard, who is the perfect dinner guest, despite his working-class origins. Richard knows about wine, and the correct way to eat asparagus or oysters, and any other tricky matters of dining etiquette—you could take him anywhere. Whereas I could see that Donna would think Sean was great eye-candy for a night out on the town but a bit of a social liability in any restaurant more classy than the local Indian. In fact, the local Indian is called the Viceroy, and Sean once referred to it as the Vicky-Roy.

Donna did see him, just once—I sneaked her up to the gym and surreptitiously pointed him out when she'd brought the twins for their tae kwon do class in the dance studio. I was a bit disappointed that she didn't seem to share my views on how gorgeous he is—I suppose it was a bit unfortunate that we caught him sort of preening in front of the big mirrors by the free weights. All she said was, 'Bet he has those massive tubs of protein powder in his kitchen cupboards.' She can be a bit of a snob, can Donna.

It was pretty obvious that she believed my relationship with Sean was pure rebound, a reaction to what I perceived as being wrong with Richard. She thinks I ditched the small, skinny intellectual platonic friend-husband for the huge, muscly passionate meathead lover.

I suppose she'd be right.

Wait—Donna knows about Claudio too! I've just remembered: we talked about him last time we went swimming—she asked if I'd been on any more dates lately. She specifically asked about Claudio! And when I smiled secretively, she got all excited.

'*What*? You have? You're in love with Claudio? Come on, spill the beans!' She ruffled up the water around us with exaggerated enthusiasm and it reminded me of her fifteen-year-old self. I laughed and told her to calm down, that we were going on another date but I wasn't exactly crazy about him, I was just seeing how it went. Then we got on to the subject of internet dating.

'The whole dating thing makes me laugh,' I said. 'It's fun. I like meeting new people. I like the attention, and the anticipation, and the whole rigmarole of getting ready to go out on a date and all the different sorts of characters you meet. I need fun in my life. Do you remember that song that went *There's an army of lovers/ Just waiting to meet you*? That's what it feels like—internet dating anyway. That, or online grocery shopping: browse the products, click on the ones you like, add them to your basket, proceed to checkout . . .'

I don't feel like that any more.

'You do need some fun,' Donna agreed, laughing too. 'Henry thinks you're mad to do internet dating, you know. He's convinced the websites are bulging with married men looking for a bit on the side, and white slave traffickers or, at the very least, ruthless sex maniacs preying on vulnerable single women . . .'

'Well, the only really bad experience I've had so far was with that nutter Gerald—you know, the one who told me I was a stuck-up whore of Babylon. But he was the exception—I hope. It's not like that any more. Everyone does it these days,' I said.

I always thought Henry was such a square, but I don't any more. I think he's totally sensible.

Donna continued, 'I know. I didn't tell Henry about the Whore of Babylon guy, or the wine-bottle poo guy—although you have to admit, they're great stories. And you met Claudio on the Babylon date, so it can't all be bad. I reckon those tales of doom and gloom about internet dating are like the story about swans being able to break a man's arm. Is that truth, or urban myth? Because nobody's ever actually met anybody who's had their arm broken by a swan, have they? I told Henry that, too. It's generally assumed to be a dubious and potentially dangerous activity, but whoever heard of anybody who's been imperilled by someone they've been on a blind date with? If you're careful, and don't do anything silly like inviting them round to yours for the first date, or agreeing to go on a long walk in a remote part of the countryside, with a man who brings black bin-liners, rope, and a large curved knife "just in case . . ." And you're always so careful. You never even walk anywhere on your own after dark!'

Those words come back to me now like a kick in the teeth. I hadn't ever invited Claudio in and I'd known him since I was sixteen: he wasn't just 'some guy off the internet'. But I didn't like him then, so why didn't I just listen to my instincts?

Donna knows about Claudio. She'll come, I know she will. She has to.

But what if she doesn't? She thinks I like him. She's glad I've met someone new. I even rang her up, far too late at night, after my second date with him.

Date number two with Claudio was in Kingston, halfway between our two homes. We ate soft, salty focaccia dipped in olive oil at Carluccio's, where he then impressed me by ordering our main courses in fluent Italian. Unfortunately the waitress was obviously from New Malden or Surbiton or somewhere, and had not the faintest clue what he was saying, which was a bit of a shame. But it worked for me.

'You're a dark horse. I didn't know you could speak the language,' I said admiringly.

'The language of love,' he replied, making a corny face at me. 'I have my mother to thank for that—she insisted I grew up bilingual.'

'How is your mother?' I asked. Claudio's lip wobbled slightly, and my heart went out to him.

'Not good,' he said, after a pause. 'I offered to move back down to Brockhurst to be nearer her, but she wouldn't let me. She prefers it this way. She is very independent. But I visit her every week.' It's the most he's ever said about her.

'I'm so sorry.' I put my hand sympathetically on top of his and gave it a squeeze. He managed a brave little smile, like a small boy who's fallen off his bike. He gazed at a shelf full of packets of dried pasta and exotic oils, tears welling.

'I will miss her very much when she's gone.'

'Yes. It's so tough. But I'm sure she's really happy that you're there for her, and seeing so much of her.'

He turned his hand over and grasped mine, and for the first time I was able to fully forget the Claudio I had disliked as a teenager.

'But now I've got you, Jo, and I can't tell you how happy that makes me.'

I smiled, half-pleased, half-doubtful. Claudio reckoned he 'had me', after one-and-a-half dates? But I liked his positivity about us.

Or at least that's what I thought then.

He passed the second date test with flying colours, where you decide whether you like someone more or less than on the first date. It can so often go either way. There was something so vulnerable about him, which came out more strongly the more I talked to him; a certain strange reserve that made me think that he'd been hurt before. When I mentioned anything about previous relationships, a hooded expression came over his face and he looked depressed, almost agitated. I supposed it must be because of the woman who dumped him at the altar. Poor Claudio, I thought—it must have been bad. I was sure he'd tell me about it, in good time.

Frankly, I was just so delighted to be on a date with someone who wasn't wearing a single item of comedy clothing—no Homer Simpson tie, or Mickey Mouse waistcoat, or even Arsenal socks, all a massive turn-off—and to whom I felt more and more drawn as the evening progressed. I liked the fact that he had the kind of context that my other internet dates lacked: having known him as a kid meant that I trusted him a good deal more than I would normally be predisposed to.

By the end of the date when we said goodbye at the taxi rank, I was desperate for him to kiss me. He reached down towards my expectantly tilted-up face, I held my breath, and he brushed my lips with his and smiled. His lips felt dry but soft. The pressure of the kiss increased, and I broke out in goose bumps as his tongue slipped gently into my mouth. I wanted more, but he broke away. That was when I got a faint whiff of something rotten coming from his mouth, or stomach, and I blanched—but then dismissed it. Everyone had the odd bit of bad breath now and then.

Now I think the evil smell was coming from his *soul.*

'See you soon?' he asked, his eyes gleaming under the street lights. Two teenage girls in tiny white mini-skirts and very high heels tottered past, and one nudged the other, pointing admiringly at Claudio. It's pretty shallow, but I liked the idea of having a boyfriend whom other women would notice. Claudio wasn't gorgeous, but he definitely had something about him.

'Very soon,' I promised him and jumped into my cab, my heart thumping like a schoolgirl's at a One Direction concert.

I had to ring Donna when I got home, too drunk on red wine and excitement to let my habitual reticence kick in—reticence at least when it came to telling her about my dates. She always claimed to want to know, but somehow I got this overwhelmingly disapproving vibe off her, even as she was giving me the third degree. I felt as if she was never going to forgive me for leaving Richard and breaking up our happy foursome.

Henry answered, sounding irritated. 'Hello?'

'Hiya, Henry, it's Jo. Is Donna there?'

One of their dogs was barking in the background, wearily, as if being forced to.

Henry raised his voice slightly to be heard over it. 'Jo, she's in bed. It's midnight. Is it an emergency?'

I felt awful. Of course it was late. I hadn't even thought. How selfish of me! 'I'm really sorry. I didn't realise the time. No, no, everything's fine.' I realised, belatedly, that it was probably the ring of the telephone that had set the dog off—Donna mentioned once before that the phone always made it bark. Whoops. 'I'll call her tomorrow instead.'

I considered telling Henry to pass on the message that I thought I'd finally met someone who 'got it'. But, probably wisely, I decided against it. I wondered if Henry had had a similar conversation with Richard, in which Richard said that Wendy 'got it'?

Chapter Twenty-Three
Day 3

'What did you mean when you said Sean was contrary?' Claudio demands as soon as we sit down.

We are at least out of my bedroom, but Claudio has shackled me to him, my right wrist to his left. He has made gin and tonics and put out small bowls of nuts and olives, and I can see that he's plumped the sofa cushions and straightened the three remote controls into regimented lines on the coffee table. I can also see that he's feeling guilty for having hit me earlier.

We are of course forced to sit together on the sofa. The G&T is good, even though it's in a plastic picnic beaker. It's cold and strong and fizzes on my tongue, feeling like the first G&T I've ever had. Plus, the sheer pleasure of being in a different room, one that has actual daylight streaming around the sides of the thin, drawn curtains, is making me feel even more heady. I'm inclined to be co-operative, even though my ear is still fat and burning. He knows that I know he'll just hit me again if I do anything unexpected like trying to scream—we're at the front of the flat now, overlooking the street. I think longingly of *people,* real, non-fucked-up people two floors down, going about their business: buying cauliflower and loo paper and scratch cards from the mini-mart up the road; going home to cook dinner for their wives and kids . . .

'Like I said, Sean is in my past now,' I tell Claudio carefully. 'He dumped me six months ago, but it's like he doesn't want me to think badly of him or forget him. Possibly he still wants me to be in love with him even though he doesn't love me any more.'

It is difficult to say those words out loud.

Claudio puts his left hand, the one handcuffed to mine, on my right knee, so my own hand has no choice but to go along for the ride. 'He must be insane,' he says, without a trace of irony. 'If we were together, properly, I'd never let you go—and when we are, I won't. Was he the love of your life?'

I've thought about this before. I take a big swig of the gin before answering, carefully. 'I believed he was. He was the one I felt most passionately about, since John. But if I've only had one love of my life, it was John.'

Claudio leans back, taking me with him. I feel like a ventriloquist's dummy. 'Do you believe that people only have one true love?'

I shrug. 'I don't know. No. I think you can have more than one. My counsellor said that most people only ever truly fall in love a couple of times in their lives. You can love lots of partners over the years but there probably won't be more than one or two stand-out ones.'

'Eileen,' Claudio agrees, nodding.

I close my eyes. He knows about Eileen. 'You cancelled my appointment this week, didn't you,' I state flatly.

'Yup.'

'But I don't keep a record of them in my phone! How did you know?'

'I looked through your cheque stubs and there's a forty-pound payment to an Eileen Marks once a week. I Googled her and found out her number and who she was. Then I just texted her from your phone to say you were away for a few weeks.'

'Great.'

'Don't be like that, Jo. Tell me more about Sean. I want to know what he's got that I haven't. I'm genuinely interested. Did you cheat on Richard with him, is that why you got divorced?'

I sigh. 'I did fall in love with him while I was still married. But nothing physical happened between us until after I left Richard. It's complicated.'

'So? We've got all night.' Claudio tosses an almond into his mouth like a sea-lion catching a fish, as though he's watching a baseball match on TV rather than watching me dissect my failed relationships.

'My marriage wasn't that great at the time,' I begin reluctantly. 'We spent years and years trying to have a baby, focusing all our emotional energy on getting pregnant, doing IVF, me having loads of miscarriages . . . but we really stuck together through it. Richard was unbelievably supportive. And then when Megan finally came along, it was like we both just took our foot off the pedal with each other, like, "We're sorted now." Richard assumed that because I'd had the baby I always wanted, he didn't need to make an effort with me any more, or at least that's how it felt to me. I thought that having Megan would make us more of a family but really it made us less of one. He got a new job and worked crazy hours—we never saw him.'

'What does he do, anyway?' Claudio says it like he couldn't care less, but I see the way he holds his breath. He doesn't want Richard to be more successful than he is.

'He's got his own company: graphic design and branding.'

Claudio scowls.

'He's doing *really* well.' I can't help it.

'So you thought it would be a good idea to shag your personal trainer?'

He's getting his revenge.

'No! Not at all. I thought Sean was really attractive but I didn't for a minute want to leave Richard. I loved him. And anyway I had no idea that Sean fancied me too. He didn't give me any indication of it, not for ages.'

Claudio smiles fondly at me. 'That's one of the things I love about you, Jo. You have no idea how beautiful you are.'

You have no idea how beautiful you are. Ironically, these are the exact same words Sean also once said to me. That was the moment I first twigged that he felt the same about me as I did about him.

Up until then, our discussions during personal training were of a strictly professional nature—how much carbohydrate I ought to eat and at what times of day, when to increase the weights, how to stretch my back. But I loved the sessions. I loved waking up and knowing that I'd be seeing him later that morning. I always booked my sessions for the mornings when the gym was at its least busy—fewer other women looking at him.

I loved seeing my waistline becoming tighter and my triceps honed. I even loved the ache in my thighs and buttocks and shoulders at the end of every hour. I'd leave the gym exhausted but buzzing with adrenaline, and the next day I'd be back again—not for personal training, but just to jog along the treadmill and surreptitiously watch Sean working with his other clients.

His face began to light up every time I walked into the gym, but I didn't think anything of that. In fact, I thought I was probably imagining it. But when I did a small controlled experiment to see his reaction to other women's arrivals, it did seem that the polite smile he gave to them was different from the broad one he'd give me. He'd give me the sort of smile you'd walk over broken glass for. But I still assumed that he just liked me as a person, that was all.

Gradually, the horizons of our topics of conversation broadened beyond the gym equipment and out into more personal territory. He asked me one day how well Richard and I got on.

'Fine,' I said carefully. 'We're very good mates. Always important in a marriage.' I watched for any change in Sean's expression, not sure whether I wanted to see one or not, but none came.

'Right: hamstrings now,' was all he said.

Somehow I ended up telling him how Richard worked most evenings and many weekends, not to mention the frequent business trips and client dinners. How, since he'd started out on his own, his work had gone completely mental and the company was expanding monthly. That it was great the business was such a success, but that I'd thought it would mean he'd be around for Megan and me more often, not less often. Sean was a good listener. I wasn't moaning or bitching, but somehow he managed to extract the sort of information from me that I hadn't really even told Donna. I suppose it's that sort of relationship—one on one, intimate in a bizarre sort of way. I learned more about him, too, that he had recently split up with his girlfriend, who used to leave him on his own for hours at parties, and put him down in front of her friends. I was astonished, and said so. I couldn't imagine anybody wanting to put Sean down, literally as well as emotionally. I also couldn't quite see Sean standing on his lonesome at a bar. Somehow I visualised him with a permanent gaggle of lovelorn women surrounding him.

One day, about three months after I'd started the training programme, he said to me, casually, as I performed my end-of-session calf and quad stretches, 'So, what do you do when your husband's out all the time or away? Do you, I mean, manage to get out at all yourself? It must be quite, sort of, lonely . . .'

'Well. It's not too bad. My daughter keeps me company, and my best friend Donna doesn't live that far away.'

Was it my imagination, or did he look disappointed? He dropped his eyes, and I realised he was staring at me as I leaned sideways to stretch.

'What a waist,' he said.

I straightened up, puzzled and a little offended. I thought he was talking about my marriage. 'What's a waste?'

'You. You've got a fantastic waist,' he blurted, and blushed.

'Oh! No, I haven't really, but thanks,' I said, immediately dismissive, as I always was when given an unsolicited compliment.

'You have no idea how beautiful you are, do you?' he asked, and looked away, leaving me gaping at the side of his bright red face.

Neither of us spoke for the rest of the session, but as we were confirming the time for the following week, he said, gazing at the carpet tiles, 'Um, I was just thinking, if you ever fancied going out for a drink or anything—purely *plu*tonically, of course—you could always give me a ring . . .'

I bit my lip to try not to laugh at his misuse of the word *platonic*, but I was touched all the same. He was blushing again. It didn't seem as if the invitation had been extended 'plutonically', but I was sure that he couldn't have any ulterior motives. During the course of one of our other conversations, he'd confessed that when he was younger he'd been instrumental in breaking up a marriage by having an affair with an older woman, and it had nearly destroyed them both. He said that he would never, ever even contemplate an affair, because he'd witnessed first-hand the devastation they wrought. The conviction in his voice had been so vehement that I felt safe in the belief that he'd never let me cheat on Richard with him.

And he didn't, as it turned out—at least not physically. But there's an awful lot of emotional infidelity it's possible to commit, without actually touching somebody . . .

Perhaps that was the problem. Perhaps if we'd just had sex right at the start, I'd have felt so guilty that I'd have run straight back to

Richard and confessed, and none of this nightmare would've happened. He might have forgiven me, if I'd begged enough. But the trouble was, Sean and I waited, wordlessly, our connection growing stronger and stronger, our attraction so palpable I could almost taste it on the tip of my tongue. I would feel myself growing wet and tingly just from talking to him about the weather—there was just something in the way we looked at each other.

I thought about him constantly, day and night. I even went away on my own, to Scotland, to try to clear my head. Should've gone with Richard, really, shouldn't I? No wonder the trip away didn't have the intended effect: Sean refused to be cleared from my overwhelmed, infatuated head. I should've told Richard, confessed to the infatuation, got him to help me through it. Perhaps he and I and Megan could have moved away, perhaps even up to Scotland, near Mum and Brian. Surely if I'd never seen him again, nothing could ever have happened?

But I'd always have wondered.

Another part of me knows that it had to happen. That we'd probably already crossed the line when he invited me out that time, 'plutonically'; that there was no going back. I had to leave Richard. I couldn't stay with him, feeling the way I did about Sean—and Sean about me. It wasn't fair on any of us. I should have owned up, though, told Richard that although nothing had happened, I was in love with another man. I didn't, because I didn't want to add insult to injury. I didn't want him to feel inadequate.

Inadequate . . . As if his wife telling him she wanted a divorce could have made him feel any other way! But I really thought it would be less devastating.

By the time Sean and I finally made love it was simply too late to turn back. Even though at that stage Richard would still have made a go of things with me if I'd let him. But I couldn't. I wanted Sean with every atom of my being. All those months of anticipation, fantasy, growing closeness, pure animal attraction—it was the most mind-blowing, intense, beautiful experience I have ever had. Everything about him was perfect and fitted me perfectly.

I straddled him, on his shabby little sofa, inching down on him, gazing into his bright blue eyes. We both cried. If I could have had any idea how many more times Sean and I were to cry together—and not through pleasure—I'd have jumped off that sofa and out of that house, right back into the safety of Richard's arms, regardless of the chemistry between me and Sean.

So technically I didn't actually, physically have an affair. Might as well as done, as it turned out. Might as well have been hung for a lamb as for a sheep. Perhaps if I hadn't left Richard first; if Sean and I had had the secret, sordid affair, rolling around guiltily on rumpled bedsheets in his tiny bland house, secret liaisons in out-of-the-way pubs, the full nine yards—it would have eventually run its course, and I'd have realised that a hard body and some sweet words were not enough to make it worthwhile leaving my lovely Richard. Especially if I'd known then what I know now, that Sean was never in it for the long haul. But I didn't know that then. He told me he wanted to marry me, wake up with me every morning for the rest of his life, be the one who made me complete . . . Why would I not believe that? Of course I believed it. So I left Richard and slept with Sean. What's that expression about there being no fools like old fools? That was me—a gullible old fool.

'I made a massive mistake,' I say bleakly. 'I wish I'd never set eyes on Sean.'

Claudio, still in sympathy mode, strokes my leg with his finger. 'No you didn't,' he says fondly. 'When one door closes, another one opens. If you had stayed with Richard, we'd never even have had a chance. Now at least we have a chance . . . right, Jo?'

And here it comes. He leans towards me, eyes closed, dog-breath in full force. I grit my teeth and reciprocate the kiss as swiftly as I can, a brush on his dry lips before snatching my head away, dreading the tongue.

'That's a good way to look at it,' I say, as tenderly as I can muster. 'Always good to think positive.'

'That's my girl!' he says, beaming.

'Could I have another gin, please?' I ask, picking up my empty beaker and rattling the almost-dissolved ice cubes.

'For you, my princess, anything,' he says, standing up and taking me with him. He seems almost high on that one brief kiss.

I force myself to smile. Make him think it could happen, if he's patient enough.

'We will continue the conversation later, then. I'm really enjoying it. This is what I'd hoped for, Jo—us getting to know one another better every day. Growing together.'

Puke.

As we walk down the hallway to the kitchen like conjoined twins, he starts trying to put his arm around me but then twigs that this is a physical impossibility while we're handcuffed together. Either it would twist my arm behind my back or he'd have to step in front of me to hug me and walk backwards, like the idiot he is. He quite often does little things like this that make me realise he doesn't think things through. Like trying to open a packet of chapattis with a fork. Like kidnapping me. He must have had the Rohypnol and handcuffs already, but what if he hadn't planned any of this beyond a sudden urge to keep me for himself? I'm pretty sure he rushed out that first morning to buy the wood for the windows, so he hadn't planned that in advance. He could have chucked his power tools and suitcase into the boot of my car that night he drugged me.

Perhaps he had originally only—only!—wanted to drug and rape me, but it all got out of control. It gives me a flicker of hope, that I can somehow use this to my advantage and escape.

'Isn't it difficult, though, for you to hear me talk about other men?'

I am genuinely curious about this. Surely it must feel to Claudio like prodding a bruise? Yet he seems happier than I've seen him since we've been incarcerated here together.

We squeeze through the kitchen door side by side and he opens the fridge for the bottle of tonic.

'Yes, in a way it is painful. But I feel more sorry for you than for me. There you were, making so many mistakes over the years that caused you so much pain, when you didn't realise that all you had to do was to be with me. And here we are, so it will all turn out right in the end, I know it will.'

'Make it a large one,' I mutter, as he pours the gin.

Chapter Twenty-Four
Day 3

Back in the front room with fresh drinks, Claudio pulls out my diary from under a cushion like a magician producing a rabbit from a hat, and my heart sinks.

'So,' he says, in therapist mode, 'there's one entry that really fascinated me. Did you have it?'

I guess there's no point reminding him that he said he wouldn't read it.

'Did I have what?'

'The breast reduction operation.'

I can't help blushing. 'Yes. Eventually, a couple of years after I first started thinking about it.'

'I thought you looked different. You shouldn't have done that, Jo. Your body was perfect the way it was. I loved it.'

'I didn't think it was perfect.'

'BUT I DID!' he suddenly screams in my face and I flinch back as far as the handcuffs will allow. There are actual tears in his eyes and a catch in his voice. 'I'm sorry for shouting, Jo, but that was a terrible thing to do! Messing with your God-given beauty.

How could you have voluntarily allowed yourself to be mutilated like that? You must have terrible scars now!'

'Not any more,' I mutter. 'You can barely see them.'

There doesn't seem to be any point in explaining how much better the operation made me feel, how after Dad and John and the man in the alley it was the first thing that made me feel good about myself again.

'It's complicated, Claudio. I'm sorry you don't approve, but it was the right thing for me. I don't regret it at all.'

'Well, I don't approve. And I don't understand why, although I imagine it is connected with this very poor body image you still seem to have. You were bulimic too. Are you still?'

I cringe, utterly mortified now. I feel laid bare, stripped down to muscle and sinew, pinned open like a frog for dissection. 'God, Claudio . . . .'

'We have no secrets!' he declaims, his anger gone again in a flash. 'Don't be ashamed. I can help.'

Interesting form of therapy. I wouldn't recommend it to anyone else.

'No, I'm not bul—' I can't even say the word. 'No, I'm not. I haven't been since I got married. Can I see which diary entry you're talking about?'

Lips pursed as though he thoroughly disapproves of my (private) insecurities, despite his protestations of sympathy, he hands over my diary open at the relevant page. I take my time reading it, mostly so I don't have to speak to him for a while:

30th December 1986

I've just pierced Donna's ear. Hope it doesn't go septic. We're in our PJs and I'm writing this lying on her bed. She keeps twisting the earring in her new TCP-drenched piercing, wincing as it burns and throbs. I'll feel so responsible if it does get all pus-y.

We've just been talking about my operation, and I'm beginning to wish I hadn't told her about it at all. She can't even bring herself to say the words 'breast reduction'—she goes: 'You won't be able to go swimming for ages, will you, if you have the . . . you know?'

'So what? Why do you keep going on about it?'

'Because it's a big deal; major surgery. I mean, just this one little hole in my ear hurts like mad. I can't imagine what it would feel like to . . . . well, you know. And what would you tell Sluggage? He'd go ape if you just stopped turning up. The B team would be rubbish if you weren't in it: they rely on you. 'Specially for the butterfly. And you couldn't tell him the real reason, could you?'

'I won't tell him anything. In fact, I'll probably give it up soon anyway. I'm getting a bit bored with it, to be honest.'

'Oh Jo! Don't! You can't leave me with all those hideous boys, and Slug shouting at me, without you there to have a laugh with. And if you're not there, Daddy will just nag me to join the Pony Club instead. He thinks that I mix with the wrong sort at the swimming club. I'm sure he only lets me come because he's got such a soft spot for you.'

Hmm, well, tough titties, Don. I like swimming and all, but it's so horrible, seeing all the boys staring at my enormous chest. In my Speedo I look like I've got a uniboob. And a hunchback too—I know I hunch my shoulders forwards to try to minimise the mounds of flesh oozing round under my bloody armpits and covering my whole ribcage. It would be worth never going swimming again just to have neat little 34Cs and to be able to proudly push my shoulders back. I wouldn't want to go back after the op anyway—they'd be bound to notice the difference.

Donna tries again. 'Boys like girls with big boobs. John told me.'

She obviously hadn't heard what Nigel Weston said about me at that gala in Guildford, then. It was so embarrassing. He nudged Simon Brown and said, 'Look at the state of that . . . you'd need a Sherpa to find your way round those tits, wouldn't you?'

I reluctantly told Donna that, but she dismissed it and said Nigel Weston had said far worse things about her. Apparently he told her that she looked like Bobby Sands three weeks into his hunger strike.

'One comment by Nigel Weston is no reason to have major surgery!'

I can't tell her what's finally made me book the operation—the memory of the man with the balaclava and what he did to me in the alley.

Instead, I jumped out of bed, ran over to Donna's knicker drawer and pulled out one of her tiny little lacy bras—pink, with half an inch of mooring at the back and wisps of silk for straps. Then I found my own bra in the pile of my clothes on the floor: a great, thick, scaffolded garment with rows and rows of reinforced hooks and eyes, and straps like seatbelts that leave deep red weals on both my shoulders.

I held up the two garments, one hooked over each thumb.

'Compare and contrast.'

'Yeah . . .' said Donna pensively. 'I suppose I do see your problem.'

You don't know the half of my problem, I thought.

She still had one more go at trying to talk me out of it though, saying she'd be there for me if I did it, but to make sure I had really thought it through . . . Duh.

'Obviously! I've read about it, and talked to the doctor. I'll probably look like I've been attacked by a shark afterwards, but the scars will fade. It'll be worth it.'

I didn't tell Donna what else I've learned: that the surgeon might remove as much as two or three pounds of boob fat from each side and, more gross, that he will cut off my nipples, trimming them down to half their previous size (like a frowny-faced child cutting circles out of coloured paper with round-ended scissors), leaving them sitting in a kidney bowl in the operation theatre while he gouges around in my chest, and then sews them back on again afterwards . . . . Imagine having your own nipples lying on a table next to you! I feel sick.

Across the room, Donna shudders telepathically. 'Ugh. Well. You gotta do what you gotta do, I suppose. But don't give up swimming. You love swimming.'

'I know. But . . .'

'What?'

'Nothing.'

'You said the scars would fade. So, come on—what?'

When I finally spoke, it was a tiny sound, almost a squeak. 'I've got to walk past that alley every time I go to training.'

'Sorry, Jo. I hope they catch the bastard. But I really don't mind walking you home, it's not a problem.'

'Thanks, Don.'

I did wonder at that point whether having smaller boobs really would help me feel any differently about anything.

31st December 1986

After Donna went to sleep last night I climbed out of bed. I went next door to the attic bathroom and threw up quietly, before spraying air-freshener and flushing the toilet twice. The pipes in the wall outside Donna's bedroom clanked as I ran the tap and cleaned my teeth, my whole body tensed in fear that the noise might wake her up.

I crept back into the bedroom, smelling of mint and fake lavender, avoiding all the creaky floorboards with a practised foot, climbed back into bed again, and closed my eyes. I hate myself.

Chapter Twenty-Five
Day 3

I am humiliated to think that Claudio read that; utterly mortified. Suddenly it occurs to me that *this* is why he is doing it. Not to 'get to know me better' but to exert control over me. The thought makes me shiver so I try to dismiss it. The gins are going straight to my head, and I've not eaten much today. Claudio has mentioned dinner a couple of times but made no move towards cooking anything—he seems to be enjoying our talk too much. Either he thinks we're bonding, or he's relishing watching me squirm. I'm not sure which is worse.

'Can we talk about Sunday's date?' he asks. 'It was such a lovely evening, just what I needed. But you women are so unpredictable! There was me, thinking it was all going so well . . .'

Actually I don't mind talking about this with him, but not for the reasons he thinks. Partly because it gets him off the subject of my body dysmorphia, and partly because I need to try to get it straight in my head anyway. Because if—when—I get out of here, I'll need to be able to tell the police what happened, coherently, in a way that won't make me sound like the fantasist or deluded rejected lover Claudio claims he'll make me out to be. What he said before is haunting me—if I'm unharmed, it's my word against his.

'Can you undo these?' I rattle our wrists. 'It would be much easier to talk if I felt a bit more relaxed. I promise I won't do something silly—I swear, on Lester's life.'

'Swear on Megan's.'

I roll my eyes. 'I swear on Megan's life.'

I suppose it would depend on your definition of 'something silly'. He unlocks and separates us, and relief sweeps over me. As I rub my wrists, I decide to play the 'it's not you, it's me' card.

'It's not that I thought it went badly, Claudio. I had a nice time with you. But I'm a mess, honestly. I'm still not over my marriage, or my relationship with Sean. I feel terrible for messing you around—I really thought I was ready for a new romance but then I got cold feet. That was all.'

'Had you planned in advance to finish with me that night?'

'No! I promise I hadn't.'

This at least was true. I hadn't originally planned to go to his place that night either, but that afternoon he rang and left a message on my machine telling me he'd booked his favourite restaurant, near his flat in town, and asking if I liked Greek food. His voice sounded different, a little subdued, as if he'd got a cold, and I remember thinking, I hope he doesn't give it to me. Did that mean I was assuming we were going to get up close and personal enough for me to catch his cold? Yes, I have to admit it did. And when I took the decision to drive to Twickenham instead of coming on the train, I thought to myself that if I wanted to drink, I could stay at his flat. He'd said he had a spare room. To my shame, though, I hadn't been intending to sleep in the spare room. Normally I would have baulked at the idea of coming into London for a night out, but Richard was picking up Megan for their holiday at noon, so I didn't have to worry about getting home for the babysitter. The gods seemed to be smiling on me.

I stopped myself telling Claudio this, though. I probably should, in my bid to convince him, but I just can't in case it gives him ideas. Instead I say, 'I knew I wasn't ready for anything physical—I'm still not—but I was really looking forward to the date.'

Megan and Richard had gone and my cheek was peppered with the imprints of Megan's kisses, my ear rustling with her whispers of love, and I felt happier than I'd felt for months. It was such a treat even to have a whole afternoon to myself to prepare for the date—the thought that, if it went well, we could potentially have the whole week ahead together made me heady with excitement.

That's ironic.

I called Claudio and asked him about parking near the restaurant, and he told me I could use the residents' car park at the back of his place, and that we could have a drink together in his flat first. Excellent, I thought then, not realizing that I was sealing my own fate.

'So what went wrong? Why did you change your mind?'

I can't tell him the truth. I can't tell him that it happened as soon as he buzzed me into his flat, and I saw him on his home territory: my heart sank just a tiny, tiny bit, and I knew then—at least, I thought—that it was all over. I was so disappointed that I could hardly summon up the energy to kiss him hello. In fact, I wanted to run away, in the opposite direction: home to Lester's warm fur and the safe anticipation of thousands more fish in the sea. Fish that I didn't actually have to meet just yet.

Claudio was standing in his hallway, holding out a long-stemmed red rose wrapped in a perfect shiny cone of cellophane, and his white shirt was immaculately pressed. He looked exactly the same as he had the week before and I even felt a faint stab of lust at the memory of our almost-kiss—but no. I didn't then know why, but I knew I would never want it to go any further than that date. It wasn't just the fact that his flat looked really depressing, either; I'm sure that if I'd met him at the restaurant and not seen the flat, I'd have still felt the same.

I felt sorry for him, as he leaned forward to kiss me. I politely proffered my cheek and accepted the rose. He was beaming at me, and I saw that he had a faint tideline of red, flaky skin on his forehead at the hairline, perhaps an ebbing bout of eczema or psoriasis. I hadn't noticed it before.

'Come in, come in. What would you like to drink? I've got red wine, or gin and tonic, or juice. Here, let me take your jacket.'

He ushered me into a very bachelorish living room and towards a horrible, saggy, pink-and-grey floral sofa that looked as if it might have been inherited from an elderly great-aunt.

There was patterned wallpaper on the walls, and three large montages of photos in clip-frames of Claudio at different ages, engaged in different activities—bungee jumping, white-water rafting, hiking, surfing. There was nobody else at all featured in the pictures, no friends or family. Some of the photographs were clearly quite old; he was a lot skinnier and much more gauche-looking. They were badly arranged in the clip-frame—some had slipped sideways, others had fallen down to reveal the cheap hardboard backing. One shot in particular caught my eye: a very youthful Claudio, standing outside somewhere that I think was the Brockhurst library, with its pillars like fat legs, and the narrow steps on which I used to sit and wait for John sometimes. I didn't like seeing those steps with Claudio on them, so I looked away.

Worst of all, there was this . . . this . . . *thing* in the fireplace, just to the right of the gas fire. It was a life-size fawn, sitting curled up, with big plastic fawny eyes and little budding antlers ('amplers', as Megan calls them). It was lavishly upholstered in something akin to Fuzzy Felt. It was monstrously tacky. I wanted to shout at Claudio, 'What the hell is THAT?' although of course it was obvious what it was. What was less obvious was why. It was the most bizarre ornamental touch I've ever seen, outside of Santa's grotto. There was no way I could date a man with a plastic Bambi in his fireplace.

The air in the room smelled a little musty, as if it needed a good airing. I felt uncomfortable there and even more sure that this relationship was over before it had begun.

'Wine would be lovely, thanks,' I said, and he vanished. I perched on the edge of the sofa—which needed a good clean—and thought about how much a person's habitat said about them. The scruffiness and decor of his flat undermined the smartness of his own appearance—in fact, invalidated it. Bambi and I tried to outstare each other. Bambi won, hooves down.

Claudio returned with a large glass of red wine. His fingers were shaking as he passed it over to me and he appeared flustered and self-conscious. He probably thinks he's getting laid tonight, I thought guiltily. I accepted the wine and took a sip. It wasn't very nice, vinegary and far too cold, so I cradled the glass in my palms to try to warm it up. They were all tiny things—cheap wine, cheap furniture, too many photos of himself, Bambi—but they were adding up into a cumulative crescendo of negativity where before I had felt so positive. I wish I wasn't so fussy. It was depressing. I really wanted this one to work.

But surely, I thought, if Claudio were right for me, these things wouldn't matter?

I felt nervous, too. Coming to Claudio's flat had seemed fine when I thought we were about to embark on a relationship, but now that I knew that we weren't, it seemed risky and unwise. There had been no indication that he was about to pounce on me, but I'm sure there was a definite tension in the air.

'What time did you book the table for?' I began, at the same time as he said, 'Did you find it all right?' We laughed mirthlessly.

'Eight o'clock.'

'Yes, thanks. I had to get out of the car to push the buzzer to raise the barrier into your car park—my arms weren't long enough to reach out of the window for it.'

I cringed at the inanity of my wittering, relieved to see on the nasty carriage clock on the mantelpiece that it was already quarter to. I took a large gulp of wine. 'Should we go, then?'

'I was going to put on some music,' Claudio said very slightly petulantly. There was definitely something a little odd about him that night, although perhaps I just think that in hindsight. I wonder now if he'd been hoping to play me that song he wrote for me. He seemed subdued and was very pale.

'Oh. OK then.'

'But if you would prefer to go, that's fine. Are you hungry?'

'Starving!' I said brightly, although I wasn't. I just wanted to get out of there.

I hadn't realised how much tension was in my body from being in Claudio's flat until I was safely outside on the pavement again and my shoulders slumped with relief. I thought then that I was just over-reacting, and now I could start to relax and hopefully enjoy the date.

I remember being quiet as we went into the restaurant and a waiter smiled and took my jacket. I shouldn't have gone through with that meal—but what could I have done? I could hardly have turned tail and left. That would have been plain rude, especially when we kind of had history. I owed him this much, I thought—he wasn't nearly as bad as that awful Gerald and his Whore of Babylon outburst. Nothing could be that bad, I thought then.

How I wish I had just been plain rude.

'Your cold has gone,' I said, as we sat down. 'But you still look a little peaky. Are you taking lots of Echinacea and vitamin C?'

'Cold? I haven't had a cold,' he replied, mystified.

'Oh! I thought you sounded like you were suffering when you left that message on my machine—you were all bunged up.'

'Suffering . . . Yes, I was. But I did not have a cold,' he said enigmatically, before changing the subject. 'So how has your day been?'

'Fine, thank you,' I replied politely. 'Enjoying my first day of freedom now that Megan's away on holiday with her dad.' If I'd still fancied him, I might have confessed that I'd had my nails done, hair blow-dried, and had a bikini wax in anticipation of tonight. But I no longer fancied him. It was as if the bulb in the light of my attraction to him had suddenly blown and no amount of tugging on the string of the switch was going to be able to illuminate that particular room again. Until the bulb was changed—which was why I wanted to rush home and find another one on the internet, to see if maybe, just maybe, I would find someone with whom a spark was mutual.

I got the distinct feeling that Claudio was waiting for me to ask what caused him to sound as if he was suffering on my answerphone, and I really wished I hadn't used such a literal turn of phrase. I realised guiltily that I didn't want to know, I didn't want to hear about his problems. If I'd liked him more, I would have done. But I didn't.

'Sorry, what did you say? I was just—er—looking at the menu.'

'I said it's lovely to see you. You look beautiful.'

I gave an instinctive self-deprecating snort, then hastily added, 'Thank you.' Eileen had been working with me on trying to accept compliments more graciously.

I hoped perhaps his sweet words might thaw me out, but nothing changed. In fact, as I looked into his face, I realised all the things about him that I'd found a turn-on at first were now adding to my disquiet. His lips, which I thought so curved and sensual, seemed miserable, and his little eyes darted unhappily around the room in a way I interpreted—correctly, as it turned out—as sinister. Suddenly I didn't want him to think me beautiful at all.

'I was so pleased to know that you were single.'

This seemed an odd thing to say. 'Well, I'd hardly have come on a date with you if I was still with Richard, would I?'

I didn't mean to sound aggressive, but it sort of came out that way.

'No. No, of course not. I just meant . . . Oh, I don't know. I'm just happy to be with you.'

He took my hand across the table, and it was all I could do not to snatch it away immediately. Instead I gave his fingers a little squeeze, then released myself and picked up my glass instead. I was livid with myself. Why, oh why couldn't I just have another relationship? Richard managed it. Sean's managed it. Here was this lovely— well, I used to think he was lovely—man, who really wanted me, and I had successfully talked myself out of it for no good reason other than a large ornamental deer.

At least now I can congratulate myself on the knowledge that it wasn't the plastic Bambi; it was my instincts being correct, for once. Claudio was the problem, not me.

If I ever get out of here, I will make sure I remember that.

We ordered and ate the usual Greek fare—warm floury pita, the rubbery saltiness of halloumi (which reminds me of Richard— he used to grill it for me. His halloumi was much better than that restaurant's), the slightly distasteful richness of taramasalata and garlicky hummus. We were having kebabs for our main course, but I wasn't sure I could sit through those too. I started planning my escape—perhaps if I went to the loo and texted Donna, she'd ring me back and concoct an emergency I'd have to leave to attend to— but what? He knew that Megan had gone on holiday with Richard that day, so I couldn't use her as an excuse.

But, fatally for me, I did thaw out a little after a glass of retsina (just the one, as I knew then that I would be driving home later after all—or at least, I thought I would be). I felt sorry for Claudio. He was talking so gratefully about how wonderful it was to have found someone he liked as much as he liked me. I wanted to let him down gently, but the more he talked, the harder I realised it would be—but the more I was determined to do it. He appeared to have built up quite a picture of us in his mind, and what's more, the picture had clearly been taking shape for many years, brushstrokes painstakingly filling in any blank corners of the canvas with whatever information he could glean. At that stage I wasn't sure whether to be flattered or slightly disturbed.

'I've been following you on Twitter for years, but you don't tweet very often, do you?'

'No. My friend Steph said I ought to join so I did, but really, I reckon life's too short. If I was constantly checking Twitter and Facebook and Instagram and watching videos of kittens on YouTube, I'd never get anything done.'

'That reminds me! You never responded to my messages to you on Facebook. I sent you a friend request about five years ago. And I've sent you several emails since. They will have gone into your Other folder since I'm not yet your friend on there.'

'I didn't know I had an Other folder . . . sorry. And I don't know what happened to the friend request. I don't remember getting it. But then I'm not very active on Facebook either.'

I didn't tell him that if I had received a friend request from him five years ago, I'd almost certainly have ignored or deleted it.

Then we talked for a while about swimming—I'd forgotten that he used to be a member of the Brockhurst swimming club at the same time as I was, and he remembered Doug the sleazy trainer and some of the other characters. After the glass of retsina, I got very slightly carried away and found myself suggesting that he, Megan and I all go swimming together some time. Then I immediately felt guilty.

I mean, proposing a swimming trip didn't exactly make me a pricktease or anything—and perhaps we still could have gone, as friends—but I probably shouldn't have said it. I remember wondering if the retsina might help me change my mind about fancying him, but by the end of the evening it still didn't seem to have done.

I felt confused by this antipathy. What was wrong with me, that I could have liked him so much the last time I saw him, and then not at all? He hadn't changed. I couldn't decide whether I had been looking at him through rose-coloured specs on our first two dates, or whether I was just being a commitmentphobe. But, I suppose, it was nothing new. It was just my habitual third-date crisis.

It never occurred to me that he was a psycho who had decided that he didn't ever want to let me go. He must have been thinking about it, plotting, in every one of our many conversational hiatuses. Whenever his eyes glazed over, he had probably been planning power tools, bolts and locks, packing a suitcase for his little holiday in my flat. The bottle containing the Rohypnol must already have been nestling in his jeans pocket.

By the end of the meal I had decided not to tell him yet. I would be a coward, and email him during the week. But I resolved not to snog him that night, or suggest any future dates, so hopefully he would get the message and not contact me again. I was OK to drive home; I hadn't had that much to drink.

Anyway, how upset could he be? We'd only had three dates, for heaven's sake. You couldn't even begin to pretend that that consti-tuted a relationship, or anything whose loss would be felt keenly for more than five minutes. He didn't even know me. He didn't know me when we were sixteen-year-olds, and he didn't know me now, however much he seemed to think he did.

Claudio was quiet that night too. He must have divined that all was not going well, even though now he says otherwise. I wonder if the Rohypnol had been an insurance policy, to be used only if it looked as though I was backing away. Which I'm sure it did— I'm not good at preventing my feelings showing. I might not have planned to tell him until after that night, but it had clearly been written all over my face.

There was an awkward lull in the conversation as we waited for our rice-strewn plates to be cleared away. I had managed to finish most of my kebab, but felt uncomfortably full. Ten years ago, I'd have excused myself and gone to the Ladies to vomit it all up. I did consider it then, as I always did after every meal, but I gritted my teeth and vowed to resist the temptation. However grim things had been, I took consolation in the fact that I hadn't let the bulimia win again.

We ordered coffees and I went to the Ladies, but just for a pee before the drive home—not knowing that I wouldn't be driving anywhere. That must have been when he slipped the Rohypnol into my espresso.

'So, do you ever hear from your ex-fiancée?' I blurted hopefully, when I got back. Tactless, perhaps, but I found I didn't care. As I well knew, the pull of an ex could change everything, ruin everything. Perhaps it would be less hurtful to him if, when I did the deed, I pretended that Sean and I were getting back together? It would be better for his ego, anyhow. Three dates couldn't compete with a year-long relationship. I entertained a brief daydream about this becoming a reality: Sean turning up on my doorstep, penitent and passionate, wrapping me in his arms and then carrying me up to bed.

Claudio gazed intently as I stirred sugar into my coffee. 'Of course not. I hate her. She is dead to me.'

His expression got darker and darker, and I began to regret asking after all.

'Do you want to talk about it?'

'No,' he said, with such vehemence that I jumped, and the waiter's head turned as he was carrying a steaming moussaka past our table. Blimey. Damaged goods, I thought (Claudio, I meant, not the moussaka. The moussaka looked nice). Then I worried that Claudio might cry.

'OK. Um. Well, perhaps I should be making tracks soon . . .' I started rummaging around in my handbag for my purse. I wanted to split the bill, so I couldn't be accused of freeloading.

'You sure you don't want dessert as well as coffee? The baklava here is excellent.'

'Oh . . . I do love baklava, but it's horrendously fattening. I'd better not.'

There was a sense of the evening slipping away that I thought then, in my unawareness of the date-rape drug that I'd already ingested, we both felt; that we were two people whose paths had just tangentially crossed, and wouldn't cross again. I remembered what Dirk said (he of the hookers and the large poo) in a phone message after I dumped him: 'This is why I hate dating.' And I suppose it is a risk, emotionally, especially internet dating—you're laying yourself open in a way that doesn't happen when you meet under 'normal' circumstances: in the gym, at a bar or a party. Knowing my luck, I thought, I'd eventually meet someone I really, really liked—and they'd say 'Sorry, but I just don't fancy you.'

'So when can we next meet?' Claudio asked, having seemingly regained his composure. His eyes were pleading, like Megan's when she wants to watch TV but I'm telling her to do her homework. The waiter brought over our bill on a little silver dish, with two After Eight mints, and I put down my credit card. I was already starting to feel a little unwell.

'Let's go fifty-fifty, shall we?' I said briskly, pretending I hadn't heard his question.

'OK.' He glanced at the amount and then put three ten-pound notes onto the tray. Then he tried again: 'When are you next free?'

Aargh. What should I do? Why couldn't he have been a little less specific and just said, 'We must do this again soon,' so I could have nodded and smiled and then let him down gently later?

I realised that I had to bite the bullet. After all, it had driven me completely insane when Sean wouldn't tell me why he didn't want us to be together any more; he just kept saying, 'I can't do this,' but not explaining why. Claudio and I had only had three dates, but he deserved more than being fobbed off with excuses and promises, the way Sean fobbed me off.

I took a deep breath, suddenly feeling boiling hot. The room had started to spin a tiny bit. 'Claudio . . .'

But he stood up and helped me into my jacket, solicitously, as if I was his mother, which made me sweat even more. 'Let's go outside.' He suddenly hugged me effusively. 'I like you so much, Jo,' he whispered into my hair.

Damn, damn, damn. I could tell he wasn't going to make this easy for me. I felt sick.

We walked awkwardly back towards his flat. His hand was twitching at his side, as if he wanted to reach out and grab mine but didn't dare. He'd lost the air of assurance and sophistication that had so impressed me at our first two meetings, and he seemed dejected, a little boy lost. His shoulders were sloping, and his shoes were scuffed. I hadn't noticed that before. He was once more the teenager I didn't like.

I wished Megan wasn't on holiday with Richard. I wanted to go home, give her a cuddle as she slept, then curl up with Lester in my own bed. I felt almost beyond despondency and into resignation, and my stomach was churning. I was feeling more and more dizzy, but even as we got to the barrier of his apartment block's car park, I still assumed it was stress at what I was about to do.

Here. I have to do it here, I thought. Why was it so hard? I barely even knew the man.

'Well!' I began, as brightly as I could.

He looked at me, mute with expectation. Then he said, 'I'm free next week. Do you fancy going to see some stand-up comedy, or maybe a concert? I could get *Time Out* and—'

'Claudio,' I said desperately. 'You're a great guy, but—'

He wheeled about, so his back was to me. 'No!'

'Pardon?'

'No. You're going to say you don't want to see me again.'

The emotion in his voice brought me up short. 'Um. Well, it's just that I think that perhaps we—'

'I think you're wrong.' He turned back towards me, looming over me. I couldn't help shrinking back against the car park barrier. Everything was whirling. I must have eaten something really dodgy in that meal, I thought.

'You don't know what I'm going to say!' I felt slightly defensive. It was all very well being told I was wrong, if I was—but in this case, I was getting surer by the minute that I wasn't. And surer by the minute that I was imminently going to puke.

'You are going to say that I am very nice company but that you don't fancy me.' His bottom lip was actually jutting out like a six-year-old's. This couldn't be normal.

'Well. I wouldn't say that I don't *fancy* you, as such, because you're very fanciable—I suppose that it's more . . . um . . . my heart doesn't skip a beat. I'm sorry.'

Oh, why was I having to do this? I remember thinking. I missed Richard. I missed the stability. I miss the comfort, the nice meals, the shared companionship. When I left him, people kept saying, 'You've done the right thing. You're too young to settle for a sexless relationship. You need someone who'll be there for you.' But right then I didn't care if I never had sex again as long as I lived. I just wanted Richard. And, anyway, we *could* have had a sexual relationship, I know we could, if we'd both wanted one. All we'd needed to do was to get some sex therapy. Where there's a willy, there a way . . .

I want my husband back. And I wanted it before I ended up as Claudio's prisoner.

I have to force myself to remember back to the date again, because the pain that sweeps over me at this realisation makes me truly believe I could die from grief.

'Very well,' said Claudio huffily. 'You've made it perfectly clear. I don't understand, though—we kissed! You seemed to enjoy that. And what about the swimming? We were going to go swimming with your daughter. What about *that*?' This last was said almost triumphantly.

'I'm sorry,' I repeated miserably. It was suddenly really difficult to formulate words. 'Listen, I'd better be going. It's quite a long drive home and to be honest I'm feeling really sick. Do I just press this button to raise the barrier again?'

He nodded, once. 'Bye, then.' I reached forwards and tried to kiss him on the cheek but I felt so dizzy that I missed and kissed his neck. I ducked under the barrier and started walking towards my car.

That was the last thing I remembered.

Chapter Twenty-Six
Day 3

Claudio locks me back in my room while he goes to cook supper, ignoring my slightly tipsy suggestion of being his sous-chef. I don't feel like watching TV or listening to the radio—I'm sick of listening to news bulletins that don't mention that I'm missing—so I do what has become my default leisure activity. I read my diary. I've become addicted to it, not least because I worry that at any moment Claudio will burn it or make me eat it, or something.

31st December 1986

I remember glancing at the big clock on the wall of the Pembroke Arms function room and seeing that it was ten o'clock, every slow click of its hands ticking away the minutes until John would be kissing someone else at midnight. It felt unbearable.

John and Gareth's party was in full swing. There was this naff homemade screen at the DJ's console, flashing red, green, and yellow like malfunctioning traffic lights in time with Booker T and the MGs, Green Onions, and a glitterball rotating above the dance floor. It kept getting stuck, then jerking round again.

The crowd was mostly Young Conservatives, Young Farmers, and sixth formers. Everyone danced, which was good, but most of the dancing was crap. They even did that sitting-down rowing dance to Oops Upside Your Head. *I hate that. Everyone was tipsy by 10 p.m., me included, because Donna got served at the bar! I couldn't believe it. She bought me a rum and black, which was yummy. Had three that night.*

I was feeling totally out of place. Most of the girls were wearing ball dresses, but I'd borrowed Donna's blue and white stripy shirt and navy ra-ra skirt. Donna was moaning about her dress. She kept hoiking up the front of it and adjusting the big silk bow at the back of the waist. The dress should have been tight across her chest, Flapper-girl style, but it gaped at the front and if she leaned over it exposed her little boobs to view. She blamed me for letting her go out in it, grumbling that she couldn't sit down because of the bow, and people could see straight down it.

I told her it looked gorgeous. 'At least you've got *a dress,' I said. No-one else was just wearing a skirt and shirt. She grabbed my arm, the dress forgotten: 'Ooh look, Gareth's over there with John and their mates. Let's go and talk to them—I bet you a pound I'll get Gareth to snog me by midnight.'*

I bet she wouldn't, and we shook hands on it. Then we headed over towards them, weaving across the dance floor, dodging flailing Sloanes as the music changed to Hi Ho Silver Lining. *A ruddy-faced Young Farmer in a too-small dinner jacket grabbed me round the waist. 'Wanna dance, sexy?' he yelled in my ear.*

I ignored him. I could see John and Gareth sitting at a table with a few others and, joy of joys, Gill was just tottering off to the Ladies, so the coast was clear.

There were three more boys at the table: Alastair Brown, Claudio Cavelli, and Gavin Pinkerton. They took no notice of Donna as she crouched down in the space between Gareth's and John's chairs, holding her top tight against her chest with her hand. But John looked up at me!

'Hi,' he said. 'Glad you could make it.'

'Thanks for letting me come.' Oh god, I said 'come', I thought. Thankfully no-one seemed to notice, and John just smiled at me, blowing cigarette smoke out of the corner of his mouth. I wanted to catch the smoke and swallow it, to appropriate something of his. He looked utterly gorgeous tonight, in his dinner suit and shiny black shoes. They matched his shiny black hair.

'Don't Cry For Me Argentina,' said Alastair, a shifty-looking blond boy with narrow eyes and thin wrists. The others groaned.

'That's pathetically obvious, you moron,' said Claudio. 'But what can we expect from someone who thought the Falklands were off Scotland? My turn.'

'What are you lot doing?' Donna hauled herself up off her knees. Grabbing an empty chair from the next table, she squeezed it in next to Gareth, and gestured for me to share it with her.

'Songs about the Falklands,' Gareth said. 'How about Ascencion Island Girl by Elton John?'

Donna gazed up at Gareth. 'That's brilliant,' she said, putting her hand on his knee. Then Gareth asked me if I had a song. 'Rainy Night in South Georgia!' I blurted triumphantly. It earned me a half-hearted round of applause and, far better, a look of respect from John. My feet tingled with delight, and in one split second I had manufactured a blissful daydream in which me and John were walking up the aisle, producing four gorgeous children, and going on lots of cruises in our retirement. 'It was your ability to produce the best Falklands-related song title at my party in '86 when I really fell for you—and I've never stopped loving you since,' quavered John passionately, aged ninety.

Gill came back from the toilet, lips coated with a fresh application of coral pink, and flung herself onto John's lap with her arms around his neck. She pulled a cigarette from John's packet and waited for him to light it.

'*Gareth, sweetie, you'll never guess who's just arrived!*' *she said, inhaling as the match was obediently sparked in front of her. 'My friend Alex, the one you met at the Hunt Ball. She's dying to see you . . .'*

Poor Donna. Gareth ripped her hand off his leg like it was radioactive, and was already charging down the room towards the bar. Donna watched him go. 'Mal Venus by Frankie Avalon,' she suggested half-heartedly, swallowing the rest of her vodka and lime, and stretching out a hand for John's cigarettes. 'Can I have one of your fags, John?'

'No, you bloody can't,' he said, snatching them back again. 'You're much too young and besides, the parents are here. They'd kill both of us.'

Donna waited until John and Gill began to canoodle, and swiped a Benson & Hedges from the packet, now abandoned on the table. 'Come with me to the loo so I can smoke it,' she whispered.

'Can't we go outside?' I was keen to get away from the sight of John with his tongue in Gill's mouth.

'No. It's too cold and someone might see me and tell Mummy.'

'Someone might see you in the loos, too.'

'I'll go into a cubicle if anyone comes in. Come on.'

The Ladies was empty, and freezing cold owing to a high window having been left open. The muffled sound of Peter Gabriel's Sledgehammer *thumped through the walls from the disco. Donna examined her appearance in a speckled full-length mirror, shivered, and goose bumps sprang up on her bare arms.*

'Claudio fancies you. Did you see the way he was staring at you?'

She pointed at her breasts, clearly outlined beneath the silk bodice of her dress. 'Look, you can see my nipples.'

Even though it was Donna, I still felt embarrassed and looked away. 'He doesn't. He never talks to me unless he's taking the piss. He's awful.'

'That's a sure sign. Bet he'll try to snog you at midnight. Look at them—it's obscene!'

Louise Voss

She retrieved the cigarette, already a little soft and creased, and then extracted a family-sized box of Bryant & Mays from her seemingly bottomless handbag.

'Blimey, Don, have you got enough matches there? You're only lighting one fag, not starting a bonfire.'

'I knew I'd need some, and they were all I could find in the kitchen.' She lit up, took a feeble drag, and blew out smoke in a huge unstructured cloud that engulfed me.

I flapped my arms and clutched my throat, coughing and pretending to choke.

'For someone as healthy as you, I can't believe you smoke. Doesn't that stop you swimming as fast as you should?'

'Oh no,' said Donna, taking another minuscule puff, 'I don't smoke many a day. Only one or two a week, actually.'

Then I noticed how ugly I look when I coughed, so I turned my back on my reflection. 'Well, I don't know why you bother, in that case. So, are you upset about Gareth and that girl?'

Donna continued to pout at herself, trying and failing dismally to blow a smoke ring. 'Nah, not really—though can we extend the bet till the end of January, just in case? Even if they get off with each other tonight, it won't last. That Alex looks like a horse—long face, all gums and big teeth, you know? And she's got an enormous bum.'

She stubbed out the only quarter-smoked cigarette in the sink and dropped it into the bin. 'Mm, I needed that,' she said, unconvincingly. 'So who are you after tonight, then? Claudio? You do know you've got no chance with John, don't you? And anyway, Gill's actually quite sweet, when you get to know her. They're mad about each other.'

Each word plunged like a dagger into my heart, but I couldn't tell her. I pretended I was over him. 'He's not the one for me. And nor is Claudio—he gives me the creeps.'

I felt like there was a marble in my throat. Why did I lie to Donna? I worship every hair on John's head, every atom of him, and I will do

188

until the day I die. To say 'he's not the one for me' is sacrilege! He is the only one for me. I wanted to poke Gill's eyes out, seal up her mouth with parcel tape so she couldn't kiss him. It wasn't fair.

'I think you should find out who rescued you, and go out with him.'

'That's the most pathetic thing I've ever heard! What if I'd been rescued by a tramp, or a . . . a . . . I dunno, a . . . punk—would you suggest I went out with him? Anyway, I don't want to talk about that.'

The door opened and Donna's mum sailed in, wearing a <u>diaphanous chiffon tent affair of many layers, like expensive pastel rags</u>. Mine and Donna's eyes darted to the bin containing the recently extinguished cigarette, as if it might suddenly re-light itself and jump back into Donna's mouth.

'Having a nice time, girls?' she said. 'I say, it's terribly parky in here, isn't it? I'm not sure if I dare bare all to spend a penny—if I'm not out in ten minutes, will you come in and chip me off the lavatory seat?' I love the way she talks; it makes me laugh.

She sniffed at Donna's head suspiciously. 'Your hair smells jolly smoky.'

'Oh, I know. Dreadful, isn't it? Jo and I were just saying how being around all these smokers really makes your clothes and hair stink, weren't we, Jo?'

I nodded obediently. Mrs B-B squeezed herself into a cubicle and shot the bolt locked. 'Ooh, what a relief,' she called gaily over the door, peeing enthusiastically. 'Before you go, Donna, can I just ask you to keep an eye on your brother? He and Gill have had a frightful ding-dong out there. You know what he's like—I don't want him getting into a tremendous sulk and drinking himself silly.'

'What do you mean? They were fine a minute ago.'

I caught a glimpse of myself in the mirror, smiling. For a split second I thought, Actually, I'm quite pretty sometimes.

'Well, you've missed all the drama, then, darling. She slapped his face and left with her gummy friend Alex. Heaven knows what he said to her—he's so tactless sometimes . . .'

Donna and I gave each other an enthusiastic thumbs-up and, for once, both scrambled for a last-minute appearance check in the mirror. I wiped a small lipstick stain off one of my teeth, and Donna huffed into her hand to check her breath, and we headed back into battle, leaving Mrs B-B talking to herself in the toilet cubicle.

Midnight came, heralded by a spittly countdown from the DJ. This was followed, in the usual fashion, by a lusty rendition of Auld Lang Syne, *party poppers, whoops, and random snogging.*

I got separated from Donna as everyone tried to drunkenly organise themselves into a circle of pumping crossed arms and eventually spotted her standing on tiptoe, her head tipped back at a ninety-degree angle so she could reach Gareth's black hole of a mouth. He appeared to be swallowing her whole. An image of a boa constrictor eating a piglet sprang to mind as I watched her fondling Gareth's cauliflower ear. Damn, that was a quid I'd lost, then.

I turned away, a low heavy feeling of misery beginning to collect in the pit of my stomach. What a great start to a New Year—no boyfriend, no Donna to celebrate with, no-one even to talk to. Only about ten million extra calories assimilating into my fat cells from all the crisps and the sticky rum and blacks I'd downed. I wished I hadn't come after all. Poor Mum was at home on her own on New Year's Eve, too. I was an unfit daughter as well as an ugly misfit.

I decided to go and phone Mum up to wish her a Happy New Year. I found a ten-pence piece in my bag, picked up my coat from underneath seven others on the same peg, and left the function room for the short walk across to the hotel reception, where I knew there was a phone.

I paused at the entrance to the hotel. Hello Dad, I thought, gazing into the clear sky. Are you up there? I'm just going to ring and check Mum's OK. Can you hear me?

'Can you hear me?' I tried it out loud, just in case.

'Yes. Can you hear me?' The voice came from behind me.

I nearly jumped out of my skin. I wheeled round, heart pounding, waiting for the guy in the balaclava to spring out from behind a tree at me. I could feel his hands heavy on my shoulders again. 'Who is it?' I said, already blind with fear and crying.

'Hey, Jo, it's only me.'

John—*John!!*—appeared from round the back of the function room. He looked dishevelled and tired and was holding a glass of champagne in one hand and an unlit cigarette in the other. 'Sorry, I didn't mean to scare you. Are you all right?'

He walked up to me and wiped a tear off my face with his thumb, putting down his glass so he could hold my cold hand in his warm one. It was the first time he'd ever touched me. My knees were shaking, from shock and anticipation, and I was aware of being mortified that he'd seen me crying. I tried to collect myself.

'I'm fine. You gave me a fright, that's all. I was just going to go into the hotel and ring my mum.'

'Well, as long as you're OK. Hey, fancy having a drink with me in the hotel bar when you've finished? I'm a bit sick of the party now.'

'Where's Gill?' My fear was forgotten. I could hardly breathe with excitement.

'Oh, she went home ages ago; stormed out. We're finished.'

My voice was a squeak. 'Really?' I tried not to sound so elated, and went for the mature, understanding approach. 'Do you want to talk about it?'

John nudged me, a little shove with his elbow in the direction of the hotel. 'Yeah. Well, maybe. Let's have a drink, anyway. Go on, make your phone call. I'll meet you in the bar.'

I think that ended up being the best night of my whole life.

Chapter Twenty-Seven
Day 3

The spirit of entente continues for a while over dinner. I ask Claudio about his friendship with John when we are once more sitting at the kitchen table and he has untied my hands. Is it my imagination or does he gently brush the tender skin of my wrists with his finger? I dismiss the thought, and greedily gulp in the brick wall view through the kitchen window with its sliver of blue evening sky above. My thoughts are still with my diary, with the look on John's face when he invited me for a drink.

I have to try hard not to let the knowledge that John and Claudio were friends sully my own memories of John.

'We were at primary school together—not in the same class, but we made friends in about the Third Year, I think. He stood up for me when some bigger kids were chucking stones at a window and blamed me. He told the head it wasn't me. After that we started hanging around together.'

Claudio has such an affectionate expression on his face that for a tiny moment I thaw and think better of him for having loved John too.

'And you stayed friends once you went up to St Edmunds?'

He nods, and busies himself getting plastic plates down. There's no music tonight, no sign of the iPad. Damn. My only hope of contact with anyone. Although he's so careful, I doubt he'd leave me on my own with it for a second, even if he got caught short and had to rush to the loo. Wishful thinking.

He serves up a pasta dish, something with bacon and, bizarrely, carrots in it. I suppose it's meant to be a sort of carbonara. I try a bit on the end of my fork and it's completely tasteless. Perhaps he couldn't be arsed to make it taste nice after last night's dinner went so badly.

I have a small internal argument with myself: would it be better to try to seduce him, to get him to let his guard down, or to attack him? The pasta is steaming hot. I could rub it into his face like a clown throwing a custard pie, but that would hardly incapacitate him long enough for me to extract the keys, unlock all the doors, and run out.

At least I get to drink some wine. I down the first glass and ask for more.

'What would your colleagues think, Claudio,' I say as he turns the little tap on top of the wine box and refills my glass, 'if they knew that you had imprisoned me like this?'

He doesn't reply.

'Seriously, I'm curious. Do you hang out with them in the pub after work? Chat about last night's *Coronation Street* around the water cooler? Do they set you up with their single friends? Do they know you're a freak, or would they be shocked?'

'Don't call me that,' he says through tight lips. He twirls a forkful of pasta too aggressively and the plastic picnic fork snaps. I have to bite the inside of my cheeks to prevent a brief snarky smile escaping, even though my hands are shaking too much for me to eat at the moment. I sit on them.

'What—a freak?' I keep my voice calm and measured.

193

'I'm not a freak.' His eyes swivel slightly in his head and he looks every inch the deranged freak. I can't think what on earth I ever saw in him. Desperation—shameful.

Anger with myself and my own bad judgement makes me niggle further.

'So, what's your plan, Claudio? I think I have a right to know, since it involves me. Richard and Megan will be home in a few days. People will be missing me already.'

Calm down, I remind myself. I moderate my tone. 'You really can't keep me here. I need some fresh air. I'm due on my period any moment. You don't want to have to go and buy tampons for me, do you?'

He visibly blanches.

'All these little practicalities, Claudio, that perhaps you haven't thought of. I've missed several work appointments that aren't in my phone's schedule. I had a meeting yesterday with Steph and a publisher about us writing a book together, on sports trivia. Steph knows there's no way I wouldn't have turned up—I've been badgering her for ages for us to collaborate on a writing project; I'm so bored with medical writing. I missed my counselling session on Monday. I always call my mum on Sunday evening. Donna and I go swimming together twice a week.'

It's once a week, but he doesn't need to know that.

'At some point very soon, Claudio, they will all realise that I'm missing—if they haven't already. There's only so long you can fob them off by sending texts from my phone. They will see my car's there, and the door's locked from the inside. Donna will get the keys off Ania and when she can't get in, she'll definitely call the police. Definitely! It's going to happen. And when it does, you will be in deeper shit than you could ever imagine.'

I have swigged the rest of my wine, and I get up abruptly to help myself to more, resisting the temptation to call him a freak again. Claudio starts, defensively rearing up out of his own chair. Perhaps he thought I was going to lunge at him. For a moment we lock eyes across the table, poised as though we are going to chase each other around and around it like cartoon characters.

'What do you *want*, Claudio?' I repeat, for what seems like the hundredth time in the past few days.

This is the first time he answers, though. He walks around the table to me and grabs the back of my head, gripping my scalp.

'You. I want you.'

He kisses me roughly and I feel bile rising as his tongue shoves its way into my mouth. It's a horrible, fat, slimy tongue that seems to fill up every millimetre of available space inside my mouth, coating my teeth, pressing down my own tongue, oozing its disgusting way towards my uvula. I try to wriggle away but he slides his other hand around my waist and pulls me against him. We are stuck together, my head clamped against his face, my breasts pressing into his hot chest. I try to release my arms, and get one free, punching him ineffectually, but I'm too close to him to get any momentum going. I try to shake my head, but can't. I'm going to be sick in his mouth. That'd get him off me, surely—I will it to happen. He moans with lust and I can feel his erection pushing against my belly, which starts churning like a tumble dryer. I become aware I'm making an odd strangled sound.

Finally he releases my head and restrains my flailing arm, so I'm pinioned. But at least his tongue is out of my face. I'm panting, and babbling.

'Not like this, Claudio, not like this. I swear I'll never love you if you force me to. If you rape me I will never talk to you again, or look at you. I will find some way to kill myself so you can't have me and then you'll be done for manslaughter if not murder . . .'

I force myself to slow down and meet his eyes. There is spittle in the corners of his mouth and I gag.

'Sorry. It's just shock. Let go of me, Claudio. Let me sit down. Let's talk. We can work something out. I don't want this and I don't believe you do either.'

To my immense relief he loosens his grip on me. I gulp in air to stop myself being sick. My pasta has congealed on the plastic plate into a solid mass and the sight of it tips me over the edge. I run over to the sink and puke into it, all over the dirty pots and pans he's left in there. The thought crosses my mind that maybe it's an effort for him to have to keep looking after me like this, doing everything for me, especially if he's a mummy's boy. Perhaps he'll get tired of it.

I glance behind me and see him hovering, a look of disgust on his stubbly face. 'Sorry,' I mumble, and turn the cold tap on full. I pick up the pasta pan and start rinsing the sick off it. It's heavy. And metal! He never thought of that, did he, with his plastic plates and picnic cutlery and no sharp objects—you can't cook pasta in a plastic saucepan. I thank God I don't have a microwave, otherwise he would have done. Before I think about what I'm doing, or give him the chance to realise, I grab the handle of the pan in my other hand and swing it out of the sink like a tennis racket, heavy bottom first, backhand towards Claudio's face. Water and sick spray around us as the pan flashes through the air and I'm aware that I'm screaming, my whole being focused on his horrible jutting chin: that's my target, I can't miss, I can't miss, I'll knock him out and—

He reaches his left hand up and grabs the pan easily before it hits him. With a deft twist, I'm disarmed, and as I lurch towards him, he lifts his right hand and hits me with his own backhand, smack across my face. My cheek explodes with pain and I fall and hit the other side of my head on the tiled floor, tiny black and silver stars popping pyrotechnically around me.

Then suddenly he is on top of me on the floor, flattening me completely, grunting, the iron pincers of his fingers grabbing between my legs like the man in the alley, only this time I'm not wearing a duffel coat and a thick dress and woolly tights, just thin pyjama bottoms because I didn't want to dress for dinner, I didn't want to indulge him, and now he's going to indulge himself and it will kill me, he's stroking me ineptly like he thinks it's foreplay but at least he's not trying to kiss me because I have sick around my mouth and he sticks his hand down my trousers and his finger inside me and it hurts and I feel his fingernail scratch me because of course he's clumsy and it's the last thing I want but my head and face hurt too much to be able to fight him off and I'm making this weird strangled moaning noise again and he rips down my pyjamas and undoes his jeans and I'm crying now because I think this is it, raped on my kitchen floor but at least not in my bedroom, and I brace myself for the thrust—

But it doesn't come. I feel something small and warm pushing against me, and I hear his yelp of frustration and anger. He's lost his erection.

Thank God, thank God, thank God. But does it mean he'll hit me again?

I put my hands on the front of his shoulders and forced myself to focus on his face.

'Claudio. Let me go back to my room. This is a mistake. You know it is. I'm sorry I tried to hit you. Let's forget this ever happened. Come on. My head really hurts. I need to lie down.'

There's a long pause, like he's working out what to do. Then he slowly shuffles backwards off me, turning away to do up his jeans. He won't meet my eyes. I sit up, my head throbbing, and wipe my mouth. The room swirls and dips as I try to stand, and I don't know which side of my head to hold harder, as if I could squeeze away the pain. I drag up my PJs with one hand. It's like the aftermath of a bomb, a stunned disbelief and knowledge that everything has changed both physically and emotionally, atoms rearranged, a void into which crowd only fear and pain. Working my way around the kitchen by clinging onto the counters, I make my way to the locked door and stand by it like a cat waiting to be let out. That's a point: where's Lester? I want him.

Claudio doesn't bother to tie my wrists up again before he unlocks the kitchen door. He can tell there's no fight left in me. He shoots me sheepish, anxious looks as he grasps my elbow and helps me back down the hall to my room.

'Do you need anything?' he asks, and I give my head a tiny brief nod that sends pain flooding and pulsing behind my eyes.

'Nurofen.'

'I'll get you some.'

He locks me in my bedroom and I hear him go into the main bathroom and rummage in the cabinets. Presumably that's where he's put all my confiscated contraband.

Lester is stretched out like a concubine on my bed and the sight of him makes tears spout out of my eyes. I sit slowly down next to him and let my hand rest on his fur.

Now I know that he would do it. He would rape me, if he could. I was just lucky that he couldn't. It adds a whole new level of horror to this fucked-up situation.

Oh, this is *so* fucked up.

When he comes back in with pills and a plastic beaker of water, I'm lying curled around Lester on the bed. I ignore him and he puts the beaker and blister pack down on the bedside table.

'Goodnight, Jo,' he says uncertainly.

I continue to ignore him.

Why the hell had I not had the sense to ignore him after our first date?

Chapter Twenty-Eight
Day 4

I took the three Nurofens left in the pack and sipped the water until the taste of sick went away. I didn't have the strength to get into the bathroom and clean my teeth or have a shower. All I wanted was to hear Lester's purring and the oblivion of sleep.

Now it's 4.00 a.m. The pounding in my head and the shock have subsided just enough for me to start relaxing towards sleep, but I realise I'm only thinking of Richard. It's a new day and I don't want to give Claudio any more head space.

Richard blames himself for the divorce. He told me so, a couple of months ago when we went for a heartbreakingly polite little drink in the pub. He said he should have seen the signs, should have done something about it before it was too late. But he couldn't. He was terrified that if he said anything, it would all come crashing down on his head.

'I never realised I was such a coward,' he said, so sadly that my throat seized up and ached with the effort of not sobbing then and there, under the horse brasses and oak beams. 'But I never thought for a second that you'd actually leave me. We thought we'd be married forever—didn't we? OK, so it might not have been the most passionate relationship in the world, but it was stable, and secure, wasn't it? I didn't think there was any doubt that we loved each other . . . not until you told me you didn't love me enough.'

I tried to protest that I was wrong, that it was how I felt at the time but not now—but he just shook his head and I knew it was too late.

He admitted that he'd put me on such a pedestal—a Nelson's Column sort of size—that even when he craned his neck and shouted up at me, I was just too far away to hear him. Because it took him so many years to win me, I had been a prize to him. Perhaps that ought to have made me proud, but all I feel now is shame.

At the time I thought he didn't make enough fuss when I said I wanted a divorce. I thought the fact that he didn't fall to his knees and beg me to stay meant that somehow he went along with my decision that we should just be friends, and not married any more. But he was in shock, and when he's in shock, he said, he goes into practical mode.

He looked at me over his pint so bitterly that I dropped my gaze. 'So, Jo, forgive me that I didn't react in the way you expected. Forgive me that I started talking about which bits of furniture I wanted to keep and when I would get to see Megan . . .'

'Don't,' I said, peeling back layers of a cardboard beer mat. 'I'm sorry.'

We had stopped sleeping together months before. Every now and then he reached for me, but I would turn my head away if he tried to kiss me.

'You looked so unhappy,' he said, the corners of his mouth wobbling. 'But I just couldn't bear to ask you what was wrong, because

I knew it was *me*. Every time I tried to talk about it, the words just solidified and I couldn't. I'm sorry.'

So many sorries.

———⌣———

I am finally just falling asleep, one hand resting on the cat, the other still clutching my head, when I hear my door being unbolted, loudly, roughly. Lester shoots up in alarm and runs into the bathroom.

Claudio is angry again. I can tell, before he even gets into my room. What's made him so mad that he needs to come storming in at 6.00 a.m.?

Chapter Twenty-Nine
Day 4

Claudio switches on the overhead light. He is wearing his horrible old-man dark stripy pyjamas, and holding a bulging Sainsbury's Bag for Life in front of him. I sit up in bed, the sudden movement making my bruised cheek throb. I want to say 'What now?' but I'm too scared.

In fact, I don't think I've ever been so scared in my whole life. It's as if he's a ball of wool and someone is pulling at the end. He is unravelling.

'This isn't going as well as I'd hoped,' he says, and I nod in submissive agreement, although I don't know what he means. But from the aggression in his voice, I can tell he's really upset about it. I suspect it's a male pride thing: he's humiliated that he lost his erection last night at the crucial moment.

'I can tell you aren't in love with me!'

No shit, Sherlock.

My heart is banging so hard in my chest that I feel breathless. 'Give me time, Claudio. It's not easy when I've been stuck in here for days, and now you've been violent towards me, when you said you wouldn't be.'

I brace myself in case he hits me again.

'That was only because you went for me!' His voice is squeaky with outrage, at the perceived unfairness of my accusation. I'm half-waiting for him to say 'It's Not Fair!' and stamp his foot.

He puts the bag on my bed and I see that it's full of photograph albums. *My* photograph albums, from the bookcase in the front room.

'So, I'm going to do something to help you along a bit.'

Sitting on the edge of my bed, he tips the bag upside down. Along with the albums, several loose enlargements of photos spill out, photos that were until recently in frames either on my wall or displayed on the mantelpiece. There is one of Richard and Megan on Megan's fourth birthday, one of Richard and me at our wedding (I keep it on display because Megan says hello to it every day), another of the three of us at a wintry bird sanctuary somewhere, Megan happy in fun-fur and mittens between us. I can't remember who took it.

Claudio has removed each one from its frame, presumably so I don't take the opportunity to smash the glass and stick a shard into his face. He bloody thinks of everything.

'I'll put them away somewhere if you don't want them out on display,' I say hastily, looking at Megan's little face with longing. She is blowing out the candles on the Barbie cake I made her for her fourth birthday. Her cheeks are perfect pink puffs and her mouth a tiny excited rosebud. Richard is standing over her, gazing so fondly down at her that I have to swallow hard to try to shift the pain at the back of my throat.

Claudio shakes his head, as if that made him sad. I hate him.

'I think it will take more than just putting them out of sight,' he says. 'Your ex—both your exes—seem to be something of a barrier, and our future happiness depends on there being no barriers. A clean slate, that's what we need. So, you're going to get rid of these. Tear them all up.'

'What? No!' Protectively, I gather my precious memories in my arms. 'I can't do that, Claudio!'

'You have to,' he replies calmly. 'And I'm going to watch you do it. So get going. I'll start you off.'

He opens Megan's baby album, lifts the sheet of clear plastic covering the photographs, and takes out the first one, a shot of me in a hospital bed with a freshly born Megan in my arms, so freshly born that I have a smear of my own blood on my nose. I am beaming from ear to ear.

He tears it in two and drops the halves onto the floor.

This is outrageous. He's doing it to punish me for what happened last night.

'No! Claudio, please don't!'

I reach out my hand to grasp his arm in entreaty, but he shakes me off and rips up the next one, Megan cradled against Richard's chest. Richard looks so proud, and so young, his face exactly the same as when he was a student.

'Wait!' I try, desperately. 'Listen, please! I accept that you don't want me to have photos of Richard, that's fair enough. But please, please, don't make me get rid of Megan's baby pictures! After all—' I take a deep breath to cover my revulsion at the words I'm about to say, '—she and I come as a package. You can't just airbrush her out of the picture. She lives with me, Claudio! You'd be her stepfather. It's not ideal but if you want to be with me, you have to accept her too. Like I said, these things don't happen overnight.'

Claudio pauses. I can see that he's capitulating.

'She'd be devastated if her baby photos were gone. She looks at them all the time.'

This is true, she does. She's slightly obsessed with her birth and 'how she came out'. I plough on. 'If you want me to love you, you can't do this. I know you're a good man really. It's absolutely crucial to me that you and Megan get on, and you don't want to get off on the wrong foot with her, do you?'

'Suppose not,' Claudio mumbles. I almost want to laugh at the absurdity of the words I'm saying. Absolutely crucial that he and Megan get on? Absolutely crucial that I fucking *kill* him before he ever sullies the air that she breathes, more like.

I don't usually swear, but knowing that he's going to make me destroy every single photograph of Richard makes me feel like screaming every obscenity I've ever heard.

'She's a sweet girl. Very pretty. Looks just like her mother,' he says, a tone of pride in his voice that makes me want to rip out his throat. He picks up one of the ten by eight prints, Megan's school portrait from last year, and examines it carefully.

'So can I keep them? All of them? She'll be just as upset if the photos of her dad are gone . . .'

I'm pushing my luck, I know. He throws the photo down onto the bed.

'No. *Those* have to go. Even if Megan's in them too. Do it.'

Tears well in my eyes. 'I can't.'

Claudio stands up. 'You will.'

I shake my head.

'If you don't, then I'm going to dump all the albums, and every single photo in the flat. It's your choice. OK? And then . . .'

I drop my head, not waiting to hear what the 'then' is. I'm trying to think how many of those photos are digital, and in folders on my computer, but when I look up again, I realise that I ought instead to have been thinking about Claudio, his ever-decreasing patience with me, and I see what the 'then' was. Because he is standing there, and from somewhere he has produced the missing belt from my towelling dressing gown, which he has wrapped around his hands and pulled taut. And he is bringing it closer to my throat . . .

I squeal in terror and back away as far as I can.

'You need to start meeting me halfway, Jo. I've got the impression lately that you don't take me seriously,' he says, his face now so close to mine that I can see the broken veins around his nose and his bloodshot eyes. 'That's a mistake, Jo. One thing you'll learn about me is that I'm utterly loyal to my loved ones. I will be the best thing that ever happened to you. But you have to take me seriously, because if you don't, I think you'll find yourself in very deep trouble. After all—'

He presses the belt hard against my throat, pushing my head back against the headboard, confirming what I already suspected.

'Let's not forget that I'm a man with nothing left to lose.'

Under Claudio's watchful eye I rip up every single photograph with Richard in it into four pieces. Once, twice. Rip, rip. Quartered and destroyed. Holidays, birthdays, Christmases, parties, dinners.

All those memories.

My photo albums are desecrated and my heart is broken. But I don't cry, and I don't say another word.

Finally, when it's done, Claudio scoops all the bits back into the Bag for Life. 'Well done, darling,' he says softly. 'That's a big step forward. It can't have been easy, but you know it's for the best. Later today you're going to call your daughter and tell her that you miss her, and you're fine, and you hope she's having a wonderful time. Just so that she doesn't worry about not having heard from you. She's left you a couple of voicemails on your phone, so I think it's important that you get back to her.'

He leaves, locking and bolting the door behind him. I sink back on the pillows, reeling.

They're only photos, I repeat inside my head. Only photos. I'm still alive. Later I will hear Megan's voice, and probably Richard's too. I have to find some way to communicate that I need help.

The trouble is, I no longer have any trouble believing absolutely that Claudio will kill me if I don't do what he wants me to.

And I can't do what he wants me to.

I am fucked. Deeply, seriously *fucked*.

Chapter Thirty
Day 4

I can't believe how devastated I am about the photographs. In my mind I see each and every torn-up scrap, trying to piece them back together and take a mental screenshot before the memories are gone forever—although it feels as though they're already gone. It must be like having Alzheimer's, that slow, jagged forgetting, then mixed-up flashes of incorrect remembering. Already I'm getting it confused in my head—that one of Megan blowing out the candles on her birthday: was that her third birthday, with Richard standing behind her in his Manic Street Preachers t-shirt, or was that from her fourth?

I think he has broken *me*, not just my heart. I feel broken.

The only thing I can think to do is to read my diary again. It's the closest thing I have to being able to talk to friends and connect with family, to remind myself that as much as I had a past, I have to believe I have a future.

Lester helps, too. He wriggles out from under the bed, where he hid when he sensed all the tension in the room, and curls up on my stomach. He is a blessing.

I force myself to count my other blessings: I have a daughter who needs me and a mum who loves me, even if I hardly ever see her. I have an ex-husband who still cares about me, and I have known love. I am healthy. I have friends.

I am fortunate. I am fortunate. I am fortunate.

1st January 1987

I thought Mum would pick up the telephone immediately. I visualised her, drink in hand, the gas fire spitting on all three bars, Big Ben and fireworks on the television. But it rang for a long time before there was an answer. I congratulated myself on my restraint at allowing more than four rings, when John was waiting for me—ME!—in the bar. I just hoped Mum wouldn't start rambling on and on about previous New Year's Eves with Dad. John might get bored of waiting and go back to the party—that would be a disaster.

'Come on, come on,' I muttered into the receiver, my breath hot and wet against the cold mouthpiece. Perhaps Mum had been invited round to one of the neighbours' houses. But eventually she picked up, and I pushed in my ten pence.

'Hello?' She sounded out of breath.

'Happy New Year, Mum!'

'Oh! Jo—Happy New Year, darling. Are you having a nice time?'

'Lovely thanks, I—'

But Mum wasn't listening. 'I'll see you in the morning, sweetheart, all right? Give me a ring and I'll come and pick you up, if Mr Barrington-Brown can't give you a lift home. Night night!'

And she was gone! I gaped at the receiver in surprise. Mum usually had to be prised off the telephone—she'd talk for hours given half a chance. Something seemed odd. Could she have had company? She's never mentioned a boyfriend. But, now that I think of it, Mum had been a bit brighter of late, and she'd started to spray perfume behind her ears before going out like she used to in the old days when Dad was still alive.

I decided I'd ask her soon (although I'm writing this a week later, and I still haven't! I don't know why it's so hard, but it is. It's impossible to imagine another man sitting at the head of the table; another man in Dad's bed—but I want Mum to be happy). No need to worry about it at that moment; I needed to go to the loo, comb my hair, get more lipstick on, and then—John! What a perfect way to start a new year. My mind raced ahead: I was meant to be staying the night with Donna anyway, so that would mean I'd get a lift there with all the Barrington-Browns, and maybe John would whisper for me to sneak out at night and over to his bedroom in the stable block, and we could listen to records and cuddle until the sun came up . . . What if he hated my big breasts, though? What if he found them repulsive, with their large pale nipples, and my plump tummy underneath? No—there was no way he could ever see my boobs; I'd only risk taking my clothes off if it was pitch, pitch dark. Maybe I'd have the op first, before I let him anywhere near me. But I'd have to explain why I was in hospital if I was going out with him . . . and, either way, he'd expect to see everything, surely. Gill and he had gone all the way, Donna told me they had. She'd apparently heard them at it, by listening underneath John's window one night. I really wish she hadn't told me that.

At that point I almost lost my nerve completely and ran away, thinking I could just lurk at the back of the function room waiting for Donna and Gareth to stop snogging. I couldn't go through with this. John was way out of my league. How could I go out with some-one that experienced when I hadn't even kissed a boy properly before? I pushed my way through the heavy fire doors and back out into the freezing car park, moving from one leg to the other, taking one step back towards John in the hotel bar and then another one forward towards the safety of the heat and noise and crush of people in the function room.

This might be your only chance, said a voice in my head. If you don't go now, you might always regret it. Dad would want you to go. Go. Go now.

I went—as, deep down, I always knew I would.

Thirty seconds later, I was in a warm, quiet, badly decorated bar with paintings of hunting scenes around the walls and fake tapestry benches and chairs. There was a strong smell of furniture polish and cigarette ash, which emphasised the fact that John and I were the only people in there, apart from a tired, overweight barman with great puffy bags under his eyes. The hotel's residents had seemingly vanished off to bed at the last chime of midnight.

All I could focus on were John's amber eyes, boring into me. When he handed me the rum and black I'd asked for (no ice, because I was still freezing), our fingers brushed. His felt hot. His skin was dark like Donna's mother's and his hair was black and shiny—he and Donna look so different, not like brother and sister at all. The backs of his hands and his wrists were covered with downy soft black hairs too, and I wanted to stroke them gently with one finger, like you stroke a kitten.

I didn't know what to say to him.

'Are you upset about Gill?' I blurted eventually, thinking I'd prefer to get it over with, if all he wanted was a shoulder to cry on. I waited for a look of grief to pass over his features, but he merely shrugged.

'Not really. To be honest, I'd been thinking of chucking her for a while. She was, you know, kind of nagging me a lot.'

She was mad, I thought. Imagine having John as your boyfriend, and not appreciating him? I just about managed not to say 'I wouldn't nag you.'

'Nice girl and everything,' he added hastily. I thought about Gill, with her haughty face and customised pencil-skirts, and decided that 'nice' wasn't the word I'd have used. 'Stuck-up' was more like it. Then I started fretting that John only went for that sort.

'Yes, she seems very nice,' I said obediently.

John laughed into his beer, his teeth clashing on the edge of the glass. I was pleased to notice that despite what Donna had said, his teeth didn't look remotely mossy.

211

'Mind you, she had a right strop with me just now. Threw a pint glass against the wall. I'm surprised you didn't hear her screaming at me.'

What did you do to her, I wanted to ask, that she would do that? But I also sort of didn't really want to know. I didn't know what to say. I changed the subject instead.

'So—Donna and Gareth? Do you reckon it'll last?'

John laughed again. He's got quite an evil sort of laugh. 'Gareth? Nah. He's never had a relationship for longer than a month.'

I saved this nugget of information up to tell Donna. Poor Don.

'She really likes him.'

'Shall I tell you something?' John said, leaning in close to me. At first I thought he was drunk and slipping and instinctively reached out my hands to push him upright again. The scent and proximity of him was so heady; he had a beautiful, mellow, musky smell. Then I realised that he was actually leaning his head on my shoulder, intentionally!!

'What?'

'I really like you.' He looked up at me playfully, and I felt heat sweep through my cold body, from feet to head and back again.

He really likes me, he really likes me, he really likes me, I couldn't believe it . . . ! I couldn't prevent a huge grin from pushing my cheeks into apples, and had to put my hand over my mouth to hide my Dracula fangs. It was the best moment of my life.

'Do you?' was all I could manage. I dared to meet his gaze back again. He is, without doubt, the most gorgeous person I've ever seen; better looking than David Essex or Harrison Ford or anyone. I could feel the side of his arm leaning against my bare one, and it felt hard and sinewy and male, more man than boy.

He glanced from side to side, as if he was about to tell me a dark secret, then very slowly moved his face towards mine, so near that I could see a cluster of blackheads around the creases of his nose and between his *eyebrows, and the faint greasy sheen of his nose. For some reason the fact that he wasn't completely perfect endeared him to me even more. Then he kissed me, so softly, on the lips. I just sort of froze, my drink clutched so tightly in my hand that it might have shattered if I hadn't forced myself to put it back on the table.*

'Do you mind me doing that?' John asked, a smile curving his mouth and in his eyes.

I shook my head, hardly daring to look at him. I was half-expecting him to recoil with horror at any moment and cry 'Oh my god, it's you—Jo! What a nightmare—I thought you were Sandra/Tracy/Helen / Lisa . . . .' But instead he brought his hand up to the side of my face and cupped my cheek with it. Then his other hand, which was chilled and damp from holding his pint, came up to my other cheek, and I swear I will never forget the strangeness of one hot and one cold palm against my skin. I closed my eyes as he kissed me again, more firmly this time, holding his lips against mine, licking them gently until it seemed the most natural thing in the world for me to part them slightly, allowing that warm tongue to slip and flutter inside, joining mine <u>with a shock which felt electric in its intensity</u>. His arms slid round me and in a moment we were pressed together, my boobs against his chest. He moaned faintly and pushed me against the tall back of the bench. It was uncomfortable, but I couldn't have cared less.

'Jo, you are so lovely . . . .'

I can't believe what I said then. I just can't believe it. I said: 'I'm a dirty little cow.' It took us both aback. I went bright red and John's eyebrows shot up almost to his hairline.

Damn, damn, why did I say that? I thought I'd ruined everything.

But he was so kind. He said, 'No you aren't. Or if you are, you're a lovely dirty little cow . . .'

'You were snogging Gill less than two hours ago,' I said. I didn't want to sound accusatory, but it sort of came out that way.

213

'She was kissing me, as it happens. But like I said, it's over now. I was wondering—well—would you like to come ice-skating with me sometime?'

'Yes. Please.' I immediately wondered what I could wear to go ice-skating. Perhaps black leggings with my long purple jumper? That came down almost to my knees; that would do . . . .

Then John kissed me again and for once in my life the perennial debate about what to wear seemed to fade into insignificance.

Chapter Thirty-One
Day 4

I wake up later that morning to the noise of Lester scratching in his litter tray in my bathroom, the diary's pages creased and stuck to my swollen cheek. In a flash it comes back to me, the lost photographs. What Claudio tried to do last night. How do I know he won't try it again? What he said about calling Megan.

I need a new strategy. I will talk to Megan as instructed—in fact, that will help my resolve, like a novice marathon runner spotting a loved one in the crowd at the twenty-five mile mark. Her voice will keep me going.

I will be normal to her, and then I'm going to pretend the effort of it has made me lose my mind. I will tell him I love him, but I won't get dressed, or bathe, or eat anything. I will rub my hair into a giant tangle. I won't use deodorant or clean my teeth. I will make myself ill.

I climb out of bed, switch on the light, and start by doing as many press-ups as I can manage—not many, in my weakened state: four full ones, then another dozen on my knees. My head still aches but I don't care. Then I hook my feet under the base of the bed and try a few sit-ups. When I close my eyes I am transported out of this gloomy bedroom and back to the neon lights and bass-boomy music of the gym. I see Sean's patient, amused face and kind eyes. I feel his hand pressing gently on my thigh to encourage me, and the slippery Lycra of his top when, after we've become a clandestine couple, I slide my arm briefly round his waist. It wasn't allowed when he was working, but I couldn't keep my hands off him.

Oh, how I wish I'd never set eyes on that man. Had I not, I'd still be with Richard and therefore, had I been in Pizza Express at all that day it would have been with him and Megan, not Whore of Babylon Gerald, and even if Claudio had been in there our encounter would merely have constituted a brief hello.

I flip over onto my hands and knees and perform the series of leg raises that are meant to tone your hips and thighs. I push myself as hard as I can, as sweat drips down my face and off the end of my nose onto the carpet. Then I do more sit-ups. My head is swimming and black spots float in front of my eyes—I'm far too hungry to be doing vigorous exercise but I keep going.

The energy I'm expending seems to be generating a new emotion in me, overriding the pain in my head and the fear in my chest.

Fury.

I swear, if he'd come in right then I'd have torn him limb from limb, or at least tried to. I want to scream and kick things, but I don't want to risk alerting him as then I'd have to *see* him and the sight of him makes my stomach heave and my throat constrict. It's him who's making me sick.

I take one of my pillows off the floor and whack it as hard as I can against the wall, again and again, imagining I'm holding that saucepan again and that the wall is Claudio's stupid head. On the fifth whack, the pillow splits down the seam and I'm enveloped in a huge cloud of soft soundless bees whirling around my head like my panic personified. It's a release, of sorts, and I sit back down on the mattress, spent. I hang my head down between my knees to attempt to combat the dizziness.

I'm definitely starting to smell already. It's so hot and airless in here with the window boarded shut and the door permanently closed that I've been having two showers a day to prevent me stinking worse than a tramp's armpit.

Not any more.

I keep my head down and the faintness gradually settles, along with the feathers around me.

Then I have a moment's doubt about my new MO. If I transform into this unlovable stinky fright, will Claudio forcibly try to wash me—or, worse, panic and just clonk me over the head and leave me for dead? The best case scenario is that he locks me in and leaves me here. I'd survive till Richard and Megan got back, I think. I've sort of lost track of the date, but as long as he didn't turn the water off at the mains, I'd be OK. I've been stockpiling food under the bed, biscuits and apples, although they wouldn't keep me going for long. How many days is it that you can live on water alone?

If he did switch off the water, I could pee in the bath and drink out of the toilet—couldn't I?

Then I have a horrific mental image of poor Megan and Richard bursting back into the flat, full of blue sky holiday tales, to find me barely alive or, worse, behind a locked and bolted bedroom door, covered in feathers and excrement.

I can't let that happen.

I still think on balance that the best available plan is to try to let myself go to the extent that it wrongfoots Claudio and he starts doubting his 'love' for me—or at least quashes his desire for us to sit down to a nice dinner every night. But surely after last night he's not going to do that again?

I slide off the bed and onto the floor and lie on my back on the carpet, my chest still heaving with exertion. Something catches my eye under the little set of drawers by the bed and I lunge for it—it's a biro! Claudio confiscated all the other ones he found in the Great Bedroom Purge, but this one has slipped through his net. I scribble on my palm and after a few scrapes, it bursts into glorious blue lines over the skin of my hand. It's not by any means an escape route, but at least I can leave instructions for the police to find in the event that Claudio clonks me over the head and dumps me in a ditch somewhere. There are a few empty pages at the back of my 1986/7 diary; I can use those.

What else could I write on? In a flash of inspiration, I crawl over to my chest of drawers and pull my tired, aching body up. I open the second drawer down. It's full of t-shirts and tops that I start to pull out and then stop—Claudio might guess what I'm up to if he came in now. Instead, I push the clothes to one side and get to what I want—the yellowy brittle lining paper that's been in there as long as I can remember, right back to my childhood when this mahogany chest of drawers belonged to Mum and Dad. Mum used to keep her baby-blue plastic Tampax case in the top drawer, and it took me years to figure out what it was when I used to go on my regular sly childhood rifles through their drawers when they were out. I'm not sure what I was looking for. Perhaps it was some kind of foresight, a premonition that one day it might save my life to remember this unexpected secret source of writing material.

In big capitals I write on the lining paper: KIDNAPPED BY CLAUDIO CAVELLI OF . . . Then I couldn't remember his address, even though I'd plugged it into my satnav when I'd driven over to his place. I rack and rack my brains but nothing comes, apart from Oak Road, Twickenham, so I write that, plus THE UGLY APART-MENT BLOCK NEAR THE CHURCH. BEEN HELD IN THIS ROOM FOR FOUR DAYS SO FAR. IF I'M NOT HERE WHEN THIS IS READ, HE'S PROBABLY KILLED ME. HIS MUM LIVES IN BROCKHURST, IN A NURSING HOME OR

HOSPICE BUT I DON'T KNOW WHERE. TELL MEGAN
AND RICHARD I LOVE THEM.

Then I pile the clothes back over the top of it, close the drawer
and sink back onto the feathery bed, succumbing to the throbbing
of my head and the aching of my muscles.

Some time later Claudio unlocks the door and comes in, with a cup
of tea too tepid for it to hurt if I threw it in his face. But I wouldn't.
I have worked out all the fury and am meek as a (malodorous) lamb
again—I want to hear my daughter's voice, and I suspect that com-
pliance is the only way forward, until after the phone call at least.

'Can I still call Megan?'

'What's been going on in here?' says Claudio, putting the tea
down on the bedside table. He glances at my bruised cheek and
quickly looks away, and then at all the feathers. 'It's a mess!'

'Can I still call Megan?' I repeat.

He sighs, regarding the feathery chaos again, like a disappointed
parent.

'Yes. But there are rules.'

I thought there might be.

'If you give even a hint that something's wrong, I will stab you,'
he continues, conversationally. 'We are going to practise. What
would you usually say to Megan when she's away?'

'We don't usually talk when she's away with Richard. She only
gets homesick and misses me when we speak, so it's easier to let her
just get on with it.'

'Then why has she been texting you, asking you to call her?' he
demands suspiciously, as though Megan has been somehow com-
plicit in plotting my escape.

'I don't know,' I say, truthfully. 'Can I see the texts?'

'No. I deleted them. I replied first, saying you would call today.'

'You replied, as me?'

'Obviously.' He looks at me as though I'm stupid.

'How did you know what to say to make her believe it's me?' Although I already know the answer.

'I just copied the style and number of kisses on your other texts to her. How old is she, seven? Bit young to have a mobile, isn't she?'

I want to tell him to fuck off—how dare he sound disapproving when he's been through and read my texts, replied to them pretending to be me? Instead, I just shrug.

'So, what will you say to her?'

I roll my eyes. 'I will tell her I love her, that I'm fine, Lester's fine, ask her what she's been up to, tell her I miss her but I'll see her very soon. That kind of stuff.'

Claudio seems satisfied. 'Tell her not to ring again as your phone's going in for repair. What about Richard, would you normally speak to him too?'

'I would usually just have a quick check with him, to make sure that Megan's OK, eating properly, getting enough sleep and so on.'

'I don't want you to talk to *him.*'

'All right, I won't. You can hang up if he comes on the line. Can I have my phone now?'

'I'll go and get it. I'm dialling the number, and holding the phone. If you try to grab it, I'll stab you. Understand?'

He leaves, bolting the door, then unbolts it again a couple of minutes later. In one hand he's holding my mobile, in the other, my biggest, sharpest Sabatier knife. The sight of both these objects has a strange effect on me, making me feel faint. I grit my teeth as he comes close and puts his right arm around my shoulders, holding the knife so that the tip of it pushes slightly in between the ribs of my right side.

'Are you ready?'

Even though he is right up next to me, he doesn't seem to have noticed how much I smell. This is disappointing. Fear is making me sweat even harder, so surely he will do so by later tonight?

I can't bear his body being this close to mine.

I nod. He taps the screen of my phone with a fat thumb to connect the call, and then holds it up against my left ear. I hear the continental ring tone. It rings and rings. *Come on, Megan, please, darling*, I beg silently. *I need to hear your voice.* But Megan doesn't answer. Tears spring into my eyes as the automatic answer message clicks on. I curse my laziness in not getting around to helping her record her own message, in her own voice.

I look at Claudio and mouth *What do I do?*

'Leave a message,' he hisses back.

At the beep, I try to speak but at first my words are lost in the croak of my voice. Claudio presses the knife harder into my side, and I somehow manage to sharpen up my tone.

'Hi, sweetie-pie, it's Mummy! How are you, my darling? I'm so sorry I've missed you . . .' It takes every ounce of self-control in me not to break down. '. . . But I just wanted to say hi, and tell you I love you, and Lester and I will see you very soon, in five days' time! That's not long, is it? I hope you're having an amazing holiday with Tilly and Jemima. Don't call me back because, er, my phone isn't working properly so I have to take it into the shop to get it fixed. It's the screen. I need to get the screen fixed. Anyway. I really love you, Megan. So much. Good-bye, angel . . . .'

Claudio abruptly snatches the phone away and terminates the call. I can't help hyperventilating. It's either that or sobbing, and I don't want to do that.

I take a big slurp of tea. Very odd experience, drinking tea with a knife sticking into your side.

'Can you take that knife away now, please?' I ask him, between pants, and he does. As he's standing up, my phone rings in his hand. We both freeze.

'Who is it?' I say, in as much of a panic as he is.

He looks at the screen. 'It's your ex-husband. You're not answering it.'

'But he knows I'm here! Megan probably just missed getting to my call, so now they're ringing me straight back from his phone! He'll smell a rat if I don't!'

Claudio hesitates, and I focus hard on getting my breathing under control. I hold out my hand for the phone. He doesn't give it to me, but does press the screen to answer the call and holds it to my ear again.

This time joy floods through me as I hear Richard's voice.

'Hi, Jo, sorry, we could hear Megan's phone ring, but didn't get to it in time. How's things?'

I swallow hard. 'Fine, thanks, Richard. All fine.'

The knife is back, pricking me menacingly as though I'm a jacket potato about to go into the oven.

'What have you been up to?'

I hesitate, and the knife goes in just a little further. I jump. 'Nothing! Had a bit of a bug, actually. Been in bed a couple of days puking. You know how it is—I always seem to come down with something when I finally get a bit of time to myself. How's the holiday?'

'Ah, sorry to hear it, Jo, that's no fun. It's great here. Sunny. Could do without the horse flies, but other than that, it's all good.'

I hear Megan in the background clamouring to speak to me.

'Mummy!' she squeals, and I manage to smile.

'Hello, my darling!'

'Tilly punched me in the bottom and got sent to bed early! I've got a *bruise*! And today we're going to have ice cream in a town that's got lots of hills.'

'Oh dear, that was naughty of Tilly, wasn't it? But good news about the ice cream. I've left you a message on your phone, too.'

'I couldn't find it. We could hear it but it was hidden underneath a cushion.'

'Ah.'

I suddenly don't know what else to say. I can't bear it any more. 'I've got to go, darling, I . . . need the toilet.'

'OK, Mummy. Well, I'll see you soon, yeah? Bye!'

'Definitely, sweetheart.' *Please, God.*

She's gone, and so has Richard.

Chapter Thirty-Two
Day 4

R ead to me, Jo,' Claudio says when he gets back from putting away the knife and removing my phone. Making sure we're safely locked in, he flops down on the disgusting bed next to me. 'Read your diary.'

I'm too upset after hearing Megan's and Richard's voices to speak. I roll onto my side away from him and stare at the boarded-up window, willing myself not to cry.

'READ TO ME!' he yells in my ear, in case I haven't heard him.

'In here?' I whisper.

'Yes of course in here,' he replies testily. 'Why not?'

'Because it stinks in here. It stinks of BO and sick.' And *despair*, I think.

I wonder if I am literally losing the will to live, until I think of Megan, her innocent peachy face and the freckles that the Italian sun will have popped out over the bridge of her nose. I want to see those freckles.

'It's a mess, yes, but I can't smell anything. I don't have a sense of smell, so it doesn't bother me. If it bothers you, clean it up.'

Well that's just great, isn't it? I've gone to all these lengths to make myself revolting and malodorous and he doesn't even notice.

He throws the diary down in front of me and I start reading from a random bit, about how surprised everyone was that Donna and Gareth were still going strong, two months after New Year . . .

'No!' he interrupts.

'What?'

'I don't want that bit. I want to hear about when you went ice-skating with John, the first time.'

'You must have already read it, then,' I comment miserably.

'I only glanced at it. I want to hear it properly, from you.' There is an odd intensity about him—more odd than usual, anyway. I am really afraid of him today. I fumble through the notebook until I find the correct entry, about halfway through, and start reading in a croaky voice.

14th March 1987

We went ice-skating as a foursome; me and John, Donna and Gareth. I got to sit in the front seat of John's bronze Lancia, sneaking sidelong glances at his profile as he drove recklessly along the dual carriageway on the outskirts of Brockhurst, with a cassette of Bat Out of Hell *blaring out at top volume. He seemed to be able to smoke, drive, laugh, and gaze lustfully at me—I was torn between feeling impressed at his ability to do it all at the same time, overjoyed at the way he was looking at me and terrified at the speed we were going. I clutched tight onto the handle above the passenger door, wondering if he would take me into his stable room again later that day. I was dying to reach my arm along the back of his seat and stroke the bristly nape of his neck.*

Donna and Gareth were snogging in the back. Over the noise of the engine, and Meat Loaf, I could just make out little smacking, slurping noises, and they made my toes curl in my new tan suede pixie boots, bought with my birthday money.

'Get a room, you two,' John yelled.

'Huh,' said Donna, surfacing. 'I'm not taking instructions from someone who plays flippin' Meat Loaf in the car. I'm ashamed to call you my brother!'

'Meat's cool, sis,' said John laconically. He looked across at me and smiled.

'Can you ice-skate, by the way?'

'Never tried. Can you?'

'Yeah,' said John. 'I've been loads of times. Don't worry. I'll hold your hand.'

'And the rest,' commented Gareth from the back seat.

'Put a sock in it, Gaz,' said Donna, slapping him affectionately across the side of the head. 'I think it's sweet, Jo. Can't imagine what you see in my stinky brother, but if he's going to go out with anyone, I'd much rather it was you than that narky old Gill.'

I don't even like to hear Gill's name mentioned in front of John. I'm permanently convinced she's going to persuade him to dump me and go out with her again. Apparently she's been telling everyone John's the love of her life and that it's just a matter of time. I hate her.

I twisted my head and glared at Donna, mouthing 'Shut up'.

'What?' said Donna, as Gareth grabbed her roughly round the neck and pulled her towards him again.

All in all, I was glad when we arrived at the car park of the ice rink. John had been driving so fast that, even though I was in the front seat, I was starting to feel very queasy, and the thudding music hadn't helped either. I was also quite nervous about the skating. What if I kept falling on my bum, and made a leg-scissoring, windmilling-armed fool of myself? Or what if someone skated over my fingers and chopped them off? I had a lurid image of the ice stained crimson in sweeping petal shapes around me, and my unattached fingers rolling across the rink, as embarrassing as tampons spilling out of a handbag.

Gareth and Donna piled out of the back seat and I took off my seatbelt, leaning forward to pull open my door handle.

'Wait a minute,' said John. He leaned sideways towards me and kissed me softly on the lips, gazing at me with his flecked amber eyes. 'You've got multi-coloured eye-tops.'

'Eyelids, John; they're called eyelids. And it's eye shadow,' I murmured back, feeling so grown up, and so turned on.

'It's pretty,' he said, his lips millimetres from mine.

Donna and Gareth banged on the passenger window, making us both jump.

'Now who needs to get a room?' Donna shouted.

'By the way,' John whispered in my ear before we got out of the car, 'don't worry about Gill. She *is* narky, and now I've got you, I don't ever want to get back with her again. OK?'

I love that boy sooooo much.

We all queued for skates, joking about smelly socks as we handed over our boots and shoes to the girl behind the counter (who, I noticed, stared openly at John, pairing up his battered black lace-ups on the counter with something approaching tenderness). John helped me get my feet into the hard blue plastic clodhoppers by pushing down on my shoulders and lacing them up for me. I gazed down at the top of his head before allowing him to escort me, both of us clumping awkwardly, to the side of the rink. John was holding my cold hand in his warm one and he led me onto the ice with such grace and confidence that it was easy to slide along next to him.

'Hey, you're a natural at this,' he said, as we swept past a dad with a dangerously wobbling toddler in tow.

I was frowning with concentration. It was difficult, but not as difficult as I had expected. The ice was desperately—and somehow surprisingly—slippery, but once you got into a rhythm, it was OK. It was the other skaters who were more of a problem, veering and lunging *towards us.* Curiosity Killed the Cat *blared tinnily over the speakers as we dodged and weaved around, our blades churning the ice into vapour trails of slush.*

'This is great!' I shouted, beaming at John. At that moment I felt a perfectly rounded and complete happiness, unlike anything else I'd ever experienced. Since Dad died and the incident in the alley, I hadn't even come close to this sensation of joy—except for New Year's Eve, of course. As if to emphasise it, John grabbed me round the waist and swung me into a hug, almost lifting me off my skates. We nearly overbalanced, but I managed to reach for the barrier at the side and hung onto it as John skated into me, pressing me against him. I breathed deeply into the oily wool of his thick sweater, and he wrapped his arms around me in a protective, silent embrace.

Donna and Gareth skated past, Gareth with panic in his eyes, resembling a huge newborn foal, and Donna assertively leading him.

'Hey, you. You do still want to go out with me, don't you?'

I was flabbergasted. I couldn't believe he'd doubt it for a second. I had to bite my tongue to stop myself saying 'Go out with you? I want to MARRY you!'

'Of course! Why, do you think I don't?'

John's chin pressed into the top of my head and he whispered into my hair. 'Thing is, I get paranoid about you dumping me . . . I like you so much but I—well, sometimes I think you and Donna are laughing at me.'

This was a different John to the John who tweaked my WHSmiths bag that time and teased me about my Final Countdown *single. That John wasn't the sort of guy that could care less if two sixteen-year-olds were laughing at him. I felt confused by this, but decided it was best not to think about it too deeply.*

'No! Never! I promise you, we weren't laughing at you.' Well, I wasn't, anyway. Donna does, all the time—but then she's his sister, and brothers and sisters always laugh at each other.

'Can I ask you a question?' Again the chin dug into my scalp. 'Can we do this again sometime?'

'Sure,' said John. 'Just the two of us next time.' He kissed me and we were both smiling inside the kiss.

Claudio laughs meanly. 'John would never have married you. He was a player. He said that to whatever girl he was going out with.'

I don't believe him. He's just jealous.

'Can I stop now? I feel sick again and I need to sleep.'

'Very well,' Claudio says. 'I have a few things I need to sort out, emails and so on. We'll take a break for an hour or so and then I will come back later.'

Great, I think sarcastically. Like this is some sort of twisted team-building exercise, in our office of two. Three, if you count Lester.

Chapter Thirty-Three
Day 4

I feel calmer once he's gone, but still nauseated. I think it might be from all the exercise this morning; or perhaps he gave me concussion when he hit me. Anyway, I was sick again. I didn't quite make it to the bathroom on time and some of it got on my bed. But that's fine, that's what I want. I want him to be so repulsed by me that he won't come near me, even if he doesn't have a sense of smell, damn it.

I couldn't get back to sleep, though, despite telling him I needed to, so I've just been sitting in the bathroom reading my diary. It really smells in my bedroom and the bathroom spotlights are brighter. Reading the diary is the only thing that takes my mind off the smell. I got really engrossed in my writing when I was reading it to Claudio, but now I'm slowing down again in the knowledge of what's coming. I start flicking through chunks instead of reading every word—this particular section seems to be a paean to John. Somehow it was easier reading the grim stuff—the bulimia, the attack, Dad's death, proof that I'd been through desperate times before and blossomed back into happiness. But I don't want to be reminded of the happiness. I feel like I'm rubbing my own nose in it, knowing how transient it turned out to be. A mere few months later in 1987 and everything would be turned upside down again, even worse than before.

I'm finding it hard to concentrate. There is vomit on the corner of my mattress and over the carpet, and the acrid sharp stink drifting through to the bathroom mingles with my own body odour. The feathers I pulled out of the pillow have settled on the puke like some kind of hideous and malodorous art installation. My bedclothes are all balled up in a corner of my bedroom. Even Lester's deserted me—he shot out at speed when Claudio last came in, even though his food bowl is in my bathroom.

The only problem with my descent into what I hope he thinks will be madness is that I don't get to leave this room—I doubt he'll cook me dinner in the kitchen when I resemble a bag lady. But I'm craving daylight so badly that at times I think I really am going crazy.

I want him to see what he's doing to me; I was wrong to indulge him before, by sitting down to dinner and making conversation with him. Surely he can't fail to notice how badly it's all going?

I haven't breathed any air outside of this room and my bathroom for two days. Maybe I'm poisoning myself with my own recycled breaths. I can't do it. I can't fake it: he'll never believe me.

I flick through the diary, trying to concentrate. Time is passing so slowly, like wading through treacle.

April 1987—I lost my virginity in John's stable-block bedroom, listening to The Jam, All Mod Cons, the loveliness of the track English Rose *flowing over us both as we flowed over each other in the dark hot space under John's slightly musty-smelling duvet.*

Needless to say I'd underlined that bit. I remember writing those diaries as novelistically as I could, but there's a pretty fine line between novelistic and pretentious . . . in fact, all the bits I'd under-lined are now the bits I'd edit out, in the unlikely event of their ever seeing the light of day.

There was the sudden sticky pain Donna told me to expect—she and Gareth were a couple of months ahead—and the strange balloony smell of the condom, but apart from this it was a good experience.

It all gets a bit X-rated from that point, which cheers me up a tiny bit:

It had seemed like such a natural progression of events. John was already regularly slipping his fingers under my skirt and curling them around the edge of my pants, touching me where it was hot and liquid after just a couple of minutes of kissing; this had been going on for months. I was embarrassed at the little squelchy sounds his finger made inside of me, but not so embarrassed that I ever wanted him to stop. I learned how to feel him in return, tentatively at first, through his jeans and then more boldly, unzipping them and sliding my hand through the gap in the front of his Y-fronts to the damp heat of the velvety-smooth hardness inside.

I hope Mum never read my diary. That brought it all back. I can picture John now, and how he felt. But it wasn't just about sex, not at all. I was amazed at how sweet he was to me. How he could happily cuddle up on the sofa with me for hours, watching television, giggling at Ronnie Corbett in *Sorry*, or leaping up and running into the kitchen to make me and Mum a cup of tea.

Mum absolutely loved John too, despite having been initially rather wary of the fact that he was two years older than me. 'Such a handsome boy,' she'd whisper, whenever he came round. 'He's so good for you!'

I'd hiss at her to be quiet, both mortified and pleased. Looking back I realise, with a thrill of awareness, that I hadn't felt the need to make myself sick for the entire time John and I were together. He said so often and with such conviction that he loved my body, and my 'huge melons'—which had made me blush—that I could even imagine a day when I'd let him make love to me with the lights on. I hadn't given up on the idea of the breast reduction, but since getting together with John, I had postponed it. I remember that it no longer seemed so important.

Mum was much happier by then too. She had indeed got a new man—bit quick, I thought at the time. He was called Brian and he was a driving instructor—*my* driving instructor! That was how they met. They were enough of an item by then that he sometimes came over and watched TV with us. They requisitioned the sofa, and John and I were relegated to the big saggy armchair, where we'd hide behind the wings of it to disguise our laughter at Brian's bliss-fully unaware scratching (he was always scratching—beard, tummy, Mum's shoulder blades).

I got a lot of free driving lessons.

15th June 1987

John asked me earlier if it bothered me that Mum had got another boyfriend so soon after Dad. We were eating takeaway chow mein in the kitchen. Mum and Brian had just gone out to the pub, to hear a blues band that Brian's mates are in. John was looking at a photograph on the pinboard, that one of me and Mum and Dad on a beach—me as a toddler in frilly plastic pants, banging a spade on a sandcastle.

I thought about the question as I ate a water chestnut. It made my heart hurt to see Dad beaming, as he was then: a young man of thirty-two who had believed he had his whole life ahead of him, when it turned out that he only had another measly fourteen years.

This is what I said to John: 'It would have bothered me if I hadn't met you. It sounds selfish, but if I wasn't with you, I think I'd feel . . . lonely, if Mum was going out the whole time, and being all lovey-dovey around another man. I do miss Dad, like anything . . . But it's sort of, well, now that I know what it feels like to be in love, I'm just happy that she's happy. If that doesn't sound too soppy.'

John pushed back his chair and came across to my side of the kitchen table. He kissed me and his tongue tasted of noodles and garlic.

'You're gorgeous, you are,' he said, pulling me down onto the lino, even though it was none too clean, and I felt grains of spilled rice sticking to my elbow. We were almost underneath the table, but I didn't care about the rice, or the patch of something sticky near my face, or the fact that my neck was cricked up against one of the table legs. All I cared about was the feel of John's tongue caressing my mouth and the weight of his body on top of mine.

I just about managed to resist asking him if I was more gorgeous to him than Gill was, or any of his other ex-girlfriends. Thankfully.

Instead, I giggled and whispered, 'What are we doing down here? Why don't we go up to my room?'

'Can't wait that long,' he replied, stroking my boob, thrusting against me through our clothes, making the table shake.

'Stop it! This table's rickety. I don't want chow mein in my hair.'

'Just adds to the excitement, doesn't it, though? At any moment, one of several things could happen—I'll take your knickers off, you'll feel me pushing inside of you, or you'll get concussion from a plate on the head, and noodles all over your body . . . .'

'I'll take my chances,' I said. 'I like the sound of at least two of those options.'

John slid his hand up inside my skirt and was just, true to his word, easing my pants down over my hips, when there was the unmistakeable sound of a key in the front door, followed by Mum's high laugh.

'Shit!' John hissed, rolling off me and banging hard into the table leg. The table wobbled dangerously this time, but somehow nothing fell. I was just scrambling up from the lino when Mum came into the kitchen, delving in her handbag—which was a relief, since it prevented her noticing John hastily doing up his flies. Brian followed, hanging his head as Mum good-humouredly berated him.

'Hi, kids, it's only us. What are you doing down there, Jo? I forgot my purse, would you believe it? I think it's in here somewhere—I had it out earlier to pay the milkman. Needless to say Brian hasn't got any money. Typical, isn't it? I wanted a sugar daddy and I get a penniless driving instructor . . .'

'A resting pop-star, if you don't mind,' said Brian, pulling at his tufts of beard and trying to look dignified.

'Twenty years is a bloody long rest, if you ask me, Rip Van Winkle. Oh look, here it is. Who put a tea-towel on top of it?'

'That's what I like about you, my sweet,' said Brian, putting his arms around Mum's waist from behind. 'You keep my feet on the ground.'

John and I, who were both sitting back down again by then (John somewhat hunched over and grimacing), made faces at one another.

'Right then, we'll leave you kids to your Chinky and . . . whatever else it is that you're doing,' Mum said, with a wink and a tilt of the head in the direction of the floor. 'Be good, and if you can't be good, be careful. See you later!'

They were gone again. I buried my head in my arms on the table and groaned. 'She knew what we were up to!'

John laughed. 'She's not daft, your mum. Besides, she didn't exactly seem to mind, did she? She's cool. And it's not as if we were at it, or anything . . . . Lucky she didn't come in five minutes later, though.'

I just moaned again, blushing so hard that I was actually sweating. 'It's so embarrassing!'

John took a large mouthful of tepid chow mein and told me to for-get it. 'She might as well get used to us bonking all over the place. She's going to have to put up with it for years to come.'

He glanced sideways at me, and I think I blushed on top of my blush. 'Really?'

'Yeah. I reckon. Don't you? Mrs S'll be my mother-in-law one day.'

I just beamed back, so hard that I didn't care if my fangs were showing.

This entry makes me laugh out loud. It is like a little gift from my teenage self. I laugh harder and harder until the laughs turn into sobs, and then I lie on the bed and cry until my bare mattress has acquired more dark tear stains to add to all the other ones.

Chapter Thirty-Four
Day 4

'Did I hear you *laughing* in there earlier?' Claudio has an expression on his sallow face that's half curiosity, half disgust. He's brought me in a sandwich for dinner but I can't eat.

'Something funny on the radio,' I say sullenly. There's no way I'm going to admit to it being the diary that made me laugh, in case he makes me read it out loud to him.

'Are you all right?'

Perhaps my plan is working, even with the curveball of his lack of sense of smell. Perhaps he's going off me. He's concerned that I'm losing the plot. Good.

I shrug. 'No.'

'You look like you've been crying again.'

'So?'

'Don't be like that, Jo. I just want you to be happy.'

'Well *that's* a joke.' I blow some feathers off the mattress in a huff of irritation.

'I don't like it when you're in this sort of a mood.'

It's then I notice that he's also brought in the small chair from Megan's room, a flimsy little ladderback thing with a wicker seat.

He plonks his big arse on it next to the bed like I'm a patient he's visiting in hospital. Presumably having decided the mattress is too skanky to sit on.

'I don't like being locked in my bedroom forced to talk to you all day. Does that make us quits?'

'Is this what you're really like?'

A chink of hope splinters through me. 'Yeah actually, a lot of the time. I'm unbelievably moody, more so when I'm tired or stressed or pre-menstrual. Richard divorced me because he couldn't take my moods any more. He stopped fancying me, and then we split up when our sex life petered out completely.' I take a breath and add, pointedly, 'He'd built me up to be something I'm not, by fancying me for so long before we got together. It just took its toll, in the end.'

Claudio straightens up and examines me as though I'm something he found in his net on a nature trail. 'Really? I thought you split up because you were banging your personal trainer.'

'I wasn't *banging* him, as you so delightfully put it. Not before Richard and I separated, anyway.'

'But you wanted to.'

I pause. 'Hadn't really crossed my mind at that point.'

———⌣———

This is a complete lie. Of course it had, and not just *crossed* my mind but bulldozed a twelve-lane highway through it. It was all I could think about, until I was convinced that the reality could never be as good as it was in my imagination.

Yet when it finally happened, it was even better. It was the best sex I've ever had in my whole life, and it was here, in this bed, in this flat. It led to a Saturday morning ritual that began shortly after I moved into this flat, which Sean and I christened Tea in Pants.

On the weekends that Megan stayed at Richard's and Sean stayed over here, he would slide out of bed first thing, dress, and jog down to the twenty-four-hour Tesco for fresh croissants. He would let himself back into the flat, warm up the croissants, and make two cups of tea. From down the hall I'd hear faint sounds of clothing being removed and then, as I propped myself up on one elbow, eagerly waiting for the bedroom door to be pushed open with a shoulder, Sean would eventually appear. Two steaming cups of tea in one hand and a plate of croissants in the other, a big smile on his face and naked except for his pants.

'I can hear you rolling over to watch me coming in,' he'd say, laughing at the lust on my face.

'I can hear you taking your clothes off down the hallway. It's such a turn-on.'

The memory of his body coming into my bedroom like that was as strong as perfume: the broadness of his shoulders, his flat muscled stomach, his buttocks like two grapefruit . . . He would carefully place the tea and croissants down on the floor, and then roll on top of me in an effusive morning hug that sent Lester leaping off the bed in disgust. The tea almost always went cold before it was drunk and I was forever sweeping croissant crumbs out of the sheets, but I wouldn't have changed the ritual for anything.

Those mornings were what we were all about. The way Sean looked into my eyes as he made love to me, slowly and tenderly, with such passion, never breaking my gaze, a complete and almost spiritual connection. I've never known anything as powerful and it made me forgive everything else he did that irritated me—saying 'up London', liking Harvesters, stuffing his food, not knowing who Carole King was—none of it mattered when Sean was deep inside me, feeling like a part of me so new and wonderful that I became new and wonderful too. After all, you could talk about music and eat in posh restaurants with anybody, couldn't you? But there was only one person you could make love with, have that connection with.

As we lay there afterwards, kissing and giggling and feeding croissants to each other, I'd congratulate myself on having done the right thing. I'd had the courage to release Richard, so he could be with someone who made him feel the way Sean made me feel, and I'd freed myself to be able to make love with Sean for the rest of my life. I really couldn't imagine ever wanting to sleep with anybody else again. Actually, I still can't. I wish I could.

I'm going to try not to let Claudio's presence sully that memory, but I think it's too late.

'So, were you and Richard in touch after you left school?'

Claudio forces my thoughts back to Richard, and I feel disloyal and grubby—mentally as well as physically—for misrepresenting the facts of the collapse of our marriage. Richard deserved so much better, in all ways, than what he got from me. All he'd done for his entire adult life was love me wholeheartedly, and that was how I repaid him?

Claudio would probably argue that this was all he'd done, too. I suppose there's a fine line between stalking and wooing. Richard definitely wooed me, though.

I nod, smiling faintly at the memory. 'We became friends. I had a summer job in Boots during the uni holidays—'

'I remember,' Claudio interrupts, and I have a bizarre mental image of the pair of them hanging round outside Boots' sliding doors, waiting for me to come out and pick one. I wonder if Richard was aware that he had a competitor—not that I'd ever, in a million years, have picked Claudio over Richard anyway.

'He used to come in a lot. The first time he didn't realise I was working there. He'd just had his wisdom teeth out, the first summer after A levels, and he was really embarrassed to see me. Then it turned out my stepdad-to-be was his driving instructor as well as mine, so that was something else we had in common.'

I suppress a smile. Richard used to talk me to sleep when I woke up in the night, and I remember him telling me about driving lessons with Brian. He had a knack of recounting stories that just very slightly took the piss out of the person concerned, but never in a mean way.

I loved those stories. They were another layer of how he let me know how much he'd loved me and for how long, a deeper layer than the compilation tapes and quirky little cards that he plied me with during the months before our friendship turned into a romance.

Ignoring Claudio, I close my eyes and try to transport myself back to a long-ago night in another bedroom, a clean, freshly laundered room smelling of The White Company room scent, moonlight filtering in through the curtains, Richard's voice murmuring in my ear, his minty breath cool on my face, my big toe touching the soft hairs on his shin . . . .

'The day I failed my test,' Richard said, 'was a lovely spring day—I was leaving tyre tracks through pink cherry blossom, it was scattered like confetti over the sodding corner, the one I was supposed to reverse around but went up on the pavement instead. But honestly, all I thought when the examiner said I hadn't passed was "Great, I'll book another lesson for next week, and ask Brian if we can go and practise hill starts at the end of Jo's road."'

Claudio refuses to be ignored, though, so my reverie doesn't last long.

Perhaps he clocked the fond expression on my face when I was thinking about Richard, but he's picking at me like a scab. 'So he had driving lessons with your mum's bloke just to get closer to you? That's pretty tragic. Bet he failed on purpose.'

Not as tragic as locking me up and giving me seven days to love you, I think but wisely don't say. I don't rise to the bait.

'He did fail, but I don't think it was on purpose. He said he was gutted not to have passed the first time, but that part of him was glad too because Brian was his best link to me—this was before we became friends. Even though Brian's a bit of an old bore. Lovely guy, but obsessed with the Sixties. Richard said he used to have to keep changing the subject off Sandie Shaw and Lulu and all these other Sixties icons who had allegedly wanted to have his babies.'

'Changing the subject back to you?'

I nod. 'Apparently. Richard confessed that he found out all sorts of stuff about me and Mum by talking to Brian.'

'Like what?' Claudio looks almost as though he wishes he'd thought of that as a strategy. What is with these blokes, I wonder? I genuinely don't understand what they saw in me. It's not like I was some Kate Moss babe. I was plump and my boobs were massive and I had crooked teeth like Dracula. It must be because I only had eyes for John. It seems that playing hard to get really does work. Even when you don't want to be got.

'Oh I don't know. Stuff like, we did our grocery shopping on a Thursday. That Mum worked part-time at the Trade Union office as a secretary. That I wanted to learn the sax but Mum couldn't afford to buy me one.'

'Were you still at school then?'

'Yeah. Upper Sixth.'

'So you were with John. Why didn't Brian tell him you had a boyfriend? He must have known he was just fishing for information about you.'

I make a sound through my nose, half laugh, half huff. 'He did, in the end. After Richard failed his test. I remember Richard telling me about it. He'd been wondering, in the car, if I'd be at the joint area school disco that Friday night, and that was when Brian told him about John.'

'I'm surprised that he didn't already know you had a boyfriend if he spent so much energy following you around.'

'He didn't follow me around.'

Although he had. He'd followed me home the night of the attack.

'He just wanted to go out with me. Apparently Brian told him there were "plenty more fish in the sea" and Richard wanted to punch him.'

'Well, I suppose we have that much in common, then.' Claudio leans back in the little chair to stretch, and it creaks and cracks but doesn't give way.

———

I remember the night Richard confided in me about pumping Brian for information. We were married by then, and of course I knew he'd liked me for a really long time; he'd already told me that. He'd proved it too, by not giving up when I gave him the cold shoulder all those months after he told me he'd saved me in the alley. But there was something so raw about the way he spoke about the chat with Brian, how devastated he'd been to find out I was in love with someone else, how ridiculous the notion was of other fish in the sea. I knew how it felt, of course I did, because hadn't I felt exactly the same about John? I cuddled Richard close that night, wrapping him in my arms with gratitude and awe that someone could love me that much, for that long.

Not so different from how Claudio feels about me, I suppose, in his mind, at least. Not mine.

'Think I'll have an early night tonight,' he says eventually. 'This day feels like a bit of a write-off.'

I nod. It does. It feels like stalemate. I'm no nearer to being able to convince him I love him and I can't imagine that tomorrow will be any different.

But tomorrow, if my calculations are correct, is Day Five. Do I really only have two days left? I am thinking so hard about this as Claudio locks me in that it takes me a few moments to realise the momentous thing that has just happened and suddenly everything changes in me in a flash, as though I've been shot through with a massive charge of electricity. I lie frozen and still, heart pounding, waiting to see if he realises his mistake, but he doesn't come back. After ten minutes, when I hear the toilet flush and the door to the spare bedroom close, I bite my lip with excitement.

He left the chair behind!

Maybe this is where my luck changes!

Chapter Thirty-Five
Day 5

I pretend to be asleep when Claudio brings in my breakfast. I listen to him listening to me, trying to establish whether I'm really asleep or not. His presence in my room feels like a giant vampire bat, hovering over me with its massive rubbery wings outstretched, and I have to make a huge effort not to shudder. But I am even more excited this morning, so excited I can barely breathe. Claudio's slipped up. He still hasn't spotted that he left the chair in here. I got up in the night and threw some clothes over it in the hope of disguising it, or at least making it less obvious that it's still here.

To my joy, when he leaves, he doesn't just leave the room, but the flat. 'I'm just popping out to the chemist,' he says as he closes the door behind him. 'I've got an awful headache and you finished the Nurofen.' I hear the locks clunking and the bolt shooting. His voice sounds strained and unhappy.

As soon as I hear the front door close and lock, I leap out of bed and switch on the light.

I dash over to my chest of drawers and lean against it, trying with all my strength to push it along the wall until it is positioned directly beneath the loft hatch. But it's too heavy. I can't move it. I drag out the bottom drawer, the biggest one, and try again. It budges a couple of inches, sticking reluctantly on the carpet. This won't do.

I take out the third drawer and throw it on top of the other one, then the top drawer, so I can reach my arm inside and push as well as pulling. It works! The chest begins to judder reluctantly across the carpet. I'm sweating buckets by the time I manage to manoeuvre it underneath the hatch.

Then I lift the chair up and plonk it on the chest's smooth dark oak top, unable to suppress the thought that my mum would kill me if I got it all scratched up. It's an antique, this chest; it belonged to my granny.

I feel my grandmother cheering me on from some other world as I climb gingerly up the handy ladder made by the drawers' casings until the chair and I are both perched awkwardly on top, like two large and very out-of-place ornaments. Now comes the hard part.

I grasp the flimsy little chair and put one knee on each side of the frame—no way can I put my feet on its wicker seat: they'd go straight through. The wicker is already fraying at the edges— I'm amazed that it coped with Claudio's big arse on it last night. Gingerly, I switch from knees to feet until I'm balancing on the chair seat's frame. Standing like that reminds me briefly of those awful footpad toilets you get in parts of Europe, which you have to straddle to use.

I struggle to stop myself wobbling too much—fatigue, hunger, and adrenaline are making it difficult to keep my legs steady. But I'm now easily able to push aside the loft hatch. Cool musty air hits me, a welcome change in microclimate. I have to keep my rising excitement in check, as one wobble too far and I'll fall off the chair, off the chest, and onto the floor. It's a good seven-foot drop.

Very carefully, I finish pushing across the hatch and pull myself up into the loft, making sure I don't kick over the chair in the process. It's not too hard—the loft opening is at chest height from the chair, so I don't need to employ too much upper body strength to get in.

It's amazing to be in a different space without Claudio's oppressive presence. I pull my legs up behind me, briefly tempted to frolic like a lamb in the yellow loft insulation even though I can't stand up straight. If only this was one of those houses whose roof spaces all run into one another! I could merely pop across and down into someone else's flat to raise the alarm. But this one is bricked up, and the floor isn't boarded so I have to use the wooden struts of my bedroom ceiling as stepping stones to cross the sea of lagging.

Various items are marooned on top of the lagging—Megan's car seat, a broken stereo and—there they are! hallelujah!—the things I'd hoped against hope to find: Richard's old golf clubs. The removal men had mistakenly brought them to my flat even though my stuff had red stickers on it and Richard's had yellow. I suspect that Megan may have switched some of the stickers, intentionally or otherwise, as I ended up with a few of Richard's things and he mine. For some reason I had just bunged the golf-clubs in the loft—it had been a short-lived hobby of his some years earlier before he decided it was too middle-class for words and gave up, and we had both forgotten that I had them.

But then disaster strikes. I am so dizzy with euphoria that I miss my footing on the narrow wooden struts and stumble, dislodging the golf bag, which topples over, clubs sliding out of it and through the loft hatch, bouncing off the chest of drawers, knocking the chair off as they go. They all land on my bedroom floor, banging together like a drawerful of giant's cutlery falling, and I rush over to the hatch.

Lucky Claudio's gone ou . . .—*Wait, what's that noise?*

I pause, thinking that it's just my ears ringing from the clatter but no—to my horror, there really is a noise outside the door, the fumbling of a bunch of keys. Shit! Claudio either only pretended to go out, or I've been extremely unlucky and he forgot his wallet or something. I hear the key in the door and realise I only have a few precious seconds. I grip each side of the hatch and launch myself feet-first through it, using the chest of drawers like some kind of unyielding trampoline onto the floor. I'm fortunate I don't break my leg, but by some miracle I'm unhurt, although I fall sideways as I hit the floor, and have to right myself, panting as the wind is knocked out of my lungs.

As the outside bolt on the bedroom door starts shooting open, I just about manage to lunge for one of the clubs, a putter, and shove it under my duvet out of sight, but I can't do anything else to hide what I've been up to.

The door bursts open and he's standing there looking flabbergasted, hurt, furious—and ill. He's as white as a sheet. Perhaps that's why he came back.

'What's all this? What are you doing?' he asks in a dangerously calm voice. The handcuffs are dangling from his right hand—he must keep them right outside my bedroom door for easy access.

'Trying to escape, of course. What do you think I'm bloody doing?'

Exhaustion and disappointment make me sarcastic, despite my terror. 'This has gone far enough, Claudio: you have to let me go, now. Right now. My daughter is only seven. She and her dad will be back tomorrow. Everyone will be worried. You'll be in terrible trouble with the police. My friends will have called the police, you know. There'll be a trial, and you'll get sent to prison. Is that what you really want? Let me go now, this is enough. Enough. Let me go!'

My voice is rising with rapidly accelerating hysteria and for the first time in days the sobs come. 'LET ME GO, LET ME GO! CLAUDIO, PLEASE LET ME GO!' I launch myself at him, swinging punches and slaps, trying to kick and hurt and kill him. I swear I would have killed him if I'd had a knife in my hand. I go to grab one of the golf clubs but he disarms me as if the heavy club is nothing sturdier than a drinking straw. I notice, though, that the effort makes sweat pop out on his forehead and he's a nasty greenish colour.

He laughs meanly. 'Nice try, Jo. They aren't back tomorrow. You already told me that they were on holiday for ten days. There's another four to go. One day left for you to tell me you love me. We have *plenty* of time—well, *I* do. Yours is running out, and fast.'

I no longer care about my own safety, and, in fact, deep down I realise that this is what he's been waiting for: a reaction. We got sucked into this vortex in the spur of the moment and he's just been waiting for me to make a move of some kind. He must know that I could never love him now. His face even shows a flicker of relief as he fends off my flailing attack.

He grabs my wrists, pushing me away so that my kicks don't reach him either, and easily throws me on my back on the bed while he deftly handcuffs me to the bedpost. Then he gathers up the spilled golf clubs, wincing with pain each time he bends down, takes them out of the room with the chair so I can't get back into the loft again. He comes back in, re-locks the door, drops the keys deep into his jeans pocket, and just stands over me, glaring at me. The expression on his face is like no other I've ever seen, far worse than when I went for him with the saucepan. I can't read it, but now I am beyond scared. This is it, then. This time I'm definitely going to be raped and possibly killed. My instincts are to fight—but hey, when have my instincts ever done me any favours? Besides, if you're going to be raped, isn't it meant to be better to be passive and still and let them get it over with as soon as possible? My only hope is that he won't be able to get an erection again, like last time.

I wait to feel his weight on top of me, and him fumbling with my clothes—but instead he turns even whiter and visibly wobbles, clutching his head. Hope and joy gush in dual torrents into my chest, flooding my veins and arteries like an amphetamine. He really is ill.

I sit up. 'Are you OK, Claudio?'

'Shut up,' he says, grimacing with pain. It must be a migraine or something—excellent. He half-lies, half-flops down next to me, pulling me onto my side, so that we are facing one another. His breath stinks. I feel the hidden golf club knock against my ankle and discreetly work it further down the bed, away from Claudio's feet.

'I have something to say to you,' he begins, his eyes closed. 'Just let me lie here for a minute.'

Chapter Thirty-Six
Day 5

Claudio lies down very close—too close—to me. For a few minutes he's completely still and I long to lunge for the golf club, but I can't, not while I'm handcuffed to the bedpost. I need him to fall asleep. Then he rolls over and grips my already-restrained wrist.

'Tell me you love me,' he says, his eyes screwed up in pain. 'Tell me you want to stay here with me.'

I can't believe it, but even through the misery in his voice he actually sounds faintly hopeful, as if he thinks I might seriously ponder the question and then say, Yes, on balance, Claudio, I'd absolutely flaming well love to stay here locked in my flat for the rest of my life, with you flattening me on my fetid horrible rumpled bed, breathing your fetid horrible rumpled breath into my face . . . How could I not love such a charmer? *You stupid fetid bastard.*

'I do love you, Claudio, I swear, I do, and it will grow and grow and we could move in together and get old together and cultivate roses or keep chickens or whatever you like. I mean it! But you have to see that this is not helping. Like you said, we need a clean slate. Let me help you—you're ill. We have to be nice to each other. Please let go of my wrist. You're hurting me. If you want us to go out with each other, you have to back right off now. I mean it.'

As if! He could back off as far as the moon and he'd still never be in with a chance. But Claudio obediently lets go of my still-handcuffed wrist. I don't think he believes me, though.

I turn back to face him. Up until now, I've kind of felt as though I've been moving underwater in the twilight of this flat; nothing has seemed real. But now it is brought into sharp focus. I've broken the surface and I'm wide awake, teetering on the edge of either disaster or redemption. For the first time, I feel almost in control.

'Let me get you a cold cloth to put on your forehead. Then you can tell me what you want to tell me.'

Miraculously he lets go, takes out the bunch of keys, and unlocks my handcuffs. I think about grabbing them and whacking him round the head with them, but he locks them onto one of his belt loops. I sit up, rubbing my wrist and wondering what he suddenly needs to tell me, after all these days. I hope it isn't a confession that there are several other women underneath his floorboards back in his flat.

'I don't want you to leave me,' he says again. 'Everyone leaves me.' He has rolled onto his back and is lying with his forearms folded across his forehead, trying to press the pain away. His socked feet are dangerously close to the golf club. They smell as bad as his breath.

'Clean slate,' he mumbles. 'I've never told anyone this, Jo, never, but I can tell you because we have no secrets, do we? I know all yours. And when you know mine, you will be flattered that I confided in you, and then you won't be able to leave me, ever.'

His voice hardens, even through his evident pain. Scared of what I'm about to learn, I get off the bed and go into the bathroom. Taking a facecloth off the towel rail, I run it under the cold tap, wring it out, and take it back in to him, all the time frantically calculating whether I can make a grab for the golf club now and hit him before he notices. But it's under the duvet, and even with his headache I'm pretty sure he'll go for me if I make any sudden moves.

'You look . . . dirty,' he mumbles, taking in my grimy sweat-stained Cath Kidston short pyjamas and matted hair.

'I am. I haven't had a shower for three days. I stink. It reeks in here.'

He ignores this—since it clearly doesn't mean anything to him. I'm reminded again, with a despairing lurch, about his lack of sense of smell. All my efforts have been for nothing. Suddenly I am desperate, absolutely desperate for the sensation of clean water on my filthy, sweaty body.

He groans. 'I need Co-codamol. Is there any left in here?'

'No. You know there isn't. You took out all my painkillers. You'd better go out and get some.'

'You think I'm leaving you alone now, after what you just did? No way. Talk to me, Jo? My mother used to talk to me when I was ill.' His voice sounds blurred and unsteady and I know this is my best chance. It's the first time he's voluntarily mentioned his mum, too, so he must be feeling vulnerable.

'Richard used to talk to me when I was ill, too. And to get me to sleep at nights. Stories, memories. I do it for my daughter too.'

'Don't talk to me about him. I'm sick of hearing about him. Do it for me. Please? What do you remember?'

Slowly I start to feel powerful, finally beginning to gather up a skirt of control. I start thinking about my unfinished diary, what happened next, what has remained unwritten and unspoken for almost twenty-five years. The last entry I read—the last one in the notebook—was my second trip ice-skating with John, and that had finished abruptly, nothing but blank pages following. I had obviously changed my mind about wanting to write it all down. Or I simply hadn't been able to. I've never even talked to Richard about it.

'I remember the last time I saw John,' I say, slowly.

He knows immediately what I am talking about. 'At the ice rink. Yes. I was there too.'

For a moment, I feel as though I'm back on that rink again, sliding out of control. I freeze.

'What do you mean?'

'I was there that day.'

This throws me so much I almost jump off the bed and run back into the bathroom. I can't process it. He must have been the nameless friend that John said hi to. I don't remember him being there.

I need to maintain composure at all costs, though, so I make a colossal effort to keep my voice steady and low, forcing myself back to that day. Even just in my memory, John's presence soothes and encourages me. I miss him so much.

'I couldn't write about it—I didn't want to, because I knew every time I read it back it would rip my heart open again—but I'm going to try to remember. I remember us getting there, John reversing the Lancia into a tight space in the car park . . . His arm was draped over the back of my seat as he twisted around to steer his way in. I can remember his face, the olive skin and the black eyelashes. He was frowning with concentration . . . I told him I loved him.'

Claudio frowns too, but I'm not going to spare him the details.

'John said, "I love you too, Sweetlips," and he kissed me. He always called me Sweetlips—soppy I know, but I loved it. I breathed in the smell of him; half man, half boy, sweet sweat and cheap aftershave. I felt perfect happiness in that moment. It was the summer holidays, I was going ice-skating with my gorgeous boyfriend, exams were over, and Swing Out Sister was playing on the car radio.

'"Come on, then," he said, "Let's go and tear up that ice rink."'

I glance at Claudio and he's scowling. I can tell he doesn't like hearing this any more than he likes hearing about Richard but he still thinks he needs to. Hopefully he's feeling too ill to be able to concentrate. I make my voice stay low and soothing, willing him to relax and let it become white noise, a backdrop to oblivion.

'That second visit was much easier, technically. I got up enough confidence to really work my body into a rhythm and after only three circuits I let go of John's hand. I could swing my arms and it widened my strides. When I felt really brave, I moved in towards the faster-flowing inside of the circles of skaters. I was panting and out of breath, beaming and waving at John, who caught up with me, laughing at my enthusiasm. He dodged around an unsteady middle-aged couple in matching sweaters. I remember them because he nudged me and pointed and said, "That'll be us in a few years."

'"Good," I said. I reached out to take his hand again. "I can't wait. In fact, I might even start knitting now. That way, our jumpers might be finished in about twenty years' time."

'We skated for ages—forty minutes or so—but the rink had filled up and we had to go slower. I spotted a few people I recognised—a couple of girls from the Fifth Form, and John waved at a mate of his as he whizzed past us.'

'That was me,' Claudio mumbles.

'It might have been,' I say, reluctantly. 'I don't remember.'

'Go on.'

'John asked if I'd had enough, because I was skating more and more slowly. My feet were hurting and it felt like someone was clutching my thighs. "Let's go and have a hot chocolate," he said, squeezing my hand. "Once more round the block first?"

'I remember sighing—I'd like to have come off the ice then, that minute, could already see myself clumping back to get my shoes, leaning on John for support, trying to take the weight off my blisters—but one more circuit wouldn't hurt, not if John

255

wanted to. That's what I thought. I told him to go on ahead and I'd meet him by the exit. He called me a lightweight and swung me around with both hands round my waist. "See you in a minute," he said as he skated off, calling back over his shoulder, already picking up speed.

'Those were the last words he ever said to me. I was so busy trying to keep his red sweatshirt in sight for as long as possible that I almost got swept off my feet by three teenagers who raced past me. I wobbled and lunged for the bar at the side of the rink, and when I looked up again, John was out of sight.'

I grit my teeth with the effort of keeping my voice steady.

'I waited for him, on the ice, by the exit.'

I force myself to stroke the back of Claudio's hand, gently, like a lover would. His body is definitely starting to sink very slowly into the mattress. We are suspended in time like insects in amber. I have been inching backwards away from him across the mattress as far as I can without him noticing.

'I waited for ages. At first I thought he was playing a trick on me. Maybe even that he'd gone without me, or at least pretended to. I was getting cold, and I had cramp in one foot. I stared so hard at all the people skating towards me that my eyes went funny. I was pissed off. He'd said he was only going round one more time. But I still couldn't see him.'

It's all coming back to me, as though it happened last month. Turns out I didn't need to write it in my diary. It's been saved in a file in my head for all these years.

'There was some sort of commotion going on at the other end of the rink, but I didn't notice for quite a while, because I was too busy looking the other way, looking out for John. Then I remember the face of this woman, skating past. She looked white, and shocked. She was saying to her friend, "That poor chap! Hope he'll be all right. He came down with such a bang, didn't he?"

'It was then that I started to get worried. I turned round and saw that an area at the other end of the rink had been cordoned off. I was just in time to see someone being stretchered off the ice and outside the windows I could see the blue flashing lights of an ambulance. "Oh no," I thought, "what if he's had an accident? Lucky the hospital's so nearby." I didn't know what to do at first; I was sort of dithering about whether to skate down there, against the tide of everyone coming towards me—it didn't occur to me to go round anti-clockwise—or to take off my skates and run down the side in my socks. After all, I didn't even know that it was him. People have accidents on ice rinks all the time. They should issue helmets with the skates, I really think they should. I had visions of me running out after the ambulance, and then seeing John's face pressed up against the ice rink window from the inside, laughing at me. He was always trying to wind me up. I wouldn't have put it past him.

'Eventually I decided I had to get off the ice. I sat down and pulled off my skates, which took ages without John to help me. It was like chipping my feet out of breeze blocks and I just left the skates there, on the bench at the side of the rink—there was far too much of a queue for shoes. I remember thinking, I'll never get my shoes back, but not caring. I didn't exactly run, but I sort of hurried in the direction I'd seen the stretcher come off. There was a double door there, which said "Private", but I pushed it open and went in. It led into a concrete corridor, which was empty, apart from two girls who obviously worked there. They were about my age and they were both crying, which I thought was a bit odd—it's not unusual to see one girl crying and her friend comforting her, but you don't often see two, unless they're at a funeral or something.'

I stop for a moment, to make sure I can maintain my even tone of voice.

Claudio's eyes are two slits in his grey face under the facecloth on his head, but he's blinking quite a lot. He looks like a little boy again, struggling to stay awake. *He's a kidnapping murdering psychopath*, I remind myself, just in case I start feeling even remotely sorry for him. There's a welcome draught coming from the open loft hatch and it revives me. I take a deep breath.

'I asked the two girls if they were OK, and they wiped their faces with the backs of their hands. One of them said, "You shouldn't be in here," and I said, "I've lost my boyfriend. He told me to wait for him while he went round one more time, but that was ages ago." The girls looked at each other, and something about their faces made my heart sink. They were so young, probably a bit younger than me—in their first jobs, I expect. One was quite Goth-looking; pink eye shadow, dyed black hair, too much eyeliner. They were both wearing some sort of uniform but the Goth one had pink and black stripy tights and Doc Martens on underneath.

'"What did he look like?" said the Goth one, and I thought, No, what *does* he look like? *Does.* Not *did.* Suddenly I was having trouble getting words out, even though I couldn't believe anything really bad could have happened. They're just crying because their boyfriends have dumped them, I thought. "He's tall. Black hair. Really good-looking. Nineteen. His name's John. He's wearing a red sweatshirt and jeans." And then—this was the worst bit—they both just burst out sobbing again.

'"You need to come with us," the Goth one said. Her friend was crying too much to speak. I wasn't crying, although I can remember my heart was beating really fast and I felt sick. I asked where John was, and if he was the one I'd seen being stretchered off the ice, and she said yes, she thought it might have been him. It was sort of echoey in that corridor, and my feet were getting really cold in my socks, even though they were my thickest woolly ones. I wanted a cup of tea. I wanted John. I wanted my dad.

'"Is he concussed, then?" I asked, and then, "Why are you crying?"

'Her friend spoke, finally. She was sort of little and skinny and her nose was all red. She said, "He was just so gorgeous. It's terrible. I can't believe it. Nothing like this has ever happened here before." I was getting almost annoyed by this stage. I felt like shaking them. "Is he concussed?" I asked again, and they said, "You need to come with us." I had this image of John sitting somewhere with a big lump on his head, and an icepack pressed against it. He'd have been irritated at how uncool it was, to have to sit holding a big soppy icepack. He wouldn't have wanted me to see him like that— that's why I didn't know where he was. I looked up and down the corridor, at all the closed office doors on either side, thinking that he'd be in one of those, probably, hiding from me. Waiting till the lump went down. Thinking about how much Gareth, and all his other mates—you included, I suppose—would tease him for having a bump on his head . . . .'

I can't look at Claudio any more as I talk, willing him to fall asleep, or pass out. I hate the thought that he was in any way associated with my beautiful John; hate it, hate it. I can't bear to look, in case he's wide awake. I start at his feet, in holey, stinky once-black socks, and work my way up his legs, encased in boringly generic jeans. How can a reasonably attractive man wear such dull jeans? Then again, how can such a reasonably attractive man be enough of a psycho to keep me here when I want to leave?

I feel sick again.

'This is nice,' he mumbles, and grabs my hand. So I keep talking. *Go to sleep*, I urge him silently, the way I used to when Megan was a baby, wide-eyed and restless in the wee small hours, looking over my shoulder as if looking at the rest of the world slumbering. Except that Claudio emphatically was not, nor would he ever be, my baby. I stroke his hand again.

'So they took me down the corridor to an office behind one of the closed doors, and I was expecting to see John in there, but there was this awful man inside, with a polyester suit on. It was too big for him, and the sleeves came down to his fingers, like a little boy in a blazer at the beginning of the school year. His hair was greasy, and he was very spotty. He couldn't have been more than a year or two older than John, but I just looked at him and thought, I'm so *lucky* to have John as my boyfriend. At last, something's gone right for me. Dad might be dead, but Mum's happy now with Brian, and I don't feel half as fat and ugly as I used to—how could I, when I have this beautiful boy telling me I'm gorgeous every day? I'm so lucky . . .

'Perhaps I knew I was deluded, even then, and just couldn't admit it to myself . . . That spotty ice-rink assistant manager reminded me of the manager of Russell & Bromley, when I'd gone there for an interview for a Saturday job, a year or so earlier. I didn't get the job, and I was outraged. Even more so when Donna ended up working there later. He'd asked me what the special qualities of a leather shoe were and I had no idea, so I'd said, "It's waterproof?" and he'd looked at me pityingly, just like this ice-rink guy was doing now, and said, "No—the thing about leather is that it *isn't* water resistant," and I'd said, "Well, what's the point of making shoes out of leather, then?" I still wonder about that, you know.'

I'm aware that I'm rambling now, but rambling is good, when you're trying very hard to send someone to sleep. I should've used it as a technique on Megan as a baby, instead of singing all those fragments of songs to her: *Goodbye Yellow Brick Road*, *Wish You Were Here*, *Under the Moon of Love*, even the Creed, indelibly imprinted in my mind from years of childhood churchgoing—anything low and hypnotic and soothing. I don't quite dare to start singing the Creed now, though.

Just pretend that Claudio is a great big baby. It's not so hard—and infinitely preferable to thinking of him as a kidnapper, a potential rapist or a killer.

I dare to look into Claudio's face and sure enough, his eyes are almost completely closed. There's a movement from his direction, and I realise his head is slumping further down into the pillows. He is clearly fighting either pain or sleep really hard—just as Megan used to—but losing the battle. *Sleep, sleep, sleep*, I exhort telepathically from across the mattress.

He groans and snuffles and wakes himself up with a start, peering blearily at me. 'Why don't you come over here for a cuddle?' he asks sleepily, and I think, oh boy, now who's deluded? I hesitate, thinking that I should—but then smile tightly and shake my head. I can't. 'Suit yourself,' he replies and his eyelids start to slide again.

As I'm looking pityingly at him, his mouth beginning to fall open, I catch a glint of something shiny near his waist, and my heart lurches, adrenaline back pumping with full force through my body. It's a key, sticking out of Claudio's front jeans pocket! Only the bottom part of it, the bit with teeth. I know it's attached to the bunch, but still it gives me hope.

Suddenly I feel overcome with all the fear and anger and helplessness that I've had to suppress for the past five days, and the sight of that key, my escape route, makes grief well up inside my chest with the boiling ferocity of a volcanic eruption. But I can't let it out. I just absolutely can't, because if I make one single unexpected noise, he'll wake up, and my chance to get the key will be gone. I have to keep talking, reminding myself again that this is like some nightmarish fairytale I seem to have got myself stuck in, where the princess has to escape the evil ogre and steal the key to the castle without waking him.

This feels like the hardest thing I've ever had to do. I could help myself by speaking about something mundane and trivial, perhaps what's going on in the *Big Brother* house, or the weather, or whatever—but I can't. For some reason I feel absolutely compelled to keep talking about John and that afternoon at the ice rink when

everything in my world crumbled, and when it seems that everything I've done, said, or thought since that moment, comes back to
that day in a thousand different ways.

Well, as far as therapy goes, I'd prefer someone a bit more
qualified—I think longingly of Eileen's Sofa of Emotion—but hey,
beggars can't be choosers. Needs must, and other such clichés. I take
several deep breaths to quell the incipient storm of hysteria, and
wait until my voice is steady enough to talk again. I *have* to make
sure he's fully asleep. I'm only going to get one shot at this. It's not
the most proactive method of escape, but I don't dare do anything
else. I am, as I've realised, an inveterate coward. But I can't pass up
an opportunity like this.

'The spotty manager of the ice rink, or whatever his title was,
had this ridiculous expression on his face; kind of a mixture of sol-
emn, terrified and embarrassed, all rolled together. He asked me to
sit down, and one of the girls—it felt like the whole place was staffed
by adolescents: there we were, a room full of teenagers play-acting
at being grown-up, having to say and hear things that children
shouldn't have to; it was like a bloody Youth Theatre production—
anyway, one of the girls pulled out a chair for me. They were both
hovering, still sniffling, but clearly fascinated to be right at the heart
of the drama. They were staring at me as if they were waiting for me
to collapse, or scream, or whatever. I didn't want them to be there.
But I didn't want them to leave either—I couldn't face the thought
of being stuck in that office alone with the manager. And I think
it helped me keep it together, actually, their anticipation that I was
about to lose it. I wanted to prove them wrong.

'"I'm afraid there's been an accident," the spotty man said,
sounding so embarrassed that I even got embarrassed for him.
"Yeah," I said. "Are you sure it's John? Is he all right?" The manager cleared his throat really, really loudly—far more loudly than
he'd planned to, I think, because he looked even more mortified.

"Is your boyfriend's name John Barrington-Brown? That's what we found on the cards in his wallet."

"'Yeah,'" I said again. I was thinking about John's bedroom in the stable block, about listening to The Jam, and his breath on my face under the duvet. About how I was planning to have Donna as my chief bridesmaid and how I'd let her pick her own dress and everything.

"'I'm very sorry,'" he went on. I somehow thought he'd say it with more tact, but after all the hesitation, it came out really bluntly in the end.

"'Your boyfriend's dead.'"

Chapter Thirty-Seven
Day 5

I have to take a breather. It's the first time I have ever articulated that story. I'm no longer anywhere near crying, but the intensity of the experience is squeezing the air out of my lungs. When I stop talking, though, Claudio's eyes flicker open. Shit. I thought he was almost asleep.

'Do you really love me?' he mumbles. He probably hasn't been listening to what I've been saying, but I'm glad of the interruption.

'Yes, Claudio, I really do. We're going to be together, you wait and see. I'll look after you whenever you have a headache, or a cold, or whatever. But what I don't understand is why you want to keep me here. We have a future to start living!'

I'm trying not to sound fake or patronising, but it's hard. I take the facecloth away from his head, go into the bathroom, and run it under the cold tap again. After I've wrung it out, I replace it on his forehead, trying to stop my hand from shaking. He has taken his phone out of his pocket and is now frowning intently at the screen, his lip wobbling like a child's. I almost salivate at the sight of the phone, contact with the outside world—police, fire, ambulance, *help*. He has a very tight hold on it.

'What are you looking at? Could I see?'

I hold out my hand for the phone, hoping he'll have a momentary lapse of concentration and pass it to me. But he just turns the screen around to show me his screensaver, a photo of his mum. She looks tiny in a huge wingback chair, her wig lopsided, her jaw collapsed in on itself, raisins for eyes.

'Do you remember her from when we were in the Sixth Form?' he asks.

'No. I never went to your house.'

He looks surprised. 'Yes you did. I had a party once, for my seventeenth. December nineteen eighty-six.'

'Did I?' I have no idea, and even if I did go, I obviously hadn't thought it an event worthy of putting in my diary. Perhaps it's Claudio who's misremembering.

'Where did you live?'

'Estcourt Road, up near the fire station.'

'Um. Right, yes, I think so,' I say vaguely, not wanting to piss him off. Perhaps I do have a faint memory, but there were so many house parties back then. 'And your mum was at the party?' This would have been a bit unusual, to say the least. Claudio would've been mercilessly ribbed—no-one allowed their folks to be present at teen parties.

'Only for the first hour. She remembers you. She said you were a beautiful girl, with a face like an angel.'

How weird.

'Oh. Well, do send her my regards,' I say, half-politely, half-sarcastically.

'I can't,' said Claudio.

When I look at his face, I realise why. And why I'm being held prisoner here. He opens his mouth and confirms it.

'My mother is dead,' he bursts out, perhaps unconsciously echoing the ice-rink manager's words. He winces with pain at the sudden movement. 'My mother died six days ago and now I have nobody at all except you in the whole world. I lost my job last year. I don't have any friends. My fiancée jilted me. My mother's dead! What am I going to do? You have to help me, Jo, I need you. Please help me . . . .'

Oh no . . . I am completely thrown by this, even though I knew Mrs Cavelli had been in a nursing home or a hospice or somewhere. But he hadn't said that her demise was so imminent. And he certainly hadn't mentioned that she'd died six days ago. We must have been sitting in that Greek restaurant within hours of him receiving the news. No wonder I'd thought he was behaving strangely. He's completely flipped out.

'I'm sorry, Claudio, I'm really sorry. That's awful. But—but— why didn't you tell me? You took me out on a date the day your mum died and didn't say anything!'

Two fat tears squeeze out from behind his closed eyelids, and I glance desperately at his jeans pocket, to see if the keys are within reach. They aren't. But at least I manage to inch my way to the furthest edge of the bed and put one foot on the floor, every muscle and sinew of my body poised for flight at the first opportunity.

'I didn't want to spoil our date. Things were going so well for us and I thought that at last you were finally going to be mine . . .'

'At last? Claudio, it was only our third date!'

'I told you that you didn't understand. But perhaps you are right about one thing—it's not normal to have been in love with someone for twenty-five years . . .'

For a moment I think he's talking about me and John, and my heart jumps painfully at the reminder. I think of John's beautiful amber eyes and black hair and his long nervous fingers, and I want him more than I've ever wanted Richard and Sean put together. *Help me, John*, I implore him mentally, just in case he's managed to score the job of being my guardian angel. *Help me do the right thing to get me out of here.*

' . . . to have her, then to lose her again for so long—and then, by chance, to discover her again.'

'Who is that—the woman you nearly married?' I ask, forcing myself to concentrate. Then I wonder if he was referring to his mother. Even though I am wide awake, the underlying lack of sleep from the past few days is doing strange things to me, clouding my brain like condensation on an aeroplane window that you can't wipe away. No, obviously it can't be his mother. I stupidly wonder if this woman might be someone I knew from school—even Donna, maybe. Twenty-five years ago we were at school.

'No, Jo. It's you. Surely you know I've always been in love with you?'

Always been in love with me? I'd gathered that he fancied me when I was with John, and obviously he had now decided I was the one for him—but how could he have been obsessed with me for all those intervening years?

'Claudio, that's crazy,' I say slowly. 'I haven't seen you for over twenty years. It's not like we went out together. Or even on a date, until three weeks ago.'

He kneels up suddenly and reaches over to me at my end of the bed, grasping the sides of my arms. I recoil and so does he—the sudden movement has obviously jarred his migraine. 'But you said you loved me!'

'I do, Claudio, I do.' He doesn't believe me, I can see it—but he lets go, tears still falling down his face.

'How could you not have known that I care about you so much? I always have done. I came to your father's funeral—'

'*What?*'

'I stood at the back. At John's funeral, too. I cried for you, Jo, not for John. He never deserved you. But you were so sad. I wanted to make it all better for you, but I didn't dare. I kept nearly plucking the courage to ask you out, but something happened every time. You were with John for such a long time, till he died, and I could see you were in love. You were always polite to me, nothing more, even when I wrote you that song. Then you moved to London and your mother and her driving instructor moved away and I lost touch with you, so I left Brockhurst and moved to London too. Besides, I thought you would be cross with me . . . I told you, I need to tell you something, now we're together. I don't want us to have any more secrets: this is our clean slate. But I made a little mistake with you, you see, got a bit carried away one night. I'm so sorry, Jo, I shouldn't have done that. I thought I'd blown it then, and I didn't dare to ask you out after that. Although I expect you won't remember what I'm talking about, it was so long ago, and I didn't mean to hurt you. I felt very bad that you grazed your face on that wall . . .'

Icy realisation crackles through me, freezing me almost solid with this new horror.

'No,' I whisper, shaking my head. 'No. That's impossible. It wasn't you . . .'

I feel as if a wrecking ball has caught me in the belly, and then for a while I can't say anything else. I'm having trouble breathing, I am so frightened. I'm back in that alley again, with the tall skinny man in a black bomber jacket and a balaclava. I never thought . . . Claudio is not skinny now, but . . . Oh no. He is a violent, brutal misogynist and has been since he was a teenager.

'You do remember?' asks Claudio in a small voice. 'I am sorry, Jo. I felt very bad about it for a long time. But now I can make it up to you, I swear. I am older, and I would never do that now. It was a bad mistake. We all make mistakes, don't we, Jo? And I'm being honest now, aren't I?'

He sounds like a wheedling child.

We all make mistakes. I think of my lovely Richard; of our little family that really had been so much happier than I'd realised—although I didn't realise until it was too late. I think of Sean, the only one who's brought me even close to the passion I felt for John. I pushed them both away, because I lost John, and Dad, and ever since then, according to Eileen the therapist, I have denied myself what I've really needed. But there is something else, too, that has defined and quite possibly ruined my life for all these years, clouding my judgement and making me mistrust the instincts that could have led me to take a different path on so many occasions: that night in the alley.

The night that Claudio blithely assumes I'd probably forgotten about. He's like some kind of nightmarish Forrest Gump in my life, popping up at the centre of every major event, every trauma I've ever gone through.

'You expect that I wouldn't remember?' I find my voice, albeit in a croak. 'You think I'd forget the night that a strange man jumped on me from behind in a dark alley and tried to *rape* me? You think I'd forget that I had nightmares about it for years? That I got an eating disorder? That I had my breasts reduced because I thought that was why I got attacked? That I was afraid of men, afraid of the dark, afraid of walking anywhere on my own? You really think I'd just *forget* that?'

Without even realising, I have risen up from the bed and am standing, shaking with fury, over Claudio's sheepishly bent head. I feel really sorry for him, that his life is in such a mess—his fiancée dumped him and now his mother's dead and he's too screwed up to even mention that until I've been held hostage in my own flat for almost a week . . . but it doesn't temper the rage I'm feeling right now. I don't care if he kills me, or rapes me, or hurts me. He can't do any more harm to me than he's done already.

He looks up slowly, his mouth open, tears on his face. A waft of his breath assails me again and, unbelievably, I do finally recognise it as that same stranger's breath on my face, in the moment before Richard rescued me. My instincts scream at me that this is my chance to escape, that in this weird game of cat and mouse, my spitting rage and his migraine have finally made me the cat.

It's not only my chance to escape, it's my chance to be proactive for once: to be decisive, to do something for myself rather than do what someone else wants. I married Richard because he wanted me to. I loved Sean because his ego needed me to. But over my dead body will I stay a second longer in this bedroom lying to this deluded man about loving him when I loathe every cell of him . . .

For the first time in twenty-five years, I trust my instincts again.

'I FUCKING HATE YOU!' I scream. 'YOU'RE A PSYCHO AND I WOULDN'T GO OUT WITH YOU IF YOU WERE THE LAST MAN ON EARTH!'

Claudio's head jerks up in surprise and horror and I seize my chance. With one swift and mercifully accurate lunge, I dart towards the bed and retrieve the golf club from the bottom of the duvet. Before Claudio even has time to raise his arms to defend himself, I am screaming at the top of my lungs, wordlessly now, just white noise, lifting the club above my head and bringing it down as hard as I possibly can on the side of his skull.

Chapter Thirty-Eight
Day 5

He keels over like a solitary domino, a surprised look on his face, blood pouring out of a spot above his ear. Fortunately for him, my aim was not as good as I'd intended and I hit him with the shaft of the club, rather than the heavy end of it. I wonder if I've killed him, but at that moment, I can't stop to think about this. I've got to get out: now.

I scrabble for the bunch of keys in his jeans pocket and, my hands shaking, pull them out and unlock my bedroom door. My front door keys are on the same bunch—I recognise the fob. I run as fast as possible down the hallway, skidding on the rag-rug, feeling it ruck and slide beneath my feet, as if I was still on the ice on the day John died.

As I reach the front door, I hear a long, low moan from my bedroom. Shit, I forgot to lock and bolt it behind me in my rush to get out! I dither for a second—should I go back? But I might risk him grabbing me again, and every instinct screams at me to put as much distance as I can between us.

My hands fumble faster with the bunch of keys and I ram the biggest one into the Chubb lock. It turns immediately. I push up the snib on the Yale, twist the knob, pull the door, throw myself through it, and start half-running, half-skidding, down the stairs outside in my socks. A roar behind me makes me jump out of my skin, and I slip on the uncarpeted wooden staircase, twisting my knee so viciously that something goes 'ping' inside it and I gasp with pain as it then bangs hard against the wall on the first landing, compounding the damage. I turn to see Claudio looming at the top of the stairs, clutching his bleeding head with one hand like a zombie freshly risen from the grave. The blade of a knife—my big carving knife, the one he threatened me with when I rang Megan— glints in his other hand. Yelping with fear and pain, I try to stand, but my knee gives way and I can't. Claudio is stumbling unsteadily down the stairs towards me, ricocheting off each wall of the stair- well. Glancing in terror over my shoulder, I stagger to the top of the stairs from the ground floor. The door to the street is in sight, and I focus all my energy on it, launching myself down the staircase by bumping myself down on my bottom. Claudio is gaining on me by the second.

I reach the front door and grab the handle to drag myself up to standing on one foot. If it's locked, I'm screwed. There's no way I've got time to fumble with the keys to find the right one. Claudio is four steps away from me, four seconds at most, the knife blade only three . . . I can't see his face because it's covered with blood, but he wipes it angrily with his sleeve. He's sobbing and roaring incoher- ently, but the noise only acts as a blast of propulsion to get me out. I grit my teeth to ignore the pain in my knee, fling open the door, and thank God thank God thank God it's not locked—air! I'm out- side! The feel of fresh air in my lungs is as weird as anti-gravity, but I don't have time to think about it.

Outside. The world is going on as ever. The gum-pocked concrete is cool beneath my socked feet; that beautiful, beautiful warm city air fills my lungs, redolent of kebab and cigarettes, stale booze and exhaust fumes, but I don't have time to stop to appreciate it. The shops in the shabby high street outside my front door are all open, oblivious to the dramas that have unfolded inside my rented flat over the past week. I look frantically up and down the road, and there are people there—an Asian woman in a headscarf with a shopping trolley, an old man hobbling along on a walking stick, a traffic warden slapping a sticky notice on the windscreen of the white van parked on a single yellow line at the wrong time; normal distracted people doing a bit of shopping on a—whatever day it is—and cars and even a bus. I catch a glimpse of horrified and concerned faces staring out at me as it passes, and I must look a sight in my dirty pyjamas, hopping up the road screaming my head off as Claudio lumbers up behind me, catching me up . . .

'Help me!' I scream again, but I can't hop any more and I put my left foot down on the ground and try to run but the pain shrieks throughout my whole body and I collapse on the pavement and cover my head with my arms waiting for the cold steel to puncture my ribs and stop my heart right there outside the closed-down charity shop, opposite the betting shop and next to the convenience store that Megan and I call the Inconvenience Store because it's shut more often than it's open and the fruit's always going rotten . . .

Megan's face fills my mind, her grave blue eyes and her gappy smile, the softness of her curly hair, just as I'm thinking, with a great plunge of regret, *I'll never see you again, my darling,* and instead of the knife blade I feel a gentle hand on my shoulder and hear a kerfuffle behind me. I dare to open my eyes and see Claudio being rugby-tackled by the traffic warden, whose hat flies off as he jumps on Claudio's legs. The knife clatters across the pavement and some-one kicks it into the gutter, I don't see who. Claudio is howling and roaring still, and trying to get up, flailing at the traffic warden who looks like he's riding a bucking bronco. A terrified-looking girl pushing a screaming toddler in a pushchair is yelling into her mobile and pointing at me. More people crowd around me, but nobody else helps the traffic warden. Someone puts their coat under my head. Someone else awkwardly strokes my hair. There are questions:

'Are you hurt, love?'

'Who is he, your husband?'

'Aren't you Carol Singer's daughter Jo? I know your mother!'

'The police are coming . . .'

'Did you do that to him? He's covered in blood!' (this from a censorious-looking older lady with a white stripe through her black hair, like a badger).

I snap at her, 'He's been keeping me prisoner in my flat for nearly a week! He's off his head!' The woman who says she knows my mum clucks protectively. I don't recognise her, but Mum knew lots of people, and it's a small town.

'Don't ring my mum,' I beg her over the collective murmur of horror at my revelation, which rises to a fever pitch as Claudio, strengthened by his rage, manages to land a punch on the now-dazed traffic warden and stagger to his feet again. Several of the women around me scream, but instead of heading for me, Claudio crashes back through the still-open front door to my building and slams it behind him.

He's gone, spots of blood on the pavement and a bloody hand-print on my front door the only evidence that he's ever been there.

I hear sirens, and suddenly the pain in my knee sweeps back over me in a mighty wave. I groan in agony—but the pain feels blissful, because I'm free. I'm alive. I will see Megan again.

Everything will be fine.

⌣

The next thing I'm aware of is sitting up in the back of an ambulance, strapped to a stretcher. Someone I recognise is staring into my face. His face is kindly, and tight with shock. He's wearing a policeman's uniform.

'Jo! It's me, Henry! Oh my God, Jo, I can't believe it. I was on my way to check on you—Donna's been so worried. You'll be all right. You're safe now.'

It's Donna's husband Henry—of course. I am too dazed to speak for a moment.

'Donna's already called Richard. He's on his way. Shit, Jo, I feel awful . . . we should have done something much sooner . . .'

'Richard's in Italy,' I croak.

'He's coming back. She rang him this morning when we couldn't get hold of you. He and Megan will be back tonight.'

⌣

That's all I need to hear.

Chapter Thirty-Nine
Day 5

I spend a couple of hours in the Casualty department of Brockhurst's hospital, first having my knee strapped up and X-rayed, and then in a small private room being interviewed by two of Henry's police colleagues. I feel OK. Bit shaky, and spaced out from the painkillers the nurse gave me for my knee. I think I managed to give them the basic details about my five days' enforced house arrest. I also told them that Claudio had confessed to sexually assaulting me back in 1986.

Henry eventually comes back and drives me to his and Donna's house. Donna and Richard greet us at the front door, Donna tearfully, the dogs padding silently around her feet as I limp in on crutches. 'I'm so sorry I didn't realise sooner. I feel terrible, oh, Jo, I'm so sorry. We should have come days ago. You poor thing. Are you OK?'

I'm so knackered I can't speak. I just give her a wan smile and hug her back, then fall into Richard's outstretched arms. He holds me tight and I breathe in the scent of him. He looks tanned from the holiday, but stressed and tight with anxiety beneath the tan. Tears glimmer in his eyes too. 'Sorry you had to come back early,' I whisper.

'Don't be daft.'

'And sorry, I really stink.'

'Again, don't be daft.'

'What do you want to do, Jo?' Donna asks when Richard finally releases me. 'Megan's asleep upstairs. Glass of wine? Food? There's stew in the oven.'

I regard the staircase doubtfully. I'm desperate to see Megan but I know I won't have the energy to come down again once I've hobbled up. Tiredness is sweeping over me in great crashing waves.

'I think I just want a shower and to sleep, if you don't mind. Sorry, I know I stink.'

'Of course, no problem at all.' Donna is being slightly odd with me; formal, as though my incarceration has suddenly bestowed some sort of royal status upon me that requires her treating me with polite respect. Hope *that's* not going to last.

'Come on then, Hopalong.' Richard takes my arm and helps me upstairs to the spare bedroom where Megan is asleep, looking tiny in a double bed. At the sight of her, the jigsaw pieces of my life finally start slotting back into place.

He leaves me to shower and change into pyjamas that Donna has thoughtfully left out on the bed for me. When I climb in next to my daughter, blissfully clean again, she stirs and flops an arm possessively across me, muttering, 'Where have you been, Mummy? We came back early,' before sliding back into gentle snores.

The normality of it all almost destroys me with gratitude, and I gaze and gaze at her beautiful sleeping face, putting tendrils of her hair back from her forehead. Then Richard comes back in, sits on the edge of the bed, and does the same thing to me. The familiar feeling of his fingers on my fringe makes me shiver with nostalgia.

'Talk to me till I go to sleep, Rich?' I whisper, feeling my body start to relax next to them both. 'Tell me a bedtime story. Tell me about when you had your wisdom teeth out.'

He shifts so that he's on the other side of me, on top of the bedclothes, though, where Megan and I are beneath them. I feel him pause, to try to think how to begin—or perhaps how to do it; it's been so long since he talked me to sleep—then he starts, a small laugh in his voice.

'That was when we became friends, wasn't it? The start of it all. The summer after the first year at uni. I remember Ben calling me a purple puffer fish because my jaw was so bruised and I had cheeks like a hamster's . . . he must have been about six then.

'"Richard, be a dear and pop to Boots for me?" Mum goes. "Ben's got the runs and we're out of Diorlyte. I can't leave him. Richard, please?"'

Richard mimics his mum's high querulous voice, and it captures her perfectly. I'm in heaven. This is the best sort of therapy I could wish for. 'Go on,' I murmur.

He talks about how it was practically inevitable that he would bump into me when he looked so revolting, wearing grey sweatpants and an ancient Cure t-shirt . . . I hadn't noticed what he was wearing, but I didn't tell him that I had noticed his massive swollen cheeks, greasy hair, and the huge spot on his nose. He really looked awful—but as I didn't see him as a love interest anyway, it hadn't bothered me.

I didn't tell him that either, although I know that he knows it.

'We had a nice chat, didn't we?' I mumble instead.

'We did. You had a whole, proper chat with me, about working in Boots for the holidays, about uni, how nice it was that everyone was home for summer. Did I know that Donna and Gareth split up? That sort of thing. I couldn't get over that I was standing there, with you chatting so effortlessly to me, after all my attempts over so many years to get you to do just that. You looked so lovely, even in the white lab coat thing. You'd cut your hair short. If I was honest, I preferred it longer—like it is now—but I'd still have fancied you if you'd dyed it pink with purple spots.

'Then you said you'd better get back to work, and you held out your hand for the Diorlyte. I passed it over, with Mum's fiver and asked you if you fancied a drink some time that holiday. I nearly died of shock when you said yes.'

What had I been thinking, when I said yes? Why would I agree to a date with a boy I had never fancied? I suppose that I saw something in him, some spark of potential husband material that overrode my initial lack of sexual attraction to him. Perhaps my instincts weren't quite as crap as I'd always thought they were. Although we were friends for a long time after that before anything happened between us.

This was why I seriously thought I might be able to convince Claudio that I loved him: because when you're head over heels in love with someone, you see only what you want to see, hear what you want to hear. It didn't actually matter what I thought, with either Claudio or Richard—although God knows their motivations were very different. Claudio wanted me as some sort of consolation prize for his own desperation. Richard wanted me because he just genuinely loved me.

As I feel the soft dark pull of sleep, fear-free, deep sleep, Richard's voice starts to drift in and out of my head like a badly tuned radio. This must have been what it was like for Claudio when I was telling him about the ice rink.

'We agreed on the next day. My hands were shaking as much as my jaw was aching. All I could think about was whether or not my breath would smell as a result of the surgery, if we—finally— kissed . . . We didn't kiss the next evening, though, did we? Not for months and months after that—you wouldn't speak to me for ages, do you remember? But that first night was still insanely wonderful, out at that country pub. I drove because I couldn't drink anyway, on the painkillers. My face had subsided a little, but had turned a sickly kind of yellowy-green. I managed to shave properly, at least, and dressed up in my newest t-shirt and cleanest jeans. I contemplated borrowing some of that brown sludgy stuff my mother puts all over her face to hide her broken veins, but thankfully resisted . . . It was the best date I've ever been on, even though it was only as mates. We talked and talked—after all those years, I'd been a bit worried that we wouldn't have enough in common— but we did. You were completely awesome. And you laughed at my jokes . . . Do you remember what you said to me when we kissed goodnight, just a peck on the cheek? You said, "You've liked me for ages, haven't you?"—but you didn't say it in an arrogant kind of way.'

I nod, already dozing.

'I told you it had been years. I told you I couldn't believe you'd finally agreed to go out with me when my cheeks made me look like a hamster someone had beaten up. You said you liked me too, but it was a bit soon after John, and could we just be friends for a while . . .'

I remember that. He said OK, he'd take that. He could wait.

Richard laughs softly. 'I'd have preferred you to say that you absolutely wanted to rip my clothes off then and there and couldn't live without me, but I supposed it was a start. I wanted to tell you that I'd waited so long for you that I didn't mind how long it took now, that I was sure I was going to marry you . . . All manner of corny things were streaming through my mind: "I feel like I've come home when I look at you," or "You are the only one I will ever love," but thankfully I managed not to go that far. It would have sounded utterly ridiculous coming from someone who looked like they'd been busy storing nuts up for winter.'

'I knew, anyway,' I murmur sleepily. Richard gets up off the bed, kissing both Megan and me on the cheek. She doesn't stir.

'By the way,' he says when he gets to the door. 'I still think you're completely awesome.'

———⌣———

I dream of when Richard asked me to marry him. In real life, he'd gone down on one knee in the utility room of Mum's house, at a New Year's Eve party where the front room was full of her and Brian's friends and Richard's family, all getting giggly on cheap champagne. He had dragged me through the kitchen and out to the utility room just after the midnight countdown. I remember the ring box sitting on the top of the spin dryer. It had flecks of washing powder stuck on its black velvet carapace.

In my dream, though, Richard said, 'Jo, will you marry me? I know we don't have masses of sexual chemistry between us, but hey, let's be adults about this. I've loved you for years, you like me as a friend, and I'm sure you will love me one day because I'm a really, really good guy. And look, here's a photo of the daughter we'll eventually have together. How could you say no to that? She's called Megan. I want you so much. And if it doesn't work out, then we can get divorced. Deal?'

I looked at the photo he was holding, of Megan dancing on the sand, trailing a blue plastic spade in one hand, her curls blowing in the wind and an expression of sheer joy on her face.

'Deal,' I said.

'Great!' said Richard, turning into Sean, as he beamed at me and slipped a blood pressure cuff onto my arm, instead of a ring onto my finger. I looked up into Sean's beautiful eyes, and felt an overwhelming swell of lust through my body, followed by an even bigger swell of panic as I realised Richard had gone.

'Come back!' I shouted, and woke up crying.

Chapter Forty
Four months later

The only time I went back to the flat was to move out. I couldn't bear to spend a moment longer there than necessary, even though Donna and Ania had been in and cleaned everything, once the police had allowed them to. Poor Donna. She still felt really bad that she hadn't realised sooner that something was amiss that week.

She'd been on her way, though. She had just filed a Missing Persons report, alerted Richard in Italy, and told Henry to come to my flat to check on me, which was why he'd turned up at the very moment I escaped. Our mutual cleaner, Ania, had shown Donna the abrupt text Claudio sent her from my phone and they both agreed that it was out of character. Donna knew how much I liked Ania—I'd never have sacked her by text like that, using those words. As a result, Henry and his police colleague had been on their way over with Ania's set of keys.

So they'd have come, eventually. It helps, knowing that I *was* missed.

Megan and I are now in a two-bedroom cottage round the corner from Donna and Henry's. It's a bit ramshackle—the doors don't fit properly and there's a horrible plastic conservatory roof that you can't be under when it's raining because of the noise. But it has thick open beams, quarry-tiled, slightly sloping floors, and a sweet little garden, and we love it. Lester has spent most of the time we've been here behind the sofa in a sulk.

I found the rest of my old diaries in a box in the loft during the move and have been working through them, to remind myself that there has been so much more to my life than the events of 1986/7. I wish I'd read them before. They put a lot of things into perspective. A list caught my eye, from a few months before Richard and I split up:

- *Number of stomach crunches I did at the gym just now: 60*
- *Number of times Richard's told me he loves me this week: 78*
- *Number of times he really meant it: 78*
- *Number of times he said it through spontaneous affection: 31*
- *Number of times he said it out of fear that something's wrong, and thinking that by telling me this, everything will automatically be fixed: 41*
- *Number of times he said it out of habit: 26*
- *Number of times this week we've talked about making love: 8*
- *Number of times we made love: 0*
- *Number of times I tried but just couldn't face it: 3*

That little list made me feel sad. Our marriage hadn't been perfect—but how many marriages were? In my mind, I'd rewritten history to paint myself as the absolute ultimate bitch-betrayer, breaking up a marriage on a selfish whim, for no good reason, but that wasn't the case. I needed to stop beating myself up about it so much. Reading the diaries made me realise that we were just a normal, confused couple, muddling along, happy with some things, not at all happy with others, and yet too afraid to rock the boat by making an issue out of them. Things that were ultimately fixable, if we'd only faced up to them. Things could have gone either way, even with my feelings for Sean.

I remember once, near the end, when Richard and I hadn't touched one another for months. I knew it was a problem, but I was totally smitten by Sean and I tried to justify it by pretending things had gone to a place beyond redemption with Richard.

'We can't carry on like this,' he said, his one and only attempt to confront our problems.

'Perhaps we should go and see a sex therapist,' I replied, knowing that he'd rather walk over hot coals than do any such thing. 'You book us an appointment, and I'll come along.'

And that was the end of that. I wish I could have burrowed through that superficial layer of the longing and lust I felt for Sean, right through to the core of me, to the me who loved Richard with all my heart; who'd be so, so sorry when I'd lost him—but I couldn't. Not then. I didn't trust that little voice shouting at me not to break up the little family that meant so much to me. I didn't listen to it, because I was so used to not listening to it.

In the end I didn't have to go to court, although of course I gave lengthy statements to the police. Another advantage of there not having been a massive publicity campaign when I went missing was that the whole thing was kept out of the press. With no trial to come, there were no curious reporters wanting to know about 'my ordeal'. It was a huge relief.

Henry told me that the police had had to break down the door to get back into my flat, where they found Claudio in my bathroom, unconscious, having drunk bleach and cut his wrists. He died the next day in hospital. There'd been a note in his hand, written in wobbly letters:

TO JO, I'M SORRY. I JUST LOVE YOU AND I ALWAYS HAVE. I WAS SO HAPPY WHEN I THOUGHT I'D FOUND YOU AGAIN. BUT NOW I'VE LOST EVERYTHING AND EVERYONE.

I didn't cry for Claudio, although I felt very, very sorry for him. And bizarrely, I kept getting a mental image of the fuzzy-felt Bambi lying hooves-up in a skip somewhere. I wondered who'd have to clear out Claudio's flat. But I didn't ask, in case it turned out that I was the only person he knew, or something mad like that, and I'd feel obliged to do it myself. When I told Richard about what had happened, how Claudio had confessed to being my attacker and then said that he'd been at the ice rink the day that John died, Richard said something that made me seize up with fresh horror: 'Do you think it was him who caused the accident? Crashed into John on purpose? Easy to do, on a crowded ice rink . . .'

I couldn't speak for some time, but eventually two things occurred to me. The first was, thank *God* I didn't have that realisation when I was locked in the flat with Claudio, because I would definitely have killed him. Thank God he didn't confess to it. And the second thing was that now that he too was dead, it actually didn't matter any more. It, like Claudio himself, was in the past.

Eileen helped me come up with an image of all the pain caused by Claudio, and by Dad's and John's deaths. I put them in an imaginary metal box that I dropped from a great height into the very deepest part of the deepest lake on earth and watched the green waters close over it with a big splash. When the ripples settled and the water became glassy once more I visualised a sign sticking out of the surface. The sign read: NO FISHING. The sessions I had with Eileen over the next few months were surprisingly positive.

Something had changed in me and, with her help, I was able to analyse and utilise this change.

I realised that, after that awful year when Dad and John died and Claudio attacked me, I'd thought nothing that bad could ever happen to me again—but that very rationale was what had led to all the other bad things that had ever happened, and now I could not be passive any longer. I'd felt powerless for over twenty years, allowing myself to be swept along on a tide of fatalism. The one thing that brought it home to me with the greatest force was that my whole life had been shaped by Claudio's attack on me—and he'd assumed I wouldn't even remember it!

What a waste. Strange, but I can't hear those words without thinking of Sean saying, 'What a waist.'

Even more strange, I saw Sean last night: the evening when everything changed again.

Steph, Donna, and I met up for a girls' night out, at a salsa club in the upstairs room of a seedy pub in Brockhurst, as part of our new regime of more regular socialising. There we all were, in a line in the beginners' section, laughing, as the instructor had us take two laborious steps to the left, then two steps to the right again, whilst across the room the more experienced dancers were showing off.

Suddenly Sean and the Twelve-Year-Old walked in and headed for our group.

'Shit. It's Sean,' I hissed to Steph and Donna, who were flanking me. We were all holding fingertips with our partners: my current one was a weedy little nerd with sweaty fingers and not an ounce of rhythm.

'Oh *no*,' said Steph and Donna in unison.

'We can leave, if you want,' added Donna, as they approached.

I ducked my head in panic, my cheeks scarlet. Oh shit, oh shit, what do I do? I thought. For a moment I did want to run. Anything but to have to see Sean there with another woman—well, *girl*.

But then I thought, Hell, no, I'm not leaving. If he feels uncomfortable, he can go. I was here first.

They joined our ungainly line, holding fingertips and joining in with the left-right-left, behind, in front, behind. Sean hadn't even noticed me. My rhythm—such as it was—went right up the spout and my partner glanced at me, surprised to find that suddenly my own fingers were as clammy as his. I was trying to check out the Twelve-Year-Old up close, and to my annoyance I had to concede that she did look a bit older than I'd originally thought. Fourteen or fifteen, at least. I was pleased to see that in profile, though, she slightly resembled Princess Margaret. I wondered if she had any idea who I was.

'Change partners again!' said the instructor, and Sean was suddenly right there, holding out his hands for me to link fingertips with him. The shock of his flesh against mine again after so long made me feel vertiginous and I realised we were both holding our breath, as we had little choice but to look into each other's eyes.

I waited to feel the depth of yearning that I'd always associated with him, the desire to jump into his arms.

But nothing happened. My feet automatically did what the instructor told them to do. I could feel Steph's and Donna's anxious glances in my direction. I could see right into Sean's blue eyes—but all that was there, for both of us, was a sense of regret and embarrassment.

'Jo! You all right?' he said, and my toes curled in my high heels.

'I'm fine,' I said, forcing a smile. 'How are you?'

'Yeah. Good. Me and Michelle just got engaged, actually.'

The floor wobbled beneath my feet but I managed to remain upright. 'Oh! Good for you . . . That was quick,' I couldn't stop myself from adding as a postscript.

'Well, you know,' he said sheepishly. He opened his mouth as if to say more, but caught the eye of the Twelve-Year-Old, who was clearly trying to lip-read our exchange.

'When's the wedding?' I asked, not out of politeness but just so I could arrange to be out of the country that day.

'Dunno yet. We haven't set the date.'

'Right. Well, good luck.' I couldn't think what else to say. I felt numb, but mercifully calm. I couldn't decide whether this was just delayed shock, or whether in fact I really had moved on and didn't care any more what Sean did with his life, or with whom.

'Change partners!' called our instructor.

'Well, take care, Jo. It's nice to see you. You look great.' Sean smiled uncertainly at me. In the old days, my heart would have jumped at him saying I looked great but now, as we both moved one place to our left, it merely occurred to me that it was a mistake on his part to say his farewells, since we only had to swap partners six times before we'd be back facing each other again. I wondered if we'd have to endure this small talk each time around?

I grabbed Steph's and Donna's arms. 'Sean's getting married . . . Come to the loo with me?' I hissed. The three of us marched off the dance floor towards the Ladies, leaving Sean and two other confused-looking men without partners.

'Are you OK?' Donna asked, hugging me tightly once we got into the toilets.

I thought about it for a moment. 'Actually—yes. I think I am. After everything else that's gone on, Sean's the least of my problems. I hope he's happy with the Twelve-Year-Old. I hope I never have to see them again. But I feel all right. I'm off men, anyway . . . . I told you that I deleted my profile from the dating website, didn't I? I haven't even looked on there for ages. And seeing him tonight has made me kind of realise that I don't mind being on my own. I've got Megan. And Lester. And you two. Who needs a man?'

'That's the spirit,' said Steph, putting on lip gloss in the mirror. 'Let's get out of here, make a night of it and go clubbing. I'm sick of taking two steps to the left and two back again. It's humiliating. I feel about six years old.'

To my surprise and alarm, as we came out of the Ladies Sean was waiting for me, leaning against the wall looking anxious.

'Just wanted a really quick word, Jo,' he said, gently grabbing my elbow and steering me down the corridor towards the Mens. For a moment I thought he was going to usher me in there.

'Shall we meet you outside, Jo?' Donna asked, giving Sean the sort of look she usually reserved for one of the twins when they were misbehaving, or Henry when he left the toilet seat up. 'Or do you want us to stay?'

'No, it's fine. I'll see you outside in a second, OK?'

Donna and Steph left, both now shooting me resigned backwards glances and warning stares. But I didn't need to be warned. I found, to my interest, that I had absolutely no intention of begging Sean not to get married, or indulging in any other sort of similarly demeaning behaviour. It was such a relief.

'What is it, Sean?' I said, once we were alone. 'Where's Michelle?'

'Waiting for me in there. I said I just needed a quick chat. She's cool with that.'

'So . . . ?'

I realised that I was standing very aggressively, hip out, arms crossed, chin jutted as if I was about to head-butt him. A tempting thought.

'Jo, I just wanted to say, for what it's worth, that . . . well, I would have married you, you know. Nothing could ever come close to what we had together.'

I resisted the temptation to roll my eyes. Here we go again, I thought—and he's engaged! Is there ever going to be an end to this?

'Then why didn't you marry me?' I asked, as patiently as I could. 'Why did you dump me?'

Sean looked me in the eyes then and just for a second I felt a deep stab of passion and regret. 'That's what I wanted to tell you.

It wasn't because I went off you or anything. It was because, well, I never told you this, but it was because I knew I couldn't ever hope to compete with Richard. I know deep down you'd have gone back to him if I hadn't put pressure on you to stay with me. I just feel really bad about that, and I'm sorry. I really am, Jo. I know you loved me—but I could tell you still had feelings for him too, and I just couldn't handle it. Anyway. That's it. I just wanted to let you know. Take care.'

He turned abruptly and loped back into the bar without a farewell. I slumped against the wall, astonished and shocked. Sean had just been more honest to me in one minute than he had through the whole of our relationship. Why had he never told me that before? Of course it made sense that he was hugely threatened by my marriage, and by Richard—but at the time, I'd sincerely believed that it was Sean I loved and not Richard, and it hadn't occurred to me that Sean might doubt the depth of my feelings. Let alone doubt it with good reason . . . .

I sighed. Boy, that was two relationships I'd managed to screw up. I wondered, if I'd stayed with Sean, whether or not we'd have lasted the course. Probably not.

But still, I thought, pulling myself together and repeating my little affirmations like a mantra, it's really all in the past now. I'm fine. I'm still alive, unlike Claudio. I'm on a night out with my friends. Megan's fine. Richard seems fine, and Sean's getting married. Good luck to him.

As I walked out of the bar, Sean had his back to me, performing a hesitant and rather clumsy sort of spin with Michelle and all the other couples. Michelle saw me go, although she was pretending not to watch. I smiled at her and she gave me a tight half-smile back. I'm sure she's never been so pleased to see anybody leave.

Donna was on her mobile when I got outside and as she talked, I linked arms with her and Steph, and we set off, on our way to a bar in which, hopefully, there would be nobody I'd ever dated.

'Really?' she was saying. 'When? Really? No!' She unlinked arms with me and whispered, 'Go on ahead, I'll catch you up!'

'What did he want?' Steph asked me as we walked on, in step. 'Are you still OK?'

'I think so,' I replied. 'In fact, I think I might be more than fine. Wow . . . .' I was feeling very philosophical, in the way you tend to become after several vodka and tonics. ' . . . I think I have actually managed to Let Go.'

'Of what? Your grip on reality? Oh no, sweetie, that went years ago.'

I slapped Steph's shoulder. 'No! Well—probably—but you know what I mean. I feel so different now, like I really have moved on. I think that seeing the consequences of Claudio not being able to let go really changed things for me. That, and having the nerve to sock him one and escape. I just don't feel the sort of self-pity I used to, not any more.'

'Thank God for that,' said Stephanie bluntly. She never minced her words after a few drinks. 'You were a nightmare.'

I thought about getting offended for a moment, but couldn't. She was right, after all. And now that I realised it, I could do something to change it.

There was so much in my life that I couldn't change—choosing to walk down that dark alley, Dad dying, the decision to go skating that day with John, marrying and divorcing Richard, or falling in love with Sean. But I could change how things would be in the future.

Steph and I turned round as we heard Donna's footsteps hurrying up behind us.

'Guess what?' she said, snapping shut her mobile. 'Henry, for once in his little life, has just told me the most massive bit of gossip!'

'Ooh, what? What?' Steph and I chorused, philosophising forgotten.

'Richard's dumped Wendy!'

We all stopped in the street and stared wide-eyed at one another. 'Yes,' Donna continued conspiratorially, and for a moment I felt like I was fifteen again. 'He told Henry that he'd never loved her, not really, that it was just a comfortable sort of relationship to be in after he split up with you, Jo, but he realised that it was going nowhere and that it wasn't what he wanted. And that she deserved to be with someone who would eventually marry her, because he knew that he wouldn't.'

'Wow,' I said again, more slowly. My first thought was to hope that Richard was OK. He and I had become a lot closer since the Claudio trauma. Nothing romantic—although, strangely, I found myself really looking forward to when he picked Megan up and dropped her off again after their weekends together, and sometimes we shared a glass of wine or a cup of tea—but there was a bond between us, deeper than just our shared parenthood of Megan, and it was such a relief to rediscover it.

'He didn't mention anything to me when he came to get Megan yesterday. I wonder why not?'

At that moment, my own phone rang. Richard's name flashed up, so it was my turn to hang back from the others as I answered it. They walked on a little way and waited for me at a discreet distance, admiring the window display in Jigsaw.

'Talk of the devil! How are you?'

I had an awful thought—why was Richard ringing me at nine thirty on a Saturday night? 'Is Megan OK? Is she sick? Do you need me to come round?'

Richard's voice, so familiar and comforting, flowed into my ear. 'She's absolutely fine. Fast asleep with her bum in the air and a floppy toy tucked under each armpit. Don't worry. I was just calling to arrange when I'm dropping her off tomorrow. We didn't say a time yesterday, did we? I was wondering if you fancied meeting up at Red Peppers for an early dinner, the three of us?'

'That would be lovely,' I said with real pleasure. For Megan's sake, we were trying hard to still do some things together as a family. It wasn't exactly a hardship. We found ourselves slipping back into our old routines—sharing a bottle of the same Rioja we always used to drink, helping Megan with the word-searches on the kids' menu, playing I-Spy.

It just seemed really weird when Richard didn't come home with Megan and me afterwards.

'So, um, have you heard that Wendy and I broke up?' He sounded embarrassed. I turned my back on the others, who were cooing over some suede boots in Jigsaw's window.

'Just now, funnily enough. Henry's just rung Donna, two minutes ago, and told her.'

Richard laughed wryly. 'Not that funny really—good old Henry. I've only just got off the phone from him.'

I laughed too. 'Yes, well, I think he knows the kind of trouble he'd be in if he didn't report any gossip immediately to Donna. She got it written as a clause into their prenuptial agreement, didn't she? Anyway . . . for what it's worth, I'm really sorry, Richard. I never met Wendy, but Megan liked her and, you know, I'm sure it was good that you had someone . . . .'

I tailed off. It seemed inappropriate, if not downright arrogant, to say 'It was good that you had someone to take your mind off the fact that I left you.'

'Thanks, Jo,' he said quietly. 'Yeah. She's a great girl, but . . .'

For some strange reason, there were butterflies banging away in my stomach—butterflies! Richard had rarely given me butterflies before, but he was now, without a doubt. I felt mystified, and excited. Probably just the drink, I thought—although I wasn't all that drunk. In fact, I'd never felt more sober in my life.

He was single again. I was single again. He was my most favourite person in the whole world, apart from Megan. He was always, always there for me.

I gulped.

'Richard,' I began. 'Um . . . obviously, say no if you don't fancy me—I mean, *it*; say no if you don't fancy it, but I wondered if you'd like to go out to dinner next week? Without Megan, just the two of us, for a grown-up dinner somewhere?'

There was a pause and I found myself holding my breath. What if I'd got this all wrong? What if he'd only dumped Wendy because he had someone new? That would be so mortifying.

Steph and Donna were starting to gesticulate at me. 'Hurry up, I'm freezing,' called Donna, banging her arms against her sides and stamping her feet. 'Who is it? Call them back later!'

I made a face at her. 'Won't be long,' I mouthed back, and they rolled their eyes and went back to discussing the practicalities of cropped trousers when summer was long over.

When Richard finally replied, I could hear the smile in his voice, and joy flooded through me.

'I'd love to, Jo,' he said. 'I'd really love to.'

'Who was that?' Donna demanded once I'd got off the phone and rejoined them, beaming all over my face.

'Oh, just some hot guy I've got a date with next week,' I said airily. 'I invited him out to dinner.'

'You tart!' said Stephanie. 'I thought you said you were off all men and didn't want to date anybody?'

'Well.' I just couldn't stop smiling. 'Technically, I'm only off men that I've never been married to before . . .'

294

Acknowledgements

A huge thank you to the lovely Emilie Marneur, my editor at Thomas & Mercer, and the rest of the team, especially Sana Chebaro and Neil Hart. Particular thanks go to Katie Green for the heroic editing skills that have massively improved this book, and to Jennifer McIntyre whose copyediting comments on the manuscript often really made me laugh, as well as feel infinitely more confident about it.

Thanks to Mark Edwards for the encouragement, for being my first reader, and for coming up with the title (knowing well how rubbish I am at thinking of good titles!). Others who have been encouraging, supportive, or helpful in some way include Martin Toseland, Rachel Abbott, Lucy Vickery, Gracie Voss, Helen Russell, and my and Mark's excellent Facebook fans.

About the Author

Louise Voss was born and raised in Salisbury, England. She began her writing career in the mid-1990s when, while living in New York, she enrolled in a creative writing course.

Her first novel, *To Be Someone*, was published in 2001 by Transworld, and was the first book to come with its own CD soundtrack. This was followed by three more contemporary women's fiction novels until she switched to writing thrillers with Mark Edwards in 2011.

She and Mark were the first UK self-published authors to reach #1 on the Amazon charts with *Catch Your Death*. Their fifth co-written novel, *From the Cradle*, was published in 2014 by Thomas & Mercer.

Louise currently lives and writes near Hampton Court. She is an avid tennis player, knitter, singer, upcycler and jewellery-maker, and adds that she can stand on her head and write backwards. Although not at the same time.

She can be reached at @LouiseVoss1 on Twitter. Her website is www.vossandedwards.com.